Downtown Strut

Books by Ed Ifkovic

Edna Ferber Mysteries
Lone Star
Escape Artist
Make Believe
Downtown Strut

Downtown Strut

An Edna Ferber Mystery

Ed Ifkovic

Poisoned Pen Press

Copyright © 2013 by Ed Ifkovic

First Edition 2013

10 9 8 7 6 5 4 3 2 1

Library of Congress Catalog Card Number: 2012920286

ISBN: 9781464201554   Hardcover
       9781464201578   Trade Paperback

Poisoned Pen Press
6962 E. First Ave., Ste. 103
Scottsdale, AZ 85251
www.poisonedpenpress.com
info@poisonedpenpress.com

Printed in the United States of America

for Geraldine
and in memory of Al DeRuccio

I'll be down to get you in a taxi honey
Better be ready 'bout half past eight
I mean don't be late
Be there when the band starts playin'

Remember when you get there honey
Dance all over the floor
Dance all over my shoes
When the band plays the Jelly Roll Blues
Set 'em all alight
At the downtown strutters' ball.

—Shelton Brooks (1917)
"Downtown Strutters' Ball"
(Originally titled "Darktown Strutters' Ball")

Chapter One

As I stepped into my own living room, drawn by the excited hum of strange, eager voices, my eyes immediately caught those of a dark young man who stared back, his eyes wide and unblinking, a sloppy grin plastered on his face. I knew I'd met him before, and recently, though I had no idea where. So young—what? twenty-one, twenty-two?—with skin the color of rich mahogany, glistening and smooth. He wanted to say something to me because the carnival grin disappeared as he cleared his throat, but at that moment my housekeeper Rebecca nudged me from behind.

"Miss Edna, quite the motley bunch, no?" She laughed and nodded toward a skinny young boy who was now standing, a nervous smile on his lips.

"Mom," he began.

"Waters," Rebecca said in the same buttery chuckle, "where are your manners? You weren't raised in a barn."

I shifted my gaze from the young man with the sloppy grin to Rebecca's son, who started to stammer, "Miss Edna, I…"

"Waters," I roared like a hectoring schoolmarm, "when I'm out of town you resettle the young population of Harlem in my apartment?" But my smile gave me away. Waters, like every other gangly seventeen-year-old boy in the world, stood all raw-boned elbow and jerky wrist, bending and twisting, one foot tapping the floor.

I wasn't expected back in town for two more days, of course, but the arduous, though heady, tryouts for *Show Boat* had exhausted me. I'd checked out of my hotel early. Though the show was already headed back to New York, I'd originally planned on two days of idle shopping and lunches with friends in Philly. But I'd changed my mind.

Too many cities, each becoming a noisy blur.

I was thrilled that cosmopolitan Washington adored the new Hammerstein-Kern musical. My Lord, that first night it ran for over four hours, ending at 12:40 a.m., the audience on its feet, stomping, cheering, huzzahing. Not a soul left the theater. The excitement shook the rafters. I actually blushed, felt faint as I staggered up the aisles of the National Theater. The next morning the line for tickets circled the block. That was mid-November. We knew we had a hit on our hands.

From there the energized troupe moved to Pittsburgh's Nixon Theater, the musical now drastically and painfully cut, then on to Cleveland, and now ending a rip-roaring tryout at the Erlanger in Philadelphia. *Show Boat* would open on Broadway—a gigantic hit, everyone whispered to me—just two days after Christmas.

Foolishly, drunk on the show's evident success and awash in its riveting music and splendor, I'd become a camp follower, a schoolgirl with her first crush. It couldn't last. At one point I'd also rushed to Newark, New Jersey, and then to Atlantic City, where I watched the tryouts of *The Royal Family*, my comedy written with George S. Kaufman, scheduled to open in New York the day after *Show Boat*. It was dizzying, if wonderful.

Hidden in my hotel room, I'd become homesick, desperate for Manhattan and the quiet of my bedroom. So I boarded the train at Philly, bone weary and yet exhilarated, echoes of "Ol' Man River" reverberating in my head as the train clang-clanged into Penn Station. I wanted to be home, my door shut against the outside world. I'd lost my energy. All the pumped-up euphoria of two new shows, completed now and ready for the world to judge, left me enervated, down. It was like the morning after a successful party as you stare into your empty coffee cup and face the hollow day ahead.

When the doorman Joseph deferentially placed my suitcases inside my front door and I stepped into the living room, I didn't expect that gathering of startled, upturned Negro faces.

Waters walked toward me, half-bowed, and smiled. How much the slender, jittery little boy he seemed, with those thin shoulders and that long, stringy neck, the bony oval face with the narrow nutbrown eyes that blinked too much. A year away from college, he was a serious prep-school lad with Joe College crew-neck sweaters and starched Arrow shirts. And, he hoped, the life of a writer. "Miss Edna, you told my mother…"

I held up my hand. "Waters, please. It's no matter." My smile tried to take them all in.

But the group shuffled in their seats, nervous, ready to leave, which seemed right.

"You look tired, Miss Edna." Rebecca leaned in, shaking her head. "I'll brew you a cup of tea and then settle you in." She smiled back at the young folks sitting there. "I think these poets have rhymed enough verse for one day."

Only Waters laughed out loud, but I noticed that the lanky lad with the infectious grin widened his eyes. It bothered me. How did I know him? Something about him seemed familiar, but that made no sense: my social circle of young Negroes in their early twenties was nonexistent, really. Tall, angular, yet with a slightly pudgy, bloated face, as though he'd never fully shaken off the last of his baby fat, he was not handsome but incredibly attractive. That deep mahogany hue, yet with a sprinkle of reddish freckles around his nose and eyes that gave him a mischievous look. The eyes, yes, they looked familiar. Slatted, almost Asian perhaps, the edges lined with darker ebony, so much so that it could be stage makeup, a chorus girl's kohl-rimmed look. An amalgam of hard and soft, that face: the rigidity of his jawline at war with the puffiness of his cheeks. A gentle boy, I thought, yet when he stared at me, the eyes looked steely and fierce. I was startled.

Waters was still apologizing.

Last summer, when Waters was visiting his mother and staying with relatives in New Jersey, he scooted in and out of my apartment, the soon-to-be high-school senior always in a hurry, stacks of library books clutched to his chest—or spilling out of the overstuffed briefcase he often carried, an old-timer's briefcase with buckles and clasps and weathered leather. One afternoon he confessed a desire to be a novelist, and though I had a professional writer's dread of the amateur short story cavalierly thrust at me, I asked to read something he'd written. The short narrative he'd given me described his dead grandfather, Rebecca's father, a colorful if eccentric man everyone called Captain Tom, a towering, gaunt patriarch with straightened black hair and a thick, whiskey voice. A good man, and beloved by Waters. The piece was crude and overblown, yet it had spark, energy, verve. So I encouraged the quiet boy to spend hours reading in my personal library. There were days he never seemed to look up from a book.

Then, wandering the city streets, especially up to Harlem in search of the young writers of the new Harlem Renaissance that everyone was talking about—capitalized now, so dubbed by the *New York Herald Tribune*—he'd become friendly with a small coterie of neophyte writers and actors, young men and women who hung out at the public library on Lenox Avenue, in the lobbies of the Lafayette and Lincoln Theaters, at St. Mark's A.M.E. Church on 138th and St. Nicholas Avenue, starry-eyed young folks who hungered to be a part of the throbbing, jazz-infused world of this Negro flowering—followers of Langston Hughes, Zora Neale Hurston, Countee Cullen, and Wallace Thurman, writers not much older than they, in fact, but already established, celebrated.

Intrigued, caught by Waters' infectious excitement, I agreed to meet them one afternoon in my apartment—the first of two casual lunches I hosted. I found them refreshing and eager, brimming with enthusiasm, though a tad leery of me. Then the summer ended, and Waters returned to school and I headed to Europe for a brief sojourn.

When I left for the *Show Boat* tryouts, I'd told Rebecca that Waters, on Christmas break from his prep school in Maryland and staying across the Hudson River in New Jersey, could meet his friends in my living room one afternoon, with Rebecca serving them lunch. Waters had insisted there was no place where they could gather for a long, talkative afternoon. I had a few qualms, to be sure, because I guard my privacy and I'm covetous about my expensive rooms, but I trusted Waters. They'd be under the watchful eye of Rebecca. Frantic with concern about *Show Boat* and *The Royal Family*, I'd forgotten all about it…until I walked back into my living room.

Now, stunned into silence, they stared back at me. Waters cleared his throat. "You remember my friends…" His outstretched arm swept the room.

I remembered three of them, of course. "Sort of," I grinned.

"You remember Lawson Hicks." Waters pointed at a good-looking young man. In his early twenties, Lawson was tall and slender, very light complected, sporting richly pomaded straightened hair and a slice of manicured moustache over his full upper lip. A matinee idol, this one, I had thought the two times we'd met before, with his deep-set black eyes, his Leyendecker chin, and his baby-boy dimples. He had the habit of throwing back his head so that the overhead light accentuated the high cheekbones. Dressed in billowing creased trousers and a robin's-egg blue dress shirt, his feet shod in spiffy two-toned black-and-white shoes, he slouched on the sofa, a man comfortable with his God-given beauty. He nodded at me, smiled, then stood up and seemed ready to bow. I remembered him as the author of exquisite little poems, rhapsodic and lyrical, one of which had been published in *The Crisis*. I did remember something else—he wore his unabashed ambition so arrogantly that I imagined he could startle other souls into uncomfortable silence. A budding actor, Waters had told me. I remembered that I liked this cagey man who aimed to please, who flattered me when he didn't need to. I liked him, I supposed, because he was so good looking, fresh scrubbed, intense. A cocky lad with fire in his belly. But I suspected his talent was a narrow kingdom, genuine though limited.

"And, of course, Bella Davenport." Waters grinned foolishly and stumbled over the name. I squinted. Of course? Why? I wondered. The young woman didn't stand, but she inclined her body toward me, a soft, rumbling laugh coming from the back of her throat. Bella, an actress and playwright, statuesque and lithe, her movements self-consciously sensual, deliberate—so light-skinned she could pass for white. The one-act play I read of hers dealt with a jazz songstress dying of a cocaine overdose in the dressing room of Barron's Exclusive Club up on 134th Street and Seventh Avenue, a play titled *Snow*, which I'd learned—how could I know this?—was street lingo for the lethal drug. Dressed in a plum-colored chemise, her slender feet shod in buckled high-heeled shoes, her hair straightened and bobbed, she was a speakeasy flapper out of the pages of *The Smart Set*, albeit Negro. Bella, if I remembered, was Lawson's on-and-off lover. Like him, she was ambitious, though I sensed he was more the dreamer. She was more at home with hard-bitten reality. Bella, with the slow, calculated turn and tilt of her perfumed neck, could make men whisper inanities when their wives were conveniently out of the room. A beautiful woman, but chiseled, sleek, the ebony diamond.

"And you probably don't remember Ellie." I cast a quick glance at Waters because this last introduction seemed so dismissive. Yet Ellie took no offencs; in fact, rolling her tongue into her cheek, she appeared amused by the young boy's tactless words. Ellie, small and wrenlike, with reddish-black hair pulled back from her high forehead, had a little-girl beauty, a sharecropper Pollyanna, the girl in the room you didn't notice until she spoke…and then you found yourself wrapped around her melodic, almost falsetto timbre. She was dressed in a simple chiffon smock, though a shrill blood red in color, and, unlike Bella with her crimson lipstick, Ellie wore absolutely no make-up.

"Of course I remember Ellie," I remarked. "You wrote a poem I liked…"

Ellie was nodding her head up and down.

They all looked a little in awe of me, which is the way I wanted the whole world to be, truth be told. In my world interlopers tended to keep their distance, though they might scowl or whine. Bores ran for cover. Fools were never suffered...

Waters paused, an awkward silence filling the room, and the young man with the grin cleared his throat again.

"And then these...people," Waters ploughed on. "You *don't* know *them*." Everyone laughed nervously. "Roddy Parsons." He pointed to the young man I believed I'd met elsewhere, a man who stared at me now, a twinkle in his eyes, on the verge of telling me something. But Waters quickly moved on, pointing. "This is Harriet Porter. And this is Freddy Holder." Both of them looked ready to bolt the room, each glancing at the other. Neither smiled. Not that I expected an obsequious response whenever I entered a room, even if it was *my* room, but both of them struck me as vagabond souls who'd found themselves on the wrong subway platform. They sat together, bodies touching, though I got the impression of strangers brushing against each other in an elevator. They appeared younger than the other three, though it might have been their clothing: well-worn bulky sweaters, stretched out a bit. Harriet's dark blue one over a rag-tag skirt, Freddy's dark brown crew neck worn over wrinkled work pants, frayed at the knee. They formed a contrast to the polished look of the others, almost deliberately so, I thought. Freddy and Harriet seemed habitués of street corners. I'd seen such young souls when taxis delivered me up Broadway or Seventh Avenue toward Riverdale: high-school boys and girls who gathered in packs outside the be-bop jazz clubs and the dim-lit and poorly disguised speakeasies, their nodding heads inclined toward the jazz wailing from inside or the street corner hum of illicit boozers. Poor boys and girls, they were, mostly, and hungry to be grownup.

They glanced at each other, nervous, and the silence in the room was palpable. Waters felt a need to flesh out the history. "I heard Harriet read at a poetry reading at the Y uptown. I *liked* her poems a lot. Then Roddy heard her read somewhere—and talked about her. And then I met her friend Freddy who..."

Freddy broke in. "Sometimes doesn't write at all."

His voice alarmed me: raspy, phlegmatic, a slow drawl, yet laced with quiet anger.

"We gotta go," Harriet added, half-rising.

But no one moved, though their bodies shifted in their seats.

"Miss Edna," Rebecca said, "let me make you that pot of tea." She headed toward the kitchen.

Silence, uncomfortable.

"What are you all writing these days?" I asked.

No one answered me.

"They were talking up one of Lawson's poems," Rebecca told me, looking back over her shoulder as she walked away. "I like it. But then I like everything they write." She chuckled.

"It's very good," Waters volunteered. "It's about Jungle Alley, you know, up and down 133rd Street. Thereabouts. You know, the jazz clubs…" He breathed in. "The rhythm of…jazz beats… Folks walking the sidewalks…Saturday night at the Catagonia Club…"

Harriet spoke over his words. "I don't like it. It's…phony."

Lawson bristled.

"It's nothing new…" Harriet was going on, but stopped, unsure of herself.

"Perhaps I'll read it later." I turned away. The telephone was ringing, and I could hear Rebecca answering it in the kitchen.

Lawson spoke to my back. "Thank you."

Harriet made a grumbling sound.

Looking back, I caught a glimpse of Waters, his head nodding, gesturing. At once everyone began moving, reaching for gloves and scarves. A respectful move because he understood that I wanted to be alone in my apartment, sitting in my workroom with a cup of hot tea while I caught up with my mail. Out of the corner of my eye, I saw Lawson slipping into a tan Chesterfield overcoat.

But in that moment I noticed Bella narrowing her eyes at Ellie, her mouth set in a grim line, though she immediately turned and touched Roddy's elbow, so quick a gesture as to seem accidental. Lawson, buttoning his coat, stepped toward her.

Suddenly, jarringly, there was a confident rat-a-tat on my door, just as Rebecca stepped back into the room. "Mr. Harris is here to see you, Miss Edna. Joseph told him you were back. I insisted you'd *just* got back..." She paused. "Well, he..."

The rapping on the door swelled, insistent. An impatient man, this Jed Harris, a man used to getting his way. Rebecca hurried to open the door, and Jed stood there, one knee slightly bent, one hand cradling his feathered fedora against his chest, the other fanning a sheaf of papers. For some reason there was a scowl on his face. He stepped into the foyer, barely glanced into the room, his back turned away from the staring young folks, dismissive. "Edna, I was gonna leave the dialogue changes downstairs but the doorman said you'd returned." He frowned. "You didn't tell me you were coming back so soon."

I made a joke of it. "You didn't get my wire?" But his face was tight, the eyes unblinking. "I was tired, Jed. I..."

He kept frowning. "Thought I'd hand them to you, explain the changes. I think my changes are *important*." A sly grin covered his face. "I know you don't like changes to your words, but Ann Andrews can't deliver some of your complicated..." He stopped and for the first time turned to look at the young folks in the living room, all of them staring at him. He wasn't happy. "But it looks like you're having a party." He fairly snarled the line.

"Parties only begin when you arrive, Jed."

He narrowed his eyes. "That's because I'm the only person I enjoy talking to."

One of the young girls laughed—I think it was Harriet—and Jed flinched, threw a smoldering look in her direction.

"Leave the pages with me," I told him. "We'll talk later."

He didn't like that. He stepped back, deliberately lit a cigarette, and proceeded to blow thin wisps of blue-gray smoke into the air, purposely creating crude circles that escaped from his lips and drifted to the ceiling. A performance, I thought—one from a pouting child. "Sure," he whispered, and I knew from experience that his whispers were dangerous.

Jed was the brash, young producer of *The Royal Family*, and already he'd provided George and me with frayed nerves, bilious indigestion, and the occasional insidious migraine that puts me in bed for a day. The new and improved *wunderkind* of Broadway, Jed Harris had experienced an unparalleled string of recent SRO hits with the likes of *Coquette* and the urbane *Broadway*, and he insisted that *The Royal Family* was the ultimate hat trick.

An insomniac, he also had the misguided habit of phoning me at three or four in the morning to discuss cast changes, the disgruntled stage crew, his detestation of the actors—he famously announced that intelligence was wasted on actors—and his disaffection with my co-playwright George Kaufman. I put up with it a few times, but finally demanded he stop. With someone else, I'd have slammed down the receiver the first time he called, indignant; but Jed Harris, with the low tantalizing voice, had a way of charming me. Glib, suave, using that mesmerizing voice, he kept me on the line. Foolishly, I let him. He wooed me. I let him. I disliked the power the man had over me, and I disliked the fact that I found him—well, appealing. No one else liked him, a situation he relished. He cultivated hostility like a gardener who coveted only weeds. Ina Claire once resoundingly slapped him in the face, which immediately qualified her for Great White Way sainthood. People feared him.

But a whole part of me got quiet and scattered whenever he was around. I was too old for such puerile shenanigans. The man was a destructive imp, slick and devious. *Meshugenah*, George Kaufman insisted. Plain crazy.

Jed pushed the papers at me, but made no move to leave.

You saw a small man standing there, wiry and compact, slender as a pencil but with the suggestion of taut, high-strung muscles. Looking at him, you sensed that he was hairy, some simian creature loosed on fashionable Broadway. His dark face, that chiseled chin, and the perpetual grainy beard stubble, cast him as a faintly dissolute speakeasy dandy from a Damon Runyon tale, a man whose sartorial splendor was always impeccable, the creases in his trousers just so, cascading over his shoes just so; the shirt collar crisp; the fedora worn with the jaunty calculation of a Broadway prima donna, inclined on the small head so that it suggested an appendage acquired at birth. Worse, the hooded eyes possessed no humor, though he'd wisecrack like a smart aleck schoolboy. Not only that but, frighteningly, those black onyx eyes had a hard quartz-like polish, as though squinting at a sun no one else saw. They were the eyes of a man who was purposely evil—or just plain mad. Which didn't matter because the result was the same. "To be sexy," he once purred at me, "you've got to have menace." You avoided men like Jed. I, on the other hand, looked forward to his visits, though I hated to admit it.

He was just twenty-seven. I…well…wasn't.

While I was glancing at the typed sheets he handed me, something was happening in the room. Waters and his friends had become quiet, slipping back into their seats though most now wore their overcoats. Of course, I figured they all knew who Jed Harris was, his ferocious power on Broadway, this golden boy—but Waters, a gutsy seventeen-year-old, said something to him about seeing *Coquette*—how much he loved Helen Hayes, how much…

He stopped, sputtered, and I looked up, bothered.

Jed's icy expression stopped him cold. I found myself looking from Jed to the young folks. Jed's eyes swept over their faces, and there was nothing welcome about the look. I said something about the group of young writers and actors, talented men and women, but I realized something was wrong. A raw buzz of electricity hummed in the room. No one moved, yet everybody seemed to be in motion. Facing them, rigid, this small man took them all in. As I watched, Jed's glare moved from Roddy to Lawson to Ellie, but finally caught the eye of the beautiful Bella, tucked into a side chair, her presence partially obscured by Lawson, who was leaning forward. A tense moment, Jed and Bella holding eye contact for a brief moment—and I knew at that second that the two of them knew each other.

"Have you met…" I began, but Jed backed up, swagger in his step, and turned to leave. "Jed?"

Without saying a word he was gone, the door slammed.

The mood of the room shifted. When I glanced at Bella, she pushed herself back into the cushions of the chair, folding her body in, her long arms wrapped around her chest as though she were a child defending herself. Her striking face was flushed. She was staring across the room, seemingly fascinated by the German pewter candlesticks on my fireplace mantel. What she was doing, I realized, was avoiding Lawson, who'd turned his body so that he now faced her. His lips were drawn into a straight, disapproving line, yet when he raised a hand to his face, I noticed his fingers trembling. And the look in his eyes was both sad and curious.

At that moment Roddy stood up and hurriedly buttoned his overcoat. He glanced from Lawson to Bella, sarcasm lacing his words. "Ain't you the brave guy though?" For a moment I was confused. Yes, it was a line from the popular play *Broadway*, a tag line with faddish currency among theatergoers. Cartoon characters used it in the funny papers. It made everyone laugh. No one laughed now.

Odd, I thought, that quotation coming from this young man, and said so bitterly. A pause. Then he mentioned Jed's name, not friendly. Bella glanced at him, a sideways twist of her head that attempted to be coy but came off as apologetic. A sliver of a smile crossed her lips, but just as quickly disappeared, a feeble gesture, a little flirtatious, that told me that she liked Roddy. Lawson, meanwhile, was trembling. While I was watching this little drama, Ellie bounced up, made a dismissive grunt that seemed to take in the others, and picked up a glove she'd dropped to the floor. She turned, colliding with Freddy, standing there with his arms folded over his chest. Everyone stammered goodbye, over and over, and thanked me as they scrambled to the doorway, their arms holding bundles of their writing. In a flash, they were gone, with Freddy and Harriet doggedly following the others out the door.

Jed Harris had said not one word to any of them.

Waters, looking the baffled schoolboy he was, shot me a worried look.

"Well," I began.

In a squeaky voice he asked me, "Did something just happen here?" He opened his eyes wide, wide.

I grinned. "And I was thinking on the train ride back that it would be nice to return to my apartment where nothing ever happens."

Something had, indeed, happened.

Chapter Two

The phone woke me from a deep sleep. I glanced at the alarm clock on the nightstand: four in the morning. Good Lord, I thought, no one in Manhattan gets up at this absurd hour. Some folks were just *going* to bed. Someone had better be dead.

"Edna." Blunt, thick, a cigarette smoker's midnight voice.

I sighed. "What did I tell you about calling in the middle of the night, Jed?"

He ignored that. "You know, I'm gonna fire the cast."

My mind reeled. I sat up in bed, felt a chilly draft from the windows, wrapped my wool blanket snugly around me. What absurdity was this? "No, you're not."

A raspy chuckle, too loud, as if he held his mouth on the receiver. "I'm the producer."

"And I'm the writer." I paused. "Though your persistent and silly dialogue changes might suggest the contrary."

Again the thick unpleasant laugh. "Edna, the cast is all wrong."

"Jed, it's four in the morning. At this hour everything is wrong."

"Ann Andrews is horrible as Julie Cavendish."

True, I thought, but the wonderful actress Ethel Barrymore, on whom most believed George and I based the glamorous, enthralling Julie, not only refused to play the part, as we'd fervently and naively hoped she would, but also now planned on suing, as she'd thundered to the press on more than one occasion. We'd supposedly maligned the august Barrymore clan. Theatrical royalty. Legendary Broadway luminaries. And because of Ethel's strident pronouncement, no veteran actress would touch the central role, so we'd reluctantly settled on Ann Andrews, an old blowsy trooper who was blond and tall and filled with static— and thus all wrong for the part. A vaudeville stereotype, best at playing bawdy barkeeps. Feebly, I said into the phone, "It's too late to find someone new."

"That's why I'm closing the play down."

"No, you're not." I was getting a headache. I joked, "Isn't it bad enough that the Marx Brothers plan to sue because they suspect we based the play on *their* lives? We're becoming laughing stocks." I sighed. "Jed, I'm going to the theater this morning. We'll talk then. I haven't even looked at the changes yet." Then I added, "And then I have to be at the Ziegfeld for a meeting about *Show Boat*. Meet me at…"

"I'm headed home now, dear Edna, so I won't get up till two or three." Loud voices in the background, the tinkle of glasses, a whisper of a laugh, and a few bars of music. Jed at some midtown honky tonk—maybe the Del Ray Club or the Hotsy Totsy.

"Some people keep normal sleeping hours, Jed. I, for one, require a solid eight hours when Manhattan lies under darkness…"

He interrupted me. "Nothing good happens in Manhattan during daylight."

I was ready to hang up the phone. "I suppose you do look better in shadows, Jed."

He chuckled. "I'm closing the play."

"Meet me first."

"I'll be there at three. We'll have lunch."

"I have lunch in my workroom at one. Rebecca serves me a sandwich and…"

"I'll have lunch. You can watch me eat. I know how it thrills you."

I was shaking my head. "Don't do anything rash, Jed."

"Everything I do is rash. That's why I'm a millionaire at twenty-seven. I'm the hottest ticket on Broadway. Me, Edna. Little Jacob Horowitz from the Lower East Side. Me…"

I broke in. "Goodbye."

"Edna." A sudden change in tone, hesitant, quizzical.

"What?"

"Those Negroes in your living room. What's that all about?"

Surprised, I waited a second. "Rebecca's son Waters wants to be a writer and he's made friends with other like-minded young folks. Up in Harlem. I sat with them twice last summer, read their poems, stories, plays. I enjoyed their…exuberance, Jed. So I told Waters he could meet here when I was away. They're good sorts who…"

He whispered into the phone, a hissing that chilled me. "I wasn't pleased." He breathed in, and I could hear the intake of cigarette smoke. "I don't like Negroes."

"Good God, Jed, it has nothing to do with you." I ran my tongue over my upper lip. "You know. I had the feeling that you actually know…some of them."

He didn't answer. The lazy hum of music in the background disappeared.

"Well?" I asked.

"You shouldn't encourage people to write, Edna. It's an ignoble profession practiced by malcontents and idle dreamers."

"They have talent…"

"They have this white lady who fawns over them and promises lives they'll never have."

"Goodbye, Jed." I hung up the phone.

It was going to be a hectic day, though I knew all the days ahead of me were going to be frantic, especially the next couple of weeks through Christmas and the days immediately following, a kaleidoscope of panic, tension, and, doubtless, rising bile. Most of it would center on Jed. *Show Boat* was to open on December 27 at the new Ziegfeld Theater; one day later *The Royal Family* would open at the nearby Selwyn Theater, assuming Jed didn't slam shut the doors. Unfortunately, Jed Harris controlled its wobbly destiny.

Show Boat, the musical based on my best-selling romance of life on the turbulent Mississippi, was a very rich stepchild, though producer Flo Ziegfeld and the talented duo of Hammerstein and Kern had asked me to consult—a deplorable and empty word that meant, obviously, sit quietly in the theater and applaud and look for egregious errors that might embarrass the producer. As it turned out, Hammerstein and Kern, the imaginative creators, actually listened to me—sometimes. It was good press to have me in attendance, the winsome author lurking in the wings. Not that I minded: theater, to me, was exhilarating, vital, a life pulse. The moment a curtain rose I'd feel my heart race, my head swim. They couldn't keep me away if they wanted to. Ziegfeld would grandly escort me to Sardi's, and the tall, handsome man with the dreadfully flat voice would listen as I prattled on and on until, quite finished, he'd signal for the check and stand up, done with me.

So in the morning I didn't linger over breakfast with the *Times*, as I liked to do, nor did I take my obligatory mile-long stroll up Central Park West and down Madison or Lexington Avenue. No, Jed Harris' middle-of-the-night call propelled me into the theater at mid-morning. I sat with David Burton, director of *The Royal Family*, impatiently waiting for George Kaufman to arrive, while we discussed Jed's latest madness. Burton, a dour, serious man with a slight Russian accent, wasn't happy, but he hadn't been happy since day one when Jed, imperious and grouchy from lack of sleep, informed him that directors were lackeys in the employ of the producers and, like all lackeys throughout history, were expedient and entirely forgettable.

"He's not closing the play," Burton told me when I gave him Jed's declaration. "I'll kill him first."

"Take a number." I stood up. "Tell George I can't wait. I'll be back later this afternoon. When Jed swaggers in, beard stubble and all, with a Lucky Strike cloud over his head and cognac on his breath, tell him I need to see him."

Burton shrugged.

Outside, I rushed through Schubert Alley, feeling closed in among the jostling walkers and the dim midday light. Unlike the Selwyn, where the orderly and mechanical rehearsals ran from eleven till five daily, the Ziegfeld Theater was frantic with noise and movement, with crews scurrying all over the place. *Show Boat* was now being installed in the new New York theater. I had a brief meeting scheduled with Flo Ziegfeld's assistant who wanted to review some notes I'd assembled after watching tryouts on the road. I hoped to be back in my apartment by early afternoon.

But the minute I arrived, one of Hammerstein's aides told me, out of breath and avoiding eye contact, that the assistant was still in Philadelphia, horribly and apologetically delayed because the trains weren't running, and my meeting had to be rescheduled.

Grumbling, I turned to leave, but found myself observing the hurly-burly activity in the new, gleaming theater. In the middle of this delightful chaos, the musical director was reading notes to a group of young hopefuls who were auditioning for replacement parts in the Negro Chorus. Illness had plagued the traveling chorus, along with difficulties booking Negro singers into segregated hotels in Washington and elsewhere.

One hefty baritone, off to the side, was loudly practicing the majestic *basso profundo* of "Ol' Man River," sitting in a straight-backed chair, rocking back and forth. A young girl, thin as a rail, was humming to herself in a corner. Fascinated, I watched as the auditions began, the musical director standing alongside a gaunt, hook-nosed piano player. I was thrilled knowing that Broadway finally allowed Negroes and whites on the same stage, though the pairing still was not commonplace—nor sanctioned. Of course, blacks and whites, in some quarters, still could not share a scene together, insane as that struck me, but thanks to Eugene O'Neill's insistence and resolve, that was changing. With *All God's Chillun Got Wings* he hammered down the barrier, despite protestors on the sidewalks who thought American civilization was now in jeopardy. I remember George Kaufman's wry comment to me: "All God's chillun may got wings, but on the American stage only light-skinned folks are allowed to fly over the proscenium."

As I tucked myself into a seat, comfortable in the middle of the unlit orchestra, the young director, a stringy man with colicky fair hair, was telling the singers that they'd be hiring only two performers, one male, one female. Some actors groaned. "Sorry," the man apologized and called out a name. A chubby girl nervously walked onto the stage. Within minutes the pianist struck a chord, and her rich soprano filled the room. I found myself nodding, pleased. One by one, the successive voices swelled and echoed in the hall, and a chill swept up my spine. I closed my eyes, reveled in the sweep of spiritual and plantation work songs, transformed magically by the lyrical mastery of Jerome Kern.

During a break between auditions, I fiddled with a notepad, reviewing the comments I'd jotted down on the road. I needed to leave, but the intoxicating music…

At that moment I sensed someone slip into a seat behind me.

"Miss Ferber." A high, rumbling voice.

I turned and stared into the face of the young man with the sloppy grin. What was his name? Randy? No. Roddy. That's how Waters had introduced him to me yesterday. Roddy Parsons.

"Roddy," I said.

His lazy eyes got wide. "You remember my name?"

"I remember everything, young man."

He grinned and I saw one broken tooth. It gave him a huckleberry-boy look, a Peck's bad boy of the neighborhood. "I'm not that memorable."

"That remains to be seen."

I liked his looks. His slightly puffy cheeks were set against a precise jawline, with lazy, drifting eyes below a high, flat forehead. An expansive face, honest and eager, though a little wary; but it was the eyes, intelligent and deep, a rich mocha brown, that held you, invited you in, made you want to share confidences. And, of course, that lopsided grin. He wore his hair close-cropped and neat, almost military, and probably not popular these days of conked and slicked-down hair. His long body looked graceful as he leaned against the seat. I compared him to Waters, the awkward, skinny boy with the narrow, curious face; and with Lawson, the riveting matinee idol whose look was calculated and sure. There was naturalness about Roddy, a baffling blend of innocence and—what?—not experience, but a suggestion of worldliness. It made for an appealing man, seductive yet aloof. You wanted to hug him. I imagined women found the combination irresistible.

"I wanted to say hello to you yesterday."

I squirmed. "Do we know each other? I know I just said that I remember everything, but I lied. I *felt* I'd met you before."

The smile disappeared from his face for a second. "Washington D.C. Well, you didn't *meet* me, but you stood a few feet away. And you looked right at me."

"When I saw you in my living room yesterday, I thought…"

Again, the captivating smile. Yes, I thought, it must be easy for girls to follow him around, but that powerful grin could well disguise the life behind it. Roddy could be someone easy to misread. Here was a man who might harbor secrets and no one would ever suspect. Now, tilting his head, he pointed to the stage. "I was in the Negro Chorus in Washington. You were at one of the rehearsals. But I took sick, bouts of laryngitis, couldn't go on, so I had to leave the company, come back to New York." He bit his lip. "If I project my voice, I lose it. Doctors figure it's some virus." A hint of a smile. "So, for now, the world can't hear my rich baritone singing your songs."

"Well, not *my* songs. Jerome Kern, I think, would take issue with that."

He laughed. "Everything about *Show Boat* comes from you, Miss Ferber."

Said, the line had sweetness to it. I was used to the blatant flattery, unctuous praise, and the vapid posturing of the slick and glittery Broadway crowd. Or the rich Park Avenue matrons and their dollar-sign husbands, squired around the city in silver-colored Pierce-Arrows or sleek Stutz Bearcats, inviting me to candlelight dinners or to weekends on Long Island. Yet this line, said so softly, had about it a sincerity that momentarily silenced me. But he didn't pause. "So I'm out of the show, but…I don't know, I like being here. So I sit here, in the back row"—he pointed behind us, dramatically—"and listen to the

Negro Chorus. No one tells me to go away. I think they feel sorry for me."

Onstage the hopeful Negro singers began to audition again, this time all of them singing together, in harmony, and I strained to hear Roddy's soft voice speaking into my ear. He leaned in to me and twisted his body. I rose and motioned for him to follow me, which he did, though he seemed hesitant. Once in the lobby, the two of us facing each other, he looked awkward, stepping away from me, plunging his hands into his pockets and then pulling them out. He was the squirrelly schoolboy compelled to socialize with a distant relative, the hectoring spinster aunt. Yet his quiet voice, when he leaned in to me, was lively and questioning, as though afraid he might miss something. I liked his deferential manner, I liked the bright intelligent eyes, and I liked that goofy grin. He stood there, spine erect, though the tilt of his head seemed almost girlish, coy.

"Roddy," I began, "please join me for lunch. There's a coffee shop at the end of the block…" I stopped. My words, delivered so casually, slapped him into silence, the good-looking face closing up, his eyes now shrouded and distant. He glanced quickly over his shoulder, as if seeking a way to flee. Immediately I understood my error. How many workaday eateries in the theater district would gladly entertain a middle-aged white woman sharing a cup of coffee and a tuna salad on rye with a twenty-year-old Negro? Unseemly, perhaps, given the cruel fact that Negroes could not sit alongside whites in theaters, compelled to slink away in the distant balconies, the viciously named "nigger heaven." While we might actually get seated in some grubby little restaurant, there was no guarantee we'd be served. Hostile, disapproving eyes would watch, narrowed. Probably more in tune with contemporary America than I was, at least an America that didn't reside in doorman buildings on the Upper East Side, Roddy understood the simple but awful calculus of a Negro youth having a cup of bad coffee in plain sight of censorious eyes. My heart went out to the strapping lad, standing there fumbling with a loose button on his jacket.

I wanted to talk to this young man, though I wasn't certain why.

I spoke with one of Hammerstein's aides who'd been eying me from an appropriate distance, doubtless having been given the charge of seeing to the untoward and frivolous demands of the temperamental novelist. She'd stepped out into the lobby when Roddy and I left the theater, but she leaned nonchalantly against a back wall, feigning interest in the texture of the wood. When I looked in her direction, she scurried over. "My name is Lorna," she volunteered. She avoided looking at Roddy. Now, hesitantly, she steered Roddy and me into a small dressing room, actually pulled up chairs for us, and miraculously, or so it seemed to me, she wheeled in a tray of covered salads and sandwiches wrapped in waxed paper, as well as a pot of steaming coffee. But she didn't look happy. When I said thank you, she gasped, as though I'd cursed her with a particularly offensive obscenity, and, turning on her heels, she muttered, "No, thank *you*!" That made no sense. Her stern eye moved to Roddy, who purposely avoided eye contact with the skittish woman, though he managed a polite "Thank you" which she failed to respond to. She whispered to me that the food was intended for the absent Ziegfeld assistant—and for me. "In case you wanted lunch. This was for the two of you." She pointed to the spread of food, glancing at Roddy as if he'd usurped a decent man's final meal. I ignored her, and when she blathered on about something, I turned away. She left us alone.

Roddy and I sat at a small table, just feet apart from each other, and I could see he was anxious.

"I'm making you nervous."

"No, you're not," he lied.

"Tell me about yourself, Roddy."

He stammered a bit but grinned. "I don't know what to say, Miss Ferber. Yesterday, you know, when I sat in your living room, I actually believed for a minute that someday I'd be a writer…like you. I mean, Waters invited me to your home, and I sat there… you know…" His face darkened, and he glanced away. "Foolish,

maybe." As he spoke, he seemed to sink into the uncomfortable chair, his arms folding gracefully and his neck bending. He
reminded me of a hardy flower, now suddenly wilting.

"What do you write?" I asked him.

"Poetry, mainly. Short stories." A pause. "I mean, I try to
write…" Another pause. "When Waters asked me to be a part
of his group, I told him no."

"Why?"

He shrugged. "Well, I haven't published anything yet." He
blinked nervously. "And I don't like to show people my stuff.
I'm never…*sure* about it."

"No matter, Roddy."

He held up his hand, a gesture of resignation. "Lawson had a
poem in *The Crisis*. Beautiful. Bella had a one-act play produced
up in Harlem. At a drama workshop at the Lincoln. Everyone
loved it…So I said no, I can't be a part of the group, but Lawson
kept pushing me. He said—why not? Do it, do it. C'mon." He
grinned. "So I did it. Here I am now, sitting with the woman
who wrote *So Big*."

"Will you show *me* your writing? I know you said you don't
like to but…" I stopped. He glanced down at his hands, then
looked over my shoulder. "Last summer, when I sat down with
Waters' friends, I enjoyed reading their work. There's something
about their…energy."

Again the grin. "They told me they were terrified of you."

Now I laughed out loud. "I'm not an ogre, Roddy."

Hurriedly he said, "No, no, it's not that. It's just that, you
know, we all write and talk to each other, but suddenly we were
headed south of 125th Street and into your apartment. And
we're thinking *So Big*, *Show Boat*, Pulitzer Prize. And you were
right there…"

"Well, I hope they've lost their fear of me."

He waited a bit. "I doubt that. A little fear is a good thing, no?"

I nodded. "Good point. Usually I *demand* it in the folks I
encounter. I like people to tremble when I stroll into a room."

For the first time he laughed loudly, a hearty, throaty roar. He threw back his head but then thought better of it, stopping abruptly and looking serious. "I'm sorry."

"For what?"

He didn't say anything for a while. "I'm a little uncomfortable with you, I have to tell you."

"The ogre part of me?"

The sheepish smile. "No, the part of me that's always scared around people."

"Well, I'm glad you're part of the group," I said. "You're a charming young man, smart, and these days I find most young men boors, clods, bounders."

"You don't know me, Miss Ferber."

"I doubt if you fit into any of those three categories." I took a sip of coffee. "I'm glad Lawson is pushing you…"

"Lawson is my cousin, you know. A distant cousin. I read his stuff and I think I can't *do* that."

"Let me judge…"

He was shaking his head furiously. "Not yet. I don't have anything I'm ready to show you. Just yet. Maybe later…"

"Are you sure?" I grinned. "Every day there are budding writers at my door, clamoring for me to read their work. They hand me poems as I step out of taxis."

He was still shaking his head. "No." Emphatic, strong. "Not yet." A sly grin. "Maybe. Someday."

"Lawson is a confident young man." I smiled. "And so is Bella. Confident *woman*, that is."

"That's because they're clever, talented, and they're both so good looking. Everyone falls in love with Lawson. It's like a curse for him." He leaned in, pretending to share a confidence. "The other side of my family. The ones with the better genes. We live together, you know. Uptown in a cheap apartment. I work at a smelly, oily warehouse and Lawson is a hotel janitor. We talk all the time about where we'll end up. He dreams of being downtown on Broadway—the first important Negro playwright—and my most recent dream was singing in the Negro Chorus of *Show Boat*."

"Maybe you'll get your chance again."

"Maybe someone has to die for me to get back up there." Idly, he pointed through the wall toward the unseen stage. "Not worth it. Anyhow, my singing is not the best. There are other opportunities. You know, this whole Harlem Renaissance going on. That's what got us going, Miss Ferber. That's what sparked our group to meet. Harlem is filled with life now. Just sixty or so years after slavery, well, Harlem is a place where black folks have their…their own world. It's like a…Negro kingdom there. The jazz, the shows, it never stops. Harlem is jam-packed with writers and artists and…" His voice rose as his words ended. "Uptown. It's…it's unstoppable."

He hadn't touched the sandwich I'd given him, but now, tentatively, he sipped his coffee. His fingers, long and delicate and dark, trembled a bit as he touched the cup, and I thought: *he's still nervous.* This conversation was a novelty for him—maybe even a violation of some sort. The nosy novelist was making him nervous.

"One time I saw Langston Hughes walking on 136th Street," he said, a hint of awe in his voice. "Ever since he published *The Weary Blues* poems last year, well, he's our hero. The way he uses jazz rhythms…" Roddy's fingers tapped lightly on the table.

I smiled. "Would you believe I met him recently at a party at Carl Van Vechten's apartment? He told me he takes the train in from Pennsylvania, where he's living these days. We had a nice chat, very brief, before he was called away, but he has a way of inviting confidences. I asked him about his poetry, but within minutes he had me talking about growing up in Appleton, Wisconsin. Quite a talent, I thought."

Roddy laughed but looked away, glancing at the closed door. "I should go back. I believe in being as visible as possible. I want them to be aware of the overgrown boy in the back row. Maybe I'll be hired as an understudy. I don't know." Again, he glanced at the door. "And Ellie's meeting me later. She was hoping they might need another girl for the Negro Chorus. You remember Ellie."

"Of course. The quiet girl who sat next to Lawson. The sonneteer. I remember her one sonnet last summer."

"You know, quiet little Ellie with the freckles on her nose is also a wonderful chanteuse. She has an angel's voice."

"A jazz singer?"

Nodding, Roddy stared into my face for the first time. "She's wonderful. Like...like Florence Mills. Sweet but, you know, tough."

"She looks so quiet, Roddy. I can't imagine her on a stage."

"She sings in Negro clubs uptown but they don't pay a hill of beans, Miss Ferber. Especially someone just starting out. But tonight she's singing a few numbers in the early show at a club for white folks. Small's Paradise. You heard of that place? Her big break. Maybe." He reached down into a leather satchel he'd carried over his shoulder and had placed on the floor, and rifled through some papers. He handed me a small flyer, smudged black-and-white type on cheap yellow paper. "We got these done to, well, promote her. Her friends. Me and Lawson, actually. For her brief set at Small's Paradise up on Seventh Avenue. A real important nightclub, you know."

I stared at the crude sheet, and read: "Ellie Payne, Songstress, with the Charlie Johnson Band." A snippet of a review below a grainy snapshot of her. "A jazz singer with a tear in her voice." The quote was from some magazine I'd never read. Roddy saw me reading it. "We made that up," he confessed. "Actually Lawson said it, but no one's heard of Lawson—yet."

"I like it."

"You should come hear her," Roddy said now. "Everyone comes up to Small's Paradise at night. Up to Harlem, I mean. The clubs there."

Everyone except me. The current fad of well-heeled white nightclubers flocking uptown in ermine and pearls held no appeal for me. Lines of sleek limousines idling at curbs, while downtown businessmen ogled the light-skinned showgirls at the Cotton Club or Connie's Inn. Once or twice I'd been escorted by Noël Coward or Aleck Woollcott or Robert Benchley to glitzy nightclubs where syncopated orchestras played New Orleans ragtime or jazz. One time Noël actually got me dancing and a photographer from the *Tribune* snapped my picture. I feared I'd see it published one day…to my utter embarrassment. Fun, those times, but not addictive. Giddy flappers with Dutch-boy bobs and batik scarves looked like errant schoolboys at recess. I tried to ignore the current fascination with hidden-away taboo speakeasies and flowing bootleg bathtub gin and the drunken cheers of "twenty-three-skidoo" and "oh-you-kid." Cat's meow, my foot.

I shook my head. "I spend my evenings in bed with a good book." I reached out to touch his wrist, and he was tempted, I sensed, to pull his hand away. "Maybe someday that book will be written by you."

"You're more of a dreamer than the rest of us, Miss Ferber."

"It's not a bad dream, Roddy."

He was already standing. "That, and five cents will get me a ride on the subway headed downtown."

◇◇◇

Yet, an hour later, as I sat with Jed Harris at the Selwyn Theater, I found myself showing him the cheap flyer.

Jed had arrived at the theater just as a full dress rehearsal ended and the director Burton was reading his notes to the cast. Hearing the menacing stomp of feet behind him, Burton turned, and I saw his face tighten, his lips draw into a thin line. I'd been sitting in a back row seat and watched as Jed, unshaven, with a cigarette dangling from the corner of his mouth, swaggered down the aisle, announced in a truculent snarl that he didn't like what little he'd seen, and had serious doubts about the future careers of those quivering actors up onstage. Walking toward him, Burton shot him a contemptuous look that was lost on the imperious Jed. Running his tongue over his lips, Jed dramatically dropped the cigarette on the floor and crushed it, swiveled around and spotted me sitting in the back row. A sickly smile. "I want another run-through," he declared.

Burton protested. His hand swept over the cast. "But they're exhausted."

Jed was already striding toward me, though he looked back over his shoulder and yelled, "Begin!" His eyes stared, hard and unblinking, yet I swear they were illuminated by the elixir of power.

Defiantly, Burton called for a fifteen-minute break. Groaning, the troupe bristled, but readied to perform again, some stepping into the wings, others stretching their bodies, yawning. Doubled over, Haidee Wright was coughing. The veteran actress who played the domineering matriarch Fanny Cavendish had been grumbling for weeks about the cold, drafty theater, which, she announced more than once, would be the death of her.

"You're not closing the play," I told Jed emphatically.

He huffed and lit another cigarette, blew the smoke toward me, creating lopsided rings in the air. "I know."

"Then why…"

"You're looking radiant this morning," he interrupted me.

"It's not morning," I said in a curt voice.

"For me it is."

"Jed, you're a form of animal life best spotted poking its head out of a warren under a midnight moon."

"Ah, dear Edna. If only you could interject such venom into the lines of *The Royal Family*."

"I didn't know you when I wrote it," I shot back.

"I want a play that's fast-paced, hard as nails, rough-and-tumble."

"We didn't write a Buffalo Bill Wild West extravaganza. It's about a legendary Broadway acting family…"

"*Oy vey iz mir*," he snarled. "Alas, dearest Edna."

For a while, the theater was quiet as the players shuffled off for their needed break. He and I sat and talked. He was obsessed with Ann Andrews' less-than-sophisticated performance, speaking her full name with particular dislike. I kept hoping George Kaufman would show up, though I knew he despised Jed and conveniently tended to forget some of these eleventh-hour encounters with him. His recent comment, famously repeated along Broadway and especially at parties, said it all. "When I die, I want to be cremated and have my ashes thrown in Jed Harris' face." The person who enjoyed this *bon mot* the most, of course, was—Jed.

Tired of his diatribe against the hapless Ann Andrews, I mentioned that I'd come from the new Ziegfeld Theater where I'd listened to last-minute auditions for the Negro Chorus of *Show Boat*, and Jed sneered. "Lord, Edna, you and those Negroes." But he was smiling.

I fumed. "Yesterday in my apartment you seemed particularly fascinated with Bella, the ravishing beauty on the sofa." I watched him carefully.

That gave him pause and he looked over my shoulder, breathed in. "Is she the beautiful girl?"

"Come off it, Jed. You know she is. You recognized her." A pause. "And your glance suggested you'd met the others. Lawson, Roddy…"

"No," he interrupted. Flat out, brash.

"I observe the world, Jed."

"No." He turned away. "Not your business."

Which was the moment I took from my purse the flyer Roddy had given me and showed it to Jed. "One of my budding writers is a jazz songstress who'll be singing at Small's Paradise tonight. Big time. A lucky break for her." He took the sheet from me and read it. "But you probably don't remember Ellie, the quiet, unassuming girl in the corner, the one without the splashy lipstick and marcelled hair."

Snidely: "I notice all women." He leaned into me, purposely sniffed and twitched his nose. "I recognize them by the expensive perfume they wear."

"I'm not wearing perfume."

"You don't need to. You're rich."

"That makes no sense, Jed."

He fingered the sheet. "I've been to Small's Paradise. Wild, thrilling, hubba hubba. Good music, a fantastic orchestra. Good for her. It's a lively, hopping place. No one sits still there, Edna."

I took the flyer back from him. "Well, I haven't been there, Jed. But I've been to the Cotton Club. And I..."

"Tonight," he cut in, "you and me. Let's see if this Ellie can sing. My cab will be at your apartment at eight."

I shook my head. "Oh, I don't think so."

But he was standing up, dismissing me, his head already looking up at the stage where the players had started to reassemble. Walking away from me, he turned back. "Dress up, Edna. That dowdy look you favor doesn't go over in furs-and-satin Harlem. I know my way around up there."

I pursed my lips. "I'm not surprised. Jed. I just assumed alley-cat slumming was something you took to naturally."

Chapter Three

At night, 135th Street and Seventh Avenue bustled and throbbed with a cacophony of rhythmic noise and the blur of bodies in motion. The night chilly streets seemed lit by fire as storefront lights popped on and off, and the occasional wisp of sleet or ice in the air evaporated as it met the steam heat seeping up from the smoky manhole covers. There were scurrying crowds everywhere, hopping from club to club. Taxis and limos unloaded beaming, rushing white folks headed for Connie's Inn or Barron's Exclusive, expensive venues that speckled the side streets between Lenox Avenue and Seventh Avenue.

Jungle Alley, they called it.

And everywhere Negroes crammed into less fancy clubs with shabby canopies and dimly lit windows, sliding past one another, shoulders brushing, thin smiles on their faces. The night cold bothered no one. Everyone was in motion, laughing or yelling or dancing or singing. Nightclub-hopping women, both Negro and white, in red silk stockings and plush feathered hats, in sequined hip-hugging chemises, in garish purple cloches, paused to shimmy or tap or boogie the Charleston. Men watched, and bowed. Everyone roared, happy. Sophie Tucker and her entourage fairly leaped from the taxi that pulled up just before ours slid to the curb. Through the closed window of my cab, I could hear her uproarious, infectious laugh sail across the sidewalk. Fans swirled around her, autograph books open.

Stepping from the cab, Jed grasped my elbow and snuggled in close. I could smell his aftershave, a musky scent more appropriate for the great outdoors than this sleek and glittery avenue. He'd dressed in a tan cashmere Chesterfield topcoat with his usual fedora worn jauntily on his head. His shoes shone like polished agates.

"You look ready for a properly seedy speakeasy, Edna," he'd whispered when I got into the waiting cab back at my building.

Of course, I'd dressed for the evening. I read *Vanity Fair* and *The Smart Set*; I knew how to step into a swank Harlem eatery: a black velvet cloche pulled tight over my unruly curls, a sensible strand of real pearls encircling my powdered neck, and a cerise-and-black dress, low-belted in the flapper mode, cut just above the knee. A mink jacket, snug-fitting, tawny brown, my latest purchase from Gunther's Furrier on Madison. I'd seen the dancing fools at Roseland. In my bedroom mirror I'd thought: *I look like a spangled Floradora girl or a dizzy chorine from a George White Scandals revue.* But no matter. I was out on the town.

Now, pausing on the sidewalk, taking in the hustle of passersby on the jittery street, Jed lit a Lucky Strike and held the pack out to me. I shook my head: no thanks.

"I don't trust a woman who doesn't smoke," he hissed.

"I don't trust a man who lights his own cigarette first."

He narrowed his eyes, then nudged me forward.

Small's Paradise spilled its abundant life out onto the dense-packed sidewalk. I watched as chauffeur-driven limousines and town cars crawled quietly to the curb, jeweled women and top-hatted men slinking out. A slender woman, dressed for summer in a fringed metallic dress, shiny under the streetlights, reached into her escort's pocket and extracted a thin silver flask, and surreptitiously, though seen by all, sipped from the container, shivered, and then let out a peel of high unnatural laughter. Standing feet away from her, I caught her eye for a moment; she seemed rattled, as if she'd spotted her judgmental and puritanical mother. Jed was nudging me along, and we found ourselves stepping down into a cavernous cellar, low-ceilinged and shadowy.

It took me a while to get used to the lights and din of the jumping room, but I did notice Sophie Tucker and her crowd being ushered to a front table, far from where Jed and I nestled ourselves, back by the entrance. We sat at a small, wobbly table, inches from others like it, covered with a pristine white table-cloth. Jed said something but I couldn't hear it over the wailing wash of saxophone and trumpet. As the five-piece combo played, a few couples danced madly next to the waist-high barrier sepa-rating the dance floor from the tables. Jed pointed to the dancers. "Can you shimmy shawobble?" he said into my ear, purposely frivolous. I had no idea what he was babbling about, so I ignored him. Jed read my discomfort. This time, louder, in a pedantic tone: "It don't mean a thing if it ain't got that swing." The man was clearly mad. All around us tuxedo-clad waiters—tall starched Negroes, all—danced across the floor, carrying trays held high, filled with ginger ale bottles and disguised gin in innocent cups. One waiter broke into a loose-jointed Charleston—and never spilled a drop.

It took me a second to realize that Ellie, the modest, shrink-ing-violet little girl who sat on my sofa and seemed to sink into the overstuffed pillows, was onstage. Jed leaned in again. "I'm afraid we came at the end of her set."

"What?" I yelled.

He put his lips against my ear. "The headliner, in an hour, is Ethel Waters." He was grinning.

"So what?" I yelled back. "Ellie looks…amazing."

The loud music abated, and Ellie, stepping up to the micro-phone, began to sing a romantic dirge. Ellie the performer was a creature apart, vivacious, flirty, an alluring chanteuse. As she moved seductively through a haunting "Love Will Find a Way," her voice played off the saxophone player beside her, their bodies tipping seductively into each other. I was mesmerized: I thought of cool water splashed on the face, the deep intake of breath, the feel of soft velvet against powdered skin. I whispered to Jed, "My God, she's wonderful." He didn't answer, and I turned to stare into his face. His eyes were riveted to the exotic singer on

the stage, spellbound, his look displaying a raw covetousness
that jarred, alarmed. Immediately I felt deflated, shunned, the
pleasure ripped away.

At that moment, out of nowhere, I remembered the modest
love sonnet Ellie had written last summer, which she'd been
hesitant to share with her friends in my living room. It talked of
a saxophone player in a shiny powder-blue Norfolk suit and the
way he wailed his instrument, drunk in an alley, as he watched
an orange harvest moon rise over the Hudson. An Elizabethan
encomium to a failed love affair. It had given me chills then.
Now I understood why.

"Amazing," I whispered again, but to myself.

But that was her last number. She bowed a thank you, back
to being a shy schoolgirl. The sax player threw her a kiss as she
left the stage. She was followed by a raucous, whoop-di-do
combo, a band of rollicking men who shifted the tone of the
room, brought the crowd to its stomping feet; shrill whistles of
approval burst out across the floor. Sipping the last of the drink
that had mysteriously appeared on the table, I signaled to Jed that
I was ready to leave. He wasn't: he was staring off into the wings,
where, I noticed, Ellie was having a lively chat with someone.

Eventually, goading him, I got my way, though Jed fussed
and hawed as we strolled back out onto the sidewalk. "The night
is so young," he bellowed.

"We came to hear Ellie," I insisted.

"Maybe you did." He waved his arm, taking in the busy street.
"Christ, Edna, everyone's waiting for Ethel Waters. You know
what I paid to get us in there?" He sighed. "Well, we could go
to the Cotton Club or…"

"There's a cab that just emptied," I pointed out, the shrewish
party-pooper. "If we rush…"

But standing a few feet from me, tucked into the shadows of
a hardware store but positioned so that I would notice him as I
turned, was Roddy Parsons. I was surprised to see him standing
there at this late hour, and alone. I motioned him over.

"Miss Ferber. Mr. Harris." A pause. "Good evening."

Though he'd purposely got my attention, now he seemed hesitant to join us, speaking our names from the shadows while he glanced from me to Jed. Strangely, he was frowning at Jed, which baffled me. But then the frown disappeared in an instant. He smiled at me. "So you came to hear Ellie after all." He sounded pleased.

"Yes, I surprised myself, Roddy. But we only caught the last song. Though, I must say, she has a wonderful voice."

As he walked close to us, he confided, "She can make it downtown on Broadway, you know. We all say that—her friends. She's got the real stuff." He looked at Jed who was then tapping his foot, impatient. "She's new here, so they're trying her out. That's why she only does one early show. And just three numbers. It's a shame, really." He breathed in, nervous. "But she said they *like* her." Stressing the word, he glanced back to the entrance to Small's Paradise. "She should be a *headliner*."

"I sense a 'but' in your words, Roddy."

"She's so shy. She's not…aggressive. Singers got to be…you know…pushy."

"She's like one of those women you don't notice on the street but, once onstage, they seem to come alive." At that moment I was thinking of Helen Hayes, an unassuming and even mousy woman at a party, but once she stepped before blazing footlights, as in her current hit *Coquette*, she dominated, soared, seduced, and demanded your attention.

"I'm waiting to see Ellie home," he told me. "She lives uptown. Two subway stops. I do it sometimes when she does a show around here. We spend some time together." He looked over my shoulder, his eyes taking in the marquee for Small's Paradise. "I'm not allowed to go inside to wait for her." He looked back at me but immediately looked over my shoulder again, up the block. "Bella's with me. We were having coffee at Harry Chang's." He pointed back to a chop suey joint on the corner, the name "Harry Chang's" illuminated in blinking red, though the "H" and the "C" were darkened, making the grubby little eatery somewhat comic.

Out loud I read: "'arry hang's." Roddy showed me that grin.

I felt Jed stir at my side, and I sensed his discomfort. I'd forgotten to introduce him, and I didn't care to.

"Let me say hello to Bella," I said purposely.

An edge to his voice. "Edna, there's a cab," Jed pointed. "You said…"

"It's New York," I protested. He turned his body away from us, his back to Roddy. "There's always a cab, Jed."

Roddy didn't seem happy that we were joining him because his body tensed up and he kept nodding like a broken puppet. Nervously, he strode ahead, walking quickly, telling us over his shoulder that Ellie knew where to find us. When he got to the door of the chop suey joint, he opened but immediately closed it so that the bell clanged, then clanged again, and he stepped back toward us. "Bella's waiting with me." Why was he repeating the line? His face drawn, he was looking at Jed, unhappy. Said, the redundant line came across as an apology.

Inside the tiny restaurant, too brightly lit and too cluttered with stacks of cardboard boxes piled against one wall, Bella watched us approach her table. She didn't look pleased, stiffening her body and closing up her face. I saw her bite her lip. Not happy, the beautiful young woman. She was dressed in a sea-green spangled dress, something designed for a night club, and her face glowed eerily in the off-light because of the heavy makeup she'd applied: thick glossy scarlet lipstick, circles of peach-colored rouge on her cheeks, her large wonderful eyes lined with a dark shadow. I thought it strange makeup for a person not going onto a stage, though I knew many young girls now liked the excessive look, the fair sex freed from Victorian constraint and small-town girl dictates. Yet somehow it all worked because of her lithe graceful body, her velvety skin, and, I supposed, her assumption that men would naturally look at her. She offered us a faint smile that was, of course, no smile at all.

As we shuffled into wire ice-cream parlor chairs, circling her, she turned her body away from that of Jed Harris.

"Have you two met?" I began, glancing from her to Jed.

Jed spoke quickly. "At your apartment. Yesterday. Don't *you* remember?"

"Oh." My oracular monosyllable was worthy of an award. Roddy looked at me strangely.

"We can't stay," Jed added, folding his arms around his chest.

Bella ignored him and asked Roddy, "How was Ellie?" But there was an edge to her voice, hinting not only rivalry, I suspected, but outright dislike.

Watching her closely, Roddy answered by nodding his head up and down. "From what I could hear from outside the stage door—beautiful."

"Of course," Bella sneered. "Perfection."

After Roddy ordered coffee for everyone, he turned to me. "Bella is an actress, you know. Writer…*and* actress." But I already knew that, so I figured he was talking for Jed's benefit, though he never looked at him.

"A lot of good it does me." Bella pushed a plate of cold chop suey away from her—it looked as though she'd nibbled barely a corner of it—to rest in front of Jed. He stared at the congealed, unappetizing mess with disgust.

"In time," Roddy assured her. I could tell he didn't know how to maneuver this awkward small talk. The muscles on his neck pulled taut, dark.

Bella looked into my face. "Everyone promises me the stars, but I seem to get only stardust in my eyes."

"Does Ellie act, too?" I asked.

"No," Roddy answered too quickly. "But can she sing!"

Bella melodramatically rolled her eyes upward with no attempt to conceal her obvious annoyance. She reached across the table and took a cigarette from Roddy's breast pocket. Deliberately, she held it out toward Jed, pointing it at him, waiting for a light, but Jed, who'd been fidgeting with matches after lighting one of his own, didn't budge. Finally, shyly, Roddy reached into his pocket, found matches, and lit her cigarette. Bella blew smoke across the table, her mouth making a faint, whistling trill; and for a second all of us watched, enthralled, as she exhaled the thin line of gray smoke.

The front door clanged as Ellie joined us, dressed now in street clothes, her neck swathed in a bright blue wool scarf. She seemed perplexed at the unexpected visitors at the table, looking from me to Jed, worry on her face. "Is everything okay?"

"I heard you were brilliant." Bella, so snide.

Ellie ignored her, turning to Roddy. "They asked me to return in two weeks. I'm to do a longer set. Maybe midnight on a weekend. They're…" Her voice was bubbly and excited but she stopped. "I'm sorry." She looked at me, eyes bright. "I'm so up in the air."

I sipped the murky coffee an old waiter placed before me, which was a mistake. Tasteless, foul. Some oily concoction best used to lubricate one's touring car. "I only caught the last of your numbers, Ellie, but I must say, I liked it a lot. You have a lovely voice."

She shook her head up and down and whispered a quiet thank you. When she spoke, she was looking at Roddy. "You'll have to help me on a new number. That song from *Shuffle Along* really worked for me. The way you helped me *last* week…"

A curious word to stress, I thought.

Bella interrupted, a smile on her face. "Everyone wants Roddy to help with their stumbling careers." Sweetly, with no sweetness in her voice. "Roddy, you *do* remember you were going to read my play with me…"

Roddy looked from one to the other, but spoke to me. "Bella's finished a play. A full-length play. The part I read was good…" He was nodding his head a little too much.

A gentle diplomat, I thought, but his charming manner only seemed to irk the two women, who stared icily at him.

Bella waved her hand in the air, dismissing the comment.

Silence around the table. "You're all old friends?" I asked.

Bella expelled smoke. "Lawson, when he has time for me, is my boyfriend." Defiantly, Bella reached over and covered Roddy's wrist with her hand, a sudden move that made him jump. He pulled his hand away, embarrassed. Bella laughed a throaty, cigarette laugh, though no one else did.

Ellie was frowning. "Miss Ferber, all the men love Bella."

The line hung in the air, words laced with resignation.

"But end up with you," Bella shot back.

"I think we…" Roddy blathered, the failed diplomat.

"You all live in Harlem?"

Ellie said, "I live a bunch of blocks up from here with my grandfather over on Convent Avenue. Two subway stops. Bella lives with a brother and his wife over on St. Nicholas."

Roddy added, "And Lawson and I live a few blocks away from here. The super of the building is Harriet's father."

"And what about Harriet?" I asked. "She struck me as a strong-willed young woman."

Roddy showed that boyish grin. "She is that."

Bella smirked. "Roddy insisted she be a part of the group. No one asked for *my* vote. So much for democracy. She hardly fits in, trust me."

"Come on, Bella," Roddy said. "She's all right."

Ellie spoke up. "She wants to write political poetry, and she latched onto Waters at some reading, and then onto us. And she was already friendly with Freddy."

I went on. "Yes, what about Freddy? Another fascinating young man." Bella scoffed at that. "Where does he live?"

Roddy took his time answering. "No one knows. You know, we joke about it. All of us. Freddy wanders, checks in with his sister who lives next door to Ellie, sometimes sleeps on her floor. Even Harriet claims she doesn't know. He's the…well, rebel."

"Ah, young writers." I was smiling.

"All *would-be* writers," Roddy concluded. "See what Langston Hughes and Zora Neale Hurston did to us?"

"Ellie," I began, "when I heard you sing tonight, I thought of that sonnet you read in my living room last August—the one about the saxophone player in the alley."

Ellie raised her eyebrows. "Lord, you remember that?"

"I remember the rhythm, the way you played with images. Like your singing…" I paused. "I'd like to read it again."

She intrigued me, this young woman. She had a marvelous face, a pretty face. Bella was harshly beautiful, the blunt beauty of stage vixens; but Ellie had a natural loveliness with her gentle oval face, her soft hazel eyes, her dimpled chin.

I had an idea. "Why don't you have Waters gather your group again? Let's have lunch at my apartment. We'll do it soon. Is that possible?"

"Oh, I don't know," Roddy began. "It's hard to round up folks—to reach people, even by phone. Jobs, you know." He smiled. "Thank you, but..."

"Why not?" I persisted.

He bit his lip. "Well, all right." He stared from Bella to Ellie.

I nodded. "Let Waters know. He can plan it with his mother. I'll tell her about it. A nice lunch." I paused. "Bella, let me read something of your play."

Her eyes got wide. "Well, thank you." Genuine, surprised.

Jed half-stood. "Edna, we..."

I ignored him.

"Roddy, what about you?"

Bella and Ellie both smiled. "Roddy shares snippets of his stories," Ellie said. "Like little prose poems, filled with stark images of Harlem life. He writes all the time but only opens the door...a bit." She rubbed her thumb and index finger together.

"I'm not..."

"Ready," Bella blurted out.

"Roddy'll have those three words etched onto his tombstone," Ellie added.

Roddy seemed to be enjoying the casual ribbing. "I do write. All the time." He breathed in and repeated, "All the time. Really."

"Those aren't the three words," Ellie emphasized.

Roddy blushed. "An editor told me my stories were...stale."

Jed turned his chair to the side, staring absently at a chalkboard menu.

"Let me see one, Roddy," I suggested.

He shook his head. "No, I'm not...you know."

Everyone but Jed laughed. It was an honest, good moment, spontaneous, happy, the tension gone from the conversation. But it couldn't last. As the minutes passed, something else was obvious. Both women leaned toward Roddy, smiling, cavalierly touching his arm, catching his eye, nodding at him. Idle flirting. Ellie reached out and touched his wrist, and Bella flinched. By her own admission Bella was dating Lawson, though it was probably impossible to be involved with a man who understood—and relished—just how good-looking he really was. Yet Bella coyly flirted with Roddy, while Ellie seemed unable to take her eyes off him. Curious, this young trio. And also maddening, I suspected, for the two women; for Roddy, who possessed schoolboy good looks and a gather-near-me sensibility, displayed little interest in either woman. Again, the careful diplomat treading dangerous waters. His kindnesses and attentions came off as perfunctory, routinely friendly. Sensing himself mired in deadly quicksand, he'd decided to dream of rock ledges where he was isolated and safe.

Rocking in his chair, Jed had said nothing during our conversation, spending his time chain-smoking and occasionally glancing sideways at the vivacious Bella, who did likewise. He looked colossally bored. Suddenly, standing so quickly we all jumped, he grumbled, "Enough of this nonsense." Scarcely nodding at everyone, he slapped an outrageously generous five-dollar bill on the table and headed to the door.

"My ride," I commented, standing to put on my coat. "Talk to Waters," I told Roddy. "Rebecca will make a wonderful lunch. Soon."

Outside Jed hailed a cab that had pulled in front of Small's Paradise. An old man and woman had been heading toward it but stopped, startled by Jed's fierce, insistent whistle. I tottered after him.

Settled into the backseat, I turned to him. "You were rude, Jed."
"So?"
'You didn't open your mouth once."
"I figured I'd let you do all the talking for both of us."
"And you *know* them," I insisted. "Don't tell me you don't."

"Rubbish. You expect me to chitchat with that vain and beautiful girl about her jazzbo boyfriend?"

"Lawson?"

"It doesn't matter…"

"They're eager, young…"

"They're a dime a dozen."

"So are you. And me."

"You know you don't believe that, Edna. You're a famous and rich novelist and I'm a famous producer who's also rich." He grinned. "Who's also notoriously rude."

"I don't care…"

"For God's sake, Edna. Slumming in Harlem doesn't mean having coffee with the residents in a grimy chop suey slop hole."

I fumed, turned away.

The cab had been idling at a red light. Through the dusky windows I saw a young man standing across the street from the chop suey joint. I strained to see him because something about him…It was Freddy, I realized, the nomadic young man from my living room. He was standing in a doorway, leaning against a plate-glass window, partially lost in night shadows, but he was gazing, his body rigid, at the trio of friends then leaving Harry Chang's. Or, more precisely: arry hang's. As the cab jerked forward, I twisted my head back, but by now he'd disappeared into the darkness of the street.

Chapter Four

On Saturday morning, watching Waters Turpin as he helped his mother prepare lunch for the young writers, I found myself thinking about him. I'd known the sweet boy for years, of course, and liked his intelligence and civility, a lad who spoke in a soft, buttery voice and yet seemed to have a lot to say. But I hadn't realized his love of the written word until last summer when I spotted him nestled in a wing chair with one of my books in his lap. I paid attention.

For years, when he stayed with relatives during his school breaks, he'd visit his mother at my apartment. I encouraged it because I found him charming, inquisitive, and above all, respectful. I'd even paid him for an occasional chore. My dinner guests knew him not only because he helped his mother serve her delicious meals but because he sometimes bantered quietly but eagerly with the likes of George Kaufman, Aleck Woollcott, and Neysa McMein. He had no fear of celebrity, and they joyfully coddled him.

He spotted me watching him and grinned. "Thank you, Miss Edna."

With Roddy's help, he'd reached everyone, and they were free to come—and delighted with the invitation. But orchestrating this lunch got me thinking how little I knew about *who* they were, these budding writers and performers who were older than Waters and enmeshed in grown-up intrigues. Two visits last summer and that one brief encounter the other day told me little about them. In summer they'd talked about writing, all of them imbued with a kind of bright glow, intoxicated. I had little sense—I really hadn't paid it that much mind—of their differing personalities, their foibles and quirks. I did observe—it was hard not to—that Bella and Lawson were too stunning for their own good, both a little cocky with their accidental birthright; but Ellie…well, nothing at all. Not then. A pleasant enough girl, simply. The writer of the sonnet I enjoyed. I'd imagined her a breathless Emily Dickinson, sheltered among her books.

How much had changed in a day or so! The introduction of newcomer Roddy had shifted that imagined landscape. He was a lad I'd taken to, though I sensed most people were similarly drawn to him. He got me thinking about the dynamic interaction among these new characters. And, I supposed, the new equation that involved Jed Harris, whose obvious recognition at my apartment of Bella and Lawson—and possibly Roddy—suggested another story behind the story. Perhaps a story that Roddy was not privy to. Jed, the incessant yammerer, silenced in that chop suey joint uptown and on the cab ride back downtown. Ellie, transformed from the sweet literary mouse who wrote Edna St. Vincent Millay sonnets into a vampish version of Josephine Baker, though she didn't approximate Baker's notorious shimmying derriere. I was intrigued. The fatigue I experienced at the end of the *Show Boat* tryouts—that gnawing ennui that always followed the writing of a novel or a play—was evaporating.

I'd seen Jed Harris at the Selwyn Theater the following afternoon and purposely mentioned our brief interlude in Harlem—and his uncharacteristically taciturn performance. "That young Bella is a beautiful woman," I began.

His words were clipped. "Too beautiful. I don't know why you're fascinated with *her*. Frankly, Edna, just look into her eyes. That girl is all ambition and money. She wants to own the world."

"So?"

"She's a Negro girl playing with fire." He turned away but glanced back. He locked eyes with me. "Look into her eyes, Edna. What *I* see is ruthlessness. *Evil.*" The last word was icy.

I smiled. "Amazing, Jed. You got all of that from a brief moment in my apartment and a moment in Harlem?"

"She's not that complicated." Now his words were whispered, with Jed a sign that he was seething.

"Of course, but you must have met her before, no?" I probed.

"I've met everybody before. And she's, well, a type."

"That's too easy…"

He walked away.

Roddy was the first to arrive at my apartment, clumsily dropping a book and some typed sheets onto the coffee table. Waters had answered the door, hopping with excitement, and for a moment the two of them playfully bumped each other, some ritualistic testosteronic act I never understood, nor wanted to. Standing in the doorway of my workroom watching them, I heard Waters chuckling about something Bella had said about Roddy. Though Roddy narrowed his eyes at the remark, Waters seemed oblivious to his discomfort.

"She's so…stunning," Waters went on. "She's almost like Theda Bara."

I assumed he meant the outlandish eye makeup and the sultry come-hither glances she hurled at any available male. A flapper vamp, waiting for Valentino to visit her Arabian desert oasis.

I wandered into the room, paused, and foolishly spoke: "Yes, Roddy, Bella *does* seem to favor you." Said so intrusively and loudly, the line came off as hopelessly puerile, a line stolen from a previous century's parlor-room melodrama. Roddy blushed and didn't know where to look in the room. Not looking at me, he mumbled, "She's Lawson's girl, you know."

Waters spoke up. "Sometimes she is, sometimes she isn't. Off and on."

"That's because each one of them wants something the other is *not*," Roddy noted.

"What does that mean?" I asked.

He breathed in. "Lawson and Bella see their futures spent with friends other than…us. People they haven't met yet." He pointed to Waters and himself.

"That's not a testimony of friendship."

He grinned. "Everybody uses somebody else when they're young."

I smiled at him. "You'll discover that the habit doesn't disappear with advanced age, dear Roddy."

Waters wasn't through ribbing Roddy. "And little Ellie, shy as a skittish kitten, seems to have discovered Roddy's charms. Whatever they are."

Roddy shot him an affectionate look, though there was some warning in it. "I don't think Miss Ferber is interested in the twists and turns of young romance."

Now I laughed. "But it's a pleasure seeing you squirm, Roddy."

He chuckled. "I do a lot of that, Miss Ferber."

Waters went on, "Lately Ellie and Bella pull at Roddy like two uptown swells fighting over a last piece of fried chicken."

"Come on, Waters. Enough. Besides most times they *resent* me," Roddy said, an edge to his voice now.

"Why, for heaven's sake?" I asked.

He paused. "Because I don't want *any* romance…now." He shook his head briskly. "Sometimes they fight with me, bloodthirsty, like I'm their enemy. It's just real insane. Like they want to kill me."

"And you fight back?"

He waited a second, reflected on what his answer should be. "I just watch. I figure their battles over me have nothing to do with *me*." He seemed puzzled by his own words. "It's like they discovered how much they don't like each other and I'm there, stuck in the middle, so they use me as an excuse." A pause. "Maybe." He smiled that wide smile. "Although I do got me a fierce temper, Miss Ferber—if the mood is right."

"Are you at all interested in Ellie or Bella?" I asked. "A *little* bit? I'm nosy. Forgive me."

He smiled but didn't answer.

"Bella is Lawson's girl," Waters said.

Roddy, staring around the room, uncomfortable, echoed the remark. "Bella is Lawson's girl. I'm not a creeper."

Waters added, "Bella and Lawson belong together, I think. I don't mean just their movie-magazine looks. Both are real talented, I think. But both'll do anything to get downtown into the money and fame. You know, Miss Edna, Lawson has dreams of having his play produced on Broadway. The new naturalistic drama. Like a Negro Eugene O'Neill."

"And Bella would like to star in it," Roddy added. "I hate to say this, but sometimes I think she stays with him just to see if he'll make it—and carry her along. Still and all, Broadway?"

"You don't seem so sure."

Roddy sighed. "The fact of the matter is that there's only room for this many"—he held up two fingers—"Negroes down here on Broadway. This…this world is hundreds of illusionary miles from Harlem. *De*lusional miles. You know, Broadway goes up through Harlem, but that's not Broadway, if you know what I mean."

"Broadway is Times Square, the theaters," Waters added.

Roddy went on. "Broadway down here changes Negroes. You start out black but get whiter and whiter with each success. Sooner or later, you don't belong anywhere. Certainly you can't come back to Harlem."

Waters hinted, "And Lawson has made some enemies."

That surprised me. "Really? Who?"

He didn't respond, but rushed to answer knocking at the door.

Making an artful entrance, preceded by a strong whiff of heady gardenia perfume, Bella sallied in, dramatically slipping off her gloves. She paused a moment under the hall light, a self-conscious gesture, because the light threw her beautiful face into shadows, the heavily accented eyes gleaming against the skin that was almost translucent white. She was wearing a captivating Charleston flare dress, deep indigo with gold threading. Yes, I thought: *Theda Bara, temptress, exotic, definitely menacing, on the prowl.* The deliberate vamp for the jazz age. A woman ready to turkey trot the night away. She smiled at me and settled into the sofa with a sensuous twist of her body. It was, I thought, a stage entrance, and marvelous at that.

Ellie and Harriet immediately followed, both rushing in and complaining about the erratic and oily subway trains. They'd bumped into each other on an uptown Broadway platform, endured an intolerable delay at the 125th Street Elevated, and then ran all the way to Central Park West from Broadway. Out of breath, stammering, they stopped babbling when Bella, glancing up from her seat, rolled her eyes and mumbled a hideous crack about chronic Negro lateness. "C.P.T." Cynically, she translated for me. "Colored people time." Ellie, reacting as though slapped, turned away, her lips pursed, but managed to greet me with a thin smile. Harriet simply nodded at me. Bella snarled, "Just put it in a chair, girls."

We didn't wait for Lawson to arrive—"He has to sneak out of his job," Bella confided—and Harriet said that Freddy might not show up. She shrugged. "He's that way." I didn't know what that meant, but suspected Freddy, the militant Jack London socialist of this group, had little desire to spend an afternoon among my bourgeois though cherished trappings. How could he possibly tell his friends he spent an afternoon surrounded by my sumptuous lemon yellow curtains made from French-glazed chintz with the fire-red taffeta bunting?

"How do you know Freddy?"

Harriet jumped, surprised that I'd addressed a question to her.

"High school." Just two words, blunt, a student's reluctant response to an annoying teacher.

Harriet also cultivated a rebel's look with her tattered jacket, the sleeves frayed and stained. She struck me as a peculiar contrast to the others, who looked like the educated middle-class offspring of respectable, if struggling, families, the sons and daughters of barbers, teachers, store clerks. Perhaps behind the working-class Trotskyite pose, Harriet possessed a father who was a doctor or lawyer, a parent startled by the revolutionary spirit suddenly appearing nightly at the supper table. No, I remembered that Roddy said Harriet's father was the super at his apartment building. I wondered how Harriet—and the absent Freddy—fit into this loose-jointed budding writer's group.

Rebecca announced that lunch was ready. She stood there beaming, proud, this slender woman with the full, generous mouth and small, warm eyes. I noticed that she wore a new dress, a prim lilac-colored creation I'd never seen before. She looked… well, happy.

She served a lunch of chicken salad, creamy with dill and horse-radish; fluffy winter potatoes slathered in butter; and some exotic green vegetable I knew she'd picked up in Chinatown. She served steaming coffee, licorice flavored, followed by an apple Betty that reeked of clove and cinnamon. Waters scurried around, helping his mother serve, and glowing as his friends gobbled—there was no other word—the sumptuous feast. The chatty crowd, sepa-rated from their books and manuscripts, ate in monastic silence, absorbed in the rich bounty; any random remark by me was met by monosyllabic agreement. Smiling, content, I let them eat in peace.

But as the last of the coffee was poured, I looked at Harriet. "Roddy got you into this group?"

She took a long time answering, as though I were posing a trick question. She glanced at Roddy and finally pointed a finger at him. He answered for her. "Waters had told me that he heard her read at the Y. Then we met at a poetry reading at the Salem Methodist Church, and she learned that Lawson and I had just rented an apartment in the building where her father is the super. Harriet lives in the first apartment. We live just feet away in the back apartment. Weird, no?"

"*When* I live there," she added. "I didn't even know Pop had new tenants back there."

Roddy bit his lip. "Harriet and her father don't get along that great."

She smiled. "There's just the two of us now, and he wants me to go to some low-rent beauty school to be a hairdresser to all of Harlem. Making a living straightening hair and getting rich like A'Lelia Walker." She groaned. "That's when he's not quoting Jesus to me about my bad behavior. Jesus has a lot to say about my behavior, Miss Ferber." A shrug. "I want to write. And maybe to paint. I also want to work with political groups on behalf of the enslaved Negro." She held my eye, challenging. "We're not all brawling in alleys with razor blades or shooting craps while strung out on gin. 'Keep your mouth shut, girl,' Pop warns me. He thinks I'm gonna get arrested. I don't know why. But the NAACP frightens Pop who's happy shuffling along in white America, Bible in one hand, bottle of gin in the other."

She watched me closely.

"Good for you," I responded and she looked to see whether I was serious. "The artist is always an outsider and a colored artist…" I stopped, swallowed my words. "I don't need to lecture all of you."

Anger in her voice. "There are *real* Negroes outside"—she actually pointed out my noontime window—"and they got a story to tell."

Waters jumped in. "Miss Edna tells me I need to tell *that* story."

"You all do," I emphasized.

Harriet's look suggested I'd somehow usurped her vision, a coolness filling her eyes.

Quietly, Roddy whispered, "We all love Langston Hughes and Claude McKay, Miss Ferber. We carry around Hughes' *The Weary Blues* in our back pockets. Our Bible. My *only* Bible. They promise a new world, these writers up in Harlem." His voice got louder and he looked at Harriet. "Miss Ferber met…talked to Langston Hughes at a party."

"Really?" Doubt in Harriet's voice, a little disrespectful, and I could see Waters and Roddy—and even the aloof Ellie—breathing in, unhappy.

"You know," I went on, deliberately now, "he confided that when he was a young boy in Cleveland, he'd hide in the public library and read magazines for hours. He told me he read my early short stories in *American Magazine* and *Everybody's*, stories of Americans struggling to survive—workers in factories, in the stockyards, women as maids, as shop girls. Folks unsung."

I stopped and shook my head. "Enough." It was a vainglorious moment, this crowing, and uncalled for. "Let's talk of your writing." I stood up. "I want to hear your work."

Everyone nodded and looked relieved. As they filed back into the living room, I noticed Roddy saying something into Harriet's ear—and she didn't looked pleased. She shrugged him off, her head tilted. His eyes followed her, angry.

Lawson arrived as we settled into the living room. He made no apology for being late, for missing lunch, but, bounding into the room and sitting in the center of the sofa, his lap covered with notebooks and typed sheets, he did what I expected him to do: he refocused the energy of the room, realigning the planets of his solar system so that, perforce, he was the blazing sun. A raw power, that, and practiced seamlessly. His looks helped, of course—the tan-colored skin taut over high cheekbones and the rigid jaw, the deep-set black eyes with a hint of violet that were almost too large for him, the slender though muscular body evident through the snug dapper-Dan suit he wore, and the blazing cerise necktie appropriated from a page in a fashion magazine. A stunner, this lad. The last to arrive, he was the first to speak, assuming the role of moderator, the teacher calling on students.

"Do your stuff, my hero," Harriet muttered in a barely audible voice.

For the next hour, as we sipped new coffee, I reveled in the verve and spirit of these young writers, exhilarated by the sudden intensity swelling in the room. The petty tensions I sensed among them—yes, Bella and Ellie cast curt glances at each other every so often, and Harriet seemed unable to let go of her simmering distrust of me—now evaporated as each in turn, following Lawson's presumptuous direction, read a short poem or a paragraph of a story or a snippet of stage dialogue. Ellie, at my request, reprised her summer sonnet about the saxophone player, and Lawson and Harriet got into a short debate about the use of traditional literary form to capture Negro street life.

"Read Langston," Harriet said to Ellie. "Not Countee Cullen. Iambic pentameter is real bogus. Read Langston, his jazz and blues stuff. Nobody rhymes any more."

Ellie waited for the others to defend her, but no one did.

Bella read a few paragraphs from a short story she was working on, the opening scene taking place in a jazz club like Small's Paradise. Her prose was purposely choppy, rhythmic, poetic, Gatlin-gun rat-a-tat; and, surprisingly, she read her words in a lilting, affectionate voice at variance with her usual hard-boiled timbre. "He was a gambler at heart," she read her last line, "and a sweet-talking honey man, but he threw the best rent parties in the neighborhood." When she finished, Roddy and Waters clapped. Roddy praised the way she used jazz vernacular in her clipped, tight sentences to mimic street chatter and nightclub atmosphere.

Roddy read one paragraph of a short story he was beginning to sketch out: an exhausted woman swept the stairs in a tenement, her head swathed in old ripped rags, while her spoiled son, decked out in spats and a shiny razzle-dazzle green suit, maneuvered around her down the stairs. I thought it a little contrived though beautifully written, and said so. He kept nodding furiously, the nervous schoolboy, but finally conceded that he didn't know what to do with the paragraph. "I can't find the story I want to write." He shrugged his shoulders. "I don't know why I brought this piece today." He dropped the sheet into his lap, folded his hands over it.

Waters read a two-page story in a faltering, wispy voice, which surprised me. Ellie commented that she liked the way he shot immediately into the heart of the scene. He looked up, grinned at her, almost misty eyed.

Harriet got jittery when it was her turn, painfully clearing her throat and beginning over. But once she moved past her opening lines, her voice took on authority, force, almost belligerence. She read the opening paragraph of an essay she said was intended for the NAACP's *Crisis*, a rousing manifesto of the young leftist Negro in America, climbing what Langston Hughes called the "racial mountain." Finished, she sat back, triumphant, but no one commented. The look on her face said that she'd made her point.

I kept my mouth shut.

Lawson decided to stand when it was his turn. He'd purposely saved himself to the end, something not lost on everyone there. The star attraction. "Everyone expects me to read part of a scene from my play. But no, I won't. You're probably all sick of hearing about my play." He grinned. "You all know that my play can't seem to find a home on Broadway." A long, deliberate pause. "Rejected because it…it is too realistic. Rent parties with ten-gallon crocks of gin and grapefruit juice. The Victrola playing scratchy Bessie Smith records. Because it shows Negro life…"

Harriet interrupted. "Soapbox, Lawson. Get on with it."

A flash of anger. "Which is, of course, what *your* article is all about."

"Would Langston Hughes praise it?" Harriet's voice was sarcastic. And then, surprisingly, a *sotto voce* remark. "The way he praised Miss Ferber's short stories?"

It was a cruel, bitter line, hardly civil, especially since I'd just fed the young lass. Everyone in the room bristled. Waters half-rose, a chivalric knight in defense of damsel Miss Edna, and from the kitchen I could hear Rebecca *tsk tsk* as she eavesdropped on the conversation.

Lawson spoke through clenched teeth. "Could you remember where you are, Harriet?" Then he breathed in and smiled. "No, friends, I'm gonna share my fiction this time."

Bella groaned, but Lawson ignored her. What he did read, in a deep, throaty voice, was actually riveting: perhaps one hundred words about two men sitting next to each other on the "A" train, one young man irreverently humming a spiritual while the other, a disheveled old man, recalls a race riot he'd lived through as a boy. Simple, evocative prose, unsentimental.

"Those are characters from your play," Roddy noted. He looked at Lawson quizzically, mystified.

"So what?"

"I like it," I said. "What happened to your play?"

Another groan from Bella, though she followed it with a smile.

Lawson shrugged. "*Harlem River*, Miss Ferber. It's been rejected over and over, even uptown at the Lincoln. Negro producers afraid of its…rawness. I don't understand why." He was walking around now, antsy, a bead of sweat on his brow, and he moved quietly to the window. He turned to face us. "You know how it is." The line thundered in the room, stark and bold, and emphatically ended the conversation. "So now I'll go back to my novel."

Harriet grinned. "Christ, another pickanniny scribbling The Great American Novel."

Another flash of anger. "Well, why not?"

Bella was watching the fury build in Lawson. I could see some humor at the corners of her eyes. "Could I star in the film adaptation?" she asked coyly, batting her eyelashes. "Or do you insist on Clara Bow in black face for the role?" He ignored her, though I noticed his lips trembled. "You could sell it to the Famous Artists' Studio."

Lawson seethed. "I'll make it before you do, honey."

"We'll see about that."

No one said anything, but we all stared at the flash fire between the two lovers.

"It helps to be a…female," Lawson spat out.

"Just what are you saying?" Bella countered. "I'm a good girl." She turned to me. "You know, Miss Ferber, Lawson tried for a part in a Jed Harris production, and was cruelly and publicly dismissed."

"Jed? What play?" I was baffled.

Now Roddy stood up. "Ridiculous. It was not a Jed Harris production, Bella. And you know that. Just cut it out. It was a play produced by some friend of his. A musical revue with a Negro cast. Yes, Mr. Harris was there. But could we stop this bickering, you two?" He pointed to the ostentatious Steinway grand piano nearby. "Look where we *are*."

There was something comical about the moment, such innocence in the line, such foolishness, as everyone mechanically

stared at my piano. Ellie and Harriet burst out laughing. Even
Bella and Lawson, both on edge, were shaking their heads, smiling. Cathartic, the moment, yet I couldn't understand the raw,
gnawing tension between Bella and Lawson, other than the fact
that here were two worldly and ambitious young people whose
photogenic looks and native intelligences had not yet given them
lives they believed they were destined to lead.

"Everyone seems to be writing a novel," Roddy said into the
silence.

"Even you?" I asked.

"Of course." A pause. "Sort of." A chuckle. "Maybe."

Again, the laughter in the room.

"Powder room," Ellie whispered to me. Waters pointed to a
hallway. "First door on the left." She nodded and left the room.

The moment Ellie was out of the room Bella whispered to
Lawson in a biting tone, "Someone should tell her how to dress."
Lawson groaned. "I mean," Bella went on, "she looks like a rag
doll in that Victorian smock." Raw, malicious words, said fiercely,
coldly. She avoided looking at me as she crossed her legs and
revealed her own fashionable attire, the flapper dress and her
strapped high heels with the wide buckles.

Roddy defended Ellie. "For God's sake, Bella."

Bella rolled her eyes. "Roddy always defends the indefensible.
Booker T. Washington, begging and scraping, singing coon songs
on Fifth Avenue for a plug nickel."

Roddy said nothing.

Waters was shuffling his papers. "I hope I don't get this nasty
when I grow up."

The line made me laugh out loud.

Lawson spoke to Waters but he was looking at Bella. "Waters,
you're still a boy. You haven't met women as wicked as Bella
before this. I hope you never do. They're…hard-boiled eggs."
He was staring directly into Bella's face.

"Bottle it, Lawson," Bella sneered.

Someone knocked on the door, and Waters rushed to get it.
He stepped aside as Freddy walked into the room. Dressed in a

bulky military parka, a street-arab pork-pie cap pulled over his forehead, he mumbled something about losing track of time.

"It's because you can't tell time yet," Bella said.

Freddy ignored her, though he glanced at Ellie. Then, surprising me, he planted himself in the entrance to the living room, his parka still buttoned, his face still stiff with winter cold, and, uninvited, began to recite from memory a short poem, his rapid-fire rat-a-tat delivery a little spine chilling. It was rebellious verse, the lines filled with bitterness about a vicious Southern lynching of a feeble old black man, his hailstone words bouncing off my expensive walls. Cold, cold, yet under the stanza a fire that seared. Stunned, I didn't know where to look—me, the only white soul in the vast room. Freddy never looked at me. He didn't care that I was there, that it was the drawing room of Manhattan privilege and wealth and fame. My subdued kingdom, ruled by me from my red moiré armchair. He had something to say. Rebecca had stepped into the room and Freddy kept glaring at Rebecca and Waters, mother and son, back and forth, accusing, harsh, unforgiving.

When it was done, Freddy backed against the wall, arms folded over his chest, and stared across the room toward the polished windows. Out there was Central Park and yellow taxis and uniformed doormen and…and I felt foolish, sitting there in my expensive shoes and expensive haircut. I felt guilty, and I didn't savor the feeling. I didn't *believe* I was guilty, yet Freddy's insistent stare and those violent images echoing in my head made me want to apologize.

Chapter Five

On a brisk Monday morning, sleet slapping the cab window, I headed for the Ziegfeld Theater for the rescheduled meeting with Flo Ziegfeld's assistant. A waste of time, this meeting, since *Show Boat*—already pruned and polished and gussied up—was set to open. Crews were already erecting the elaborate Mississippi River scenery onstage. So…a perfunctory meeting at ten, an unnecessary review of last-minute changes, my scribbled suggestions analyzed as though they were ancient unearthed cuneiforms, the out-of-town reviews scrutinized. Window dressing, all of it, more sycophantic posturing, more blather about the musical as masterpiece. I wanted to believe all of it.

Of course, after rushing under a proffered umbrella to the stage door, I soon learned that the assistant had not arrived from her home in White Plains. Blame the inclement weather. Blame the faulty trains. No one had tried to call me. I told the frightened young man who informed me of the delay that I'd rather blame frail mankind. The young man apologized over and over, took the blame, which made no sense unless he moonlighted as the God of Thunder and Hail, and nudged me toward a coffee pot and a pile of trade magazines. "I am not an ingénue trying out for a walk-on," I sneered, and he actually trembled.

"I…"

"Never mind." I deepened my voice. "I'll remain here and stare at the peeling walls."

Which is what I did because I was meeting Waters in the lobby at eleven. I made myself an obvious nuisance, pacing the floor of the small meeting room, and the young man—"My name is Jimmy, if you need me"—a rubicund youngster with pink cheeks and a Renaissance cherub's head of curls, kept appearing at my side. "I did leave a message with your house-keeper," he said finally, which I figured he'd just done, believing in time machines and the failure of clocks in my apartment.

"Idle time spent in cramped, moldy theater quarters is a deadly sin," I told him.

Luckily, Waters showed up early, ambling in, lingering in the lobby. Jimmy reluctantly led him to me. Overjoyed, I embraced Waters in gratitude.

"You look unhappy, Miss Edna," he greeted me.

"I've been marooned on a theatrical island."

He squinted. "I thought you had a meeting."

"What gave you that idea?"

I told Waters to sit down, and immediately the Botticelli cherub asked if I needed anything. He eyed Waters with open suspicion, his pale gray eyes narrowing at the sight of the skinny Negro boy chummy with the cranky authoress. Waters was dressed in a creamy off-white Joe College V-neck sweater, volu-minous pleated brown trousers over black-and-white tie shoes. He looked ready to play nine rounds of golf at an all-white country club in Bucks County.

We sat on straight-backed chairs, paint stained, and I sipped coffee while Waters sat opposite me, hands folded decorously in his lap. It looked as if I were interviewing him for a job, one he knew he'd never get. "Relax, Waters," I insisted. "We have time to kill. Clearly my meeting is not going to take place. White Plains is obviously now located in Outer Mongolia, and thus inaccessible save by yak and muscular Sherpa."

He laughed. "No rehearsals here today?"

"I guess not. The set is going up. Hear the clamor?" We could hear banging and shuffling, which put my nerves on edge.

"Sort of creepy sitting here in this room."

"Welcome to the world of backstage." A pause as Waters looked everywhere but at me. I was impatient—and antsy. "Waters, since we have some time now, I've been meaning to ask you something." His eyes got wide, flickering, gold specks in the corners of his deep black pupils. I laughed. "Nothing *that* serious. It's just that, well, the other afternoon at my apartment there was such…such tension. The spitfire anger. Last summer everyone was so quiet and polite." I shrugged.

A heartbeat, then his soft-spoken words. "Last summer everyone was on their best behavior in your apartment."

I'd suspected that. "Well, it's a comfort knowing I can still intimidate young folks for no reason. I hope I haven't lost my power to wither a few souls. Nevertheless, the other afternoon…"

He smiled. "I'm certain that's true, Miss Edna, but, you know, things have been bubbling to the surface lately. I don't understand a lot of it. Last summer Bella was going out with Lawson, and then *not* going out with him. I think it was real casual with them. Nothing serious. Ellie rarely spoke up. There was no Harriet, no Freddy. You can tell that Bella doesn't like them in the group. They're too crude for her. They see her as phony high class. Dicty—Harriet's word. But I like them. And Roddy wasn't part of the group then. The fact of the matter is that *he's* the lightning rod."

"Roddy? But he's so…charming, unassuming…"

"Yeah, he may be that, but I'm thinking that may be the problem. He sort of likes to keep away from everyone, real private, and that makes everyone *want* to be with him. When he talks to you, it seems like you're the only person in the whole world he wants to be with. It's a strange power to have."

"Well, he certainly made me like him."

"Join the club."

"You're his good friend, no?"

He thought about his words, his eyes drifting round the room. "Well, we're friends. I don't know about the 'good' part. You get to know only bits and pieces of him. If you push him, he can get moody. I've seen him in a real bad mood. He…he explodes." He shrugged as if he had no other explanation.

"I like him."

"I repeat, Miss Edna. Everyone likes him. But no one really *knows* him." He swallowed. "Sometimes I think he likes playing games. Sometimes it's like he's so much older than the rest of us."

"What do you mean?"

"I mean, he's only twenty, I guess. I'm the kid, and Bella and Lawson are a few years older. But Roddy…it's like he knows something…" He shook his head. "I don't know what I'm talking about."

"But what is he all about?"

Waters took a long time answering. "People who smile all the time sometimes got a lot of demons inside them." He shook his head. "That's my mom talking to me."

I grinned. "Sounds like your mother."

"But it's not hard to see that in some people."

"Some people go through life and never see it, Waters." I leaned in. "But Bella seems to flirt with him—in front of Lawson, no less."

"Because Ellie *likes* him, you know. The two, back and forth, rivals. He keeps both at a distance, which means they go crazy chasing him. 'Roddy, you promised to help me with my story, my poem.' That kind of remark. Roddy this, Roddy that. I know it irritates Lawson. He's said some things to Roddy, not nice things, and Roddy stared back at him, hurt in his face, that sad puppy dog look. It's funny because Lawson found himself apologizing to Roddy, and he's not the kind of guy who likes to apologize to anyone."

I paused. "Is Roddy a good writer? That paragraph he shared the other day was beautiful, if a little stiff."

"He writes all the time—like he sings all the time—but it's only his singing that he shares with the world."

"That's strange, no?"

"It's like he doesn't trust himself, Miss Edna. Even his singing now—you know how he left *Show Boat* because his voice kept disappearing? We all wondered at that. But I heard him singing one day when no one was around. It sounded perfect to me.

Roddy believes he can only fail. It's like someone *told* him that. Just as Bella and Lawson believe they can only succeed."

"Roddy promised to show me his work when he's…"

"Ready." He finished for me. He laughed. "He says that all the time."

"Let's hope he's ready today."

Waters and I were headed uptown to pick up Roddy at his apartment. On Saturday Roddy had lingered when the lunch at my apartment was over, watching the others leave and then helping Waters and Rebecca clean up. He'd been in a chatty mood and even promised to let me read more of his fiction. "I *am* finishing some stuff," he insisted.

Waters had leaned in, joking, even poking Roddy in the side, teasing that Roddy's mysterious and long-awaited work was a satirical fiction based on his friends' lives, some contemporary hard-biting comedy of manners that centered on the young black intelligentsia of Harlem—not the famous "Niggerati Manor" on 136th Street, that rooming house with the black and red walls, where writers like Hughes and Wallace Thurman and Zora Neale Hurston lived rent-free—but a biting, cynical portrayal of undiscovered writers, a look at struggling folks like Bella and Lawson. The remark stopped Roddy as he moved with cups and saucers, and I felt Waters had punctured Roddy's secrecy. Bella and Lawson as protagonist and antagonist in a modern-day Harlem intrigue, with the delicious addition of gentle Ellie and her silver-throated jazz voice. Maybe even Harriet and Freddy, the street chorus chanting to the pulse of upper Seventh Avenue.

"Is that true?" I'd asked him then.

He didn't answer.

"I knew it," Waters exclaimed. "You better make me better looking, more talented, and…older."

"I'm not much older, Waters. Twenty."

"Well, make me the same age. No one takes a seventeen-year-old seriously."

Roddy, very soberly, "I do. That's the age I left home for good."

I found myself watching him: the casual, almost delicate gestures, the soft puppy eyes, the languid dipping of his head, the grin.

"Why did you leave home then?"

He debated what to tell me. "We were living out in Brooklyn, far out, forever by subway, so far from Manhattan it was like another country, and my Mama died around the time I turned sixteen. Papa struggled as a plumber but never had any money because he drank it, gambled it. A decent guy, maybe, but a real mean drunk, brutal. Beat me up so's I had black eyes, stuff like that. You know, he didn't *like* his kids. As each kid hit sixteen or so, out the door. He married a fierce woman who blamed me for everything, lied about me, real nasty, mocked me because I wouldn't fight her back, said I ate too much, was home too much, so I just left."

Waters was staring at him, as if hearing the story for the first time. "Roddy, how come you never told me this?"

Roddy looked into my face. "I wanted to move to Harlem anyway, where the life was. I lived here and there, with different people I met, worked dumb jobs, sold papers, a stock boy at a cigar store. You know, I never finished my last year of high school but I always had a library card. That was important to me. Last year I bumped into Lawson at the bookstore up on 136th Street, the Hobby Horse, a place that sells Negro writers' stuff. I recognized him because I'd seen him at a family funeral a couple years back." He smiled. "He's sort of memorable."

Waters looked at me. "Lawson is Roddy's cousin, Miss Edna."

I nodded. "I know. I keep being *told* that."

Roddy laughed. "Maybe because we're so different. I never got his drop-dead looks. Anyway, he'd drifted to Harlem from Philly, where his family lives still. His father is a carpenter, got his own house, I hear. Lawson came to New York to be an actor and a writer. He's a couple years older than me, you know. Well, he got thrown out of an apartment he shared with some other actors—he didn't like to pay his share, still doesn't, truth be told—and we decided to room together."

"When did you meet Bella?" Waters asked.

"Right after I came to the city."

"Was she seeing Lawson then?" I asked.

"Why?"

"Bella likes you."

He shook his head. "No, she doesn't. She thinks she does."

Looking as if he'd shared too much with a stranger, Roddy bustled off to the kitchen, and Waters looked at me, puzzled.

"What?" I asked.

"In one second you learn more about him and Lawson than I did after all this time."

"I'm a reporter, Waters. I ask questions."

"I ask questions, too. But people don't answer me."

I touched his shoulder. "That's because you're seventeen."

"My point exactly."

Before Roddy and Waters left together, I'd asked if they wanted to join me for lunch on Monday.

Which was why Waters and I, hailing a cab in front of the Ziegfeld Theater, were headed into Harlem to gather Roddy from his apartment. Flo Ziegfeld's assistant never did show up, and I left without informing the apologetic young man who'd tried to keep a watchful eye on me.

"Did you remind him we're coming?" I asked Waters as we settled into the back seat of the cab.

"No answer. Sometimes they don't pay their phone bill."

"Really?"

"Not everyone is rich, Miss Edna."

"Thank you, Waters. Now you sound like Harriet or Freddy reading a rousing manifesto in my living room."

Despite the chill and the wisps of light snow in the air, Harlem at midday was a rag-tag kaleidoscope of sidewalks crammed with strollers, folks weaving around mothers lazily pushing carriages with squawking toddlers, men and women chatting, gazing into shop windows, running to cars double-parked in the street. Outside a lunch counter a group of young men leaned into one another, two of them sporting snazzy leopard-skin overcoats.

Every head turned as a trio of pretty young women sauntered by, each one in snug-fitting coats, heads covered in cloches so red or blue or yellow the hats seemed dabs of shocking color on an artist's palette. Arms entwined, they ignored the grinning, foolish young men, though I noticed one woman glanced back over her shoulder as they passed. She tittered. One of the men bowed and did a sudden flirtatious dance step. He doffed his fedora to the woman.

Waters was looking elsewhere. "There," he yelled. "The Spot." He was pointing to a tiny eatery tucked in between a cigar store and a florist, a drab-looking place, unpretentious, the name of the restaurant announced in a bold, black-lettered sign nailed over the door, with jagged words painted below: "Where Everyone You Know Is Waiting For You." Here, I knew, whites and blacks could mingle freely together without a disapproving eye. They could sip famous-though-notoriously-bad coffee, munch on glazed raised sugar doughnuts, and, the more adventurous, a generous slice of rich sweet potato pie.

But it wasn't the abundant confections that attracted folks to the place. Here, according to the ticker-tape scribes in *Vanity Fair*, writers like Langston Hughes, Wallace Thurman, Zora Neale Hurston, and even W. E. B. Du Bois, occupied tables with famous whites folks like Carl Van Vechten. Here the painter Aaron Douglas lingered throughout the winter afternoons. Here, once, Aleck Woollcott, meeting Negro novelist Jean Fauset for lunch, drank a whopping twenty-five cups of coffee—according to him. "More like twenty-five slices of sweet potato pie," I'd jibed. Here, now, I was treating Waters and Roddy to lunch because neither had been there, though both desperately wanted to go. The problem was that The Spot made you wait for tables, customers huddled in an overheated entryway, sometimes for an hour. Once inside they paid fifteen cents for a cup of that horrid coffee. Every other eatery, even down on swank Park Avenue, charged five cents. Yet people clamored to get in. City legend maintained that our beloved jazz mayor, the Broadway dandy Jimmy Walker, once was forced to wait for a table, and wasn't happy.

The cab cruised past Small's Paradise, and I noted how drab and downright suspect it looked during harsh daylight; only nighttime, with its glitzy lights and creeping shadows and tinkling streetlights, gave the place its allure. The cab turned down 138th Street, west of Seventh Avenue, and came to a stop midway down the block. I shooed Waters out the door, told the cabbie to wait at the curb, and surveyed the building where Lawson and Roddy lived. A five-story classic brownstone, shabby and dark, with chipped and missing bricks and some cracked windows, one with a board nailed across a shattered pane; a cement stoop, much repaired, with a peeling black wrought-iron railing; and a broken light fixture hanging off loose wires over the entrance. A glass panel in the front door had shattered, a lacy spider's web. The building looked desperately poor, blighted, though once it had been a stylish structure. The midday sun glinted off the upper windows, but the lower floors lay shrouded in unrelenting shadow.

Waters was taking his time, and I kept checking my watch. The cabbie, a wiry Irish lad with mushroom carrot hair and a slough boy cap, was whistling a tune that was starting to grate. The longer we waited, the shriller the discordant tune. I knew Waters was not idly chatting with Lawson because on the ride uptown he'd mentioned that Lawson stayed most nights at Bella's, a few blocks away, where Bella's indifferent and often soused brother didn't care. He came home simply to change into his janitor's uniform before heading to work.

The super, Mr. Porter, Waters said, was a born-again Bible-thumper who frowned on young women visiting the back apartment where Lawson and Roddy lived, and more than once raised a stink. Certainly young women could not stay over. Of course, Waters confided, Roddy and Lawson often entered through a little-used back door off the back alley, sometimes with friends.

"I think it's awful myself, such goings on," Waters told me, a severe puritanical look on his face. Bella, he told me, lowering his voice, had slipped in by way of the back door one time, but the super heard her raucous laughter at two in the morning and pounded on the door. He'd dragged Bella out, somewhat dishabille, while spouting appropriate Bible verses at her. Interestingly, Roddy claimed, Mr. Porter was a drunk who spent most of his money on the working girls who were housed at Madame Turner's up on Convent Avenue. On Sundays, all day, he worshiped at the Abyssinian Baptist Church between Lenox and Seventh Avenue, where he prayed for the girls he'd entertained or who entertained him the night before.

"My, my, Waters," I'd said, "you certainly have some gossip to share! How much of this is true?"

Wide-eyed, he assured me it was all gospel.

As I was mulling over this sordid tale about the superintendent, his daughter Harriet emerged from the front entrance. Dressed in a crisp blue-and-white waitress uniform worn under an unbuttoned black cloth coat, her hair tucked under a redvisor cap with the name of a restaurant I couldn't make out, she seemed harried, stopping at the top of the stoop to adjust the slippery cap, then bounding down the steps onto the sidewalk. I was about to roll down the window to say hello and to ask whether she'd spotted Waters inside, but she hurried away, her coat flapping in the chilly breeze. For a second, as she came within feet of my idling cab, I thought she'd spotted me, my curious face pressed against the glass like an expectant birthday child. But she seemed to have no curiosity about the cab—nor the nosy white woman inside. She bent her body slightly, her face tilted toward me. Her lips were drawn into an angry line, but then, I told myself, she'd worn that same look at my apartment as she sat chummily in a green silk wing chair balancing a cup of coffee.

Twisting my head, I followed her swift movement on the sidewalk, her determined, haughty strut, as she wove around dawdling pedestrians. I didn't hear Waters approach until he knocked on the cab window. I jumped, startled. He simply stood there, frozen, his face ashen, his fingers trembling against his chest. Panicky, I rolled down the window. "What? For Lord's sake, Waters…"

He was shaking his head back and forth, his neck stiff.

"Miss Edna."

"What?" I stammered.

"Roddy is dead."

His words made no sense. I was sitting in the back seat of a yellow cab on a crisp winter day on a street where Negro children skipped by, their bodies bumping into one another, while mothers dragged tiny metal carts filled with bags of groceries. "What?"

"Murder." He could hardly say the word.

He stood there, frozen, so I jumped out of the taxi, wildly tossed some dollar bills at a disgruntled cabbie anxious to speed off, and I grasped Waters' shoulders, shaking him until he opened his eyes. He was sobbing, fat tears running down his cheeks. "Follow me." Not certain what I was doing or why, I rushed up the steps, my heart thumping. Waters was my hovering shadow, following so close to my back I could smell his hot, nervous breath. I turned to him. "It's all right," I sputtered, though I knew, to my marrow, that it wasn't—that this horrid moment would define his next few months, maybe years, perhaps a lifetime.

Inside I strode down the long narrow hallway, momentarily stopped by the acrid smell of burnt beans, old flaking paint, noxious stomach-turning disinfectant. The walls were painted a deck green, chipped, streaked; the floor was murky gunmetal gray. My eyes kept darting from wall to floor, taking in the revolting colors. Why would anyone choose to color this bleak canyon with paint that took away your spirit? I walked instinctively to an apartment I'd never visited, but at the back of the first floor, turning to the right, I spotted an open door.

Everything about it suggested a picture I didn't want to see.

What I noticed first was the doorjamb, a few pieces of splintered wood, as if someone had pried open the old lock and gouged the wood. I touched nothing. A tiny living room, boxlike and dark, with a beat-up and stained blue sofa and a straight-backed chair, turned over; a small side bureau with the top drawer pulled out and dropped onto the hardwood floor. A sparse room that looked unlived in. Two bedrooms beyond the messy kitchen: both doors wide open. In the first I could smell something sweet, unpleasant, cloying. There, sprawled in bed on his back, Roddy lay, half-covered with blankets, his bony chest exposed, the shaft of a knife planted where, I supposed, the human heart lay. His eyes were open, a look of absolute bafflement in them, his long, handsome face, convulsed now in a death grimace. Involuntarily, I cried out, and at that moment Waters began to wail.

Blindly, I sputtered, "Help! We must call…"

I staggered out of the room, trailed by Waters, and losing direction, I stumbled into the other bedroom. Lawson's room. Bureau drawers were pulled out, clothing scattered on the floor, the contents of a desk strewn willy-nilly about, with sheets of white paper, typescript, scattered across the floor as if someone, in haste, had used an impatient hand searching for something else. Waters was mumbling, but I didn't understand what he was saying.

"We need to call someone," I told him.

I followed Waters out into the hallway to the front of the building where he pounded on the super's door. Inside a radio played loud gospel music. The rasping, gargled sound Waters was making—I thought of wounded forest animals, trapped, dying—scared me. Minutes passed, unbearably so, until at last the door opened a crack. A bleary-eyed old man in a ripped undershirt, an unlit cigarette stuck in the corner of his mouth, seemed ready to berate the offender, but the sight of the pale white woman and the young Negro boy rocking at her side doubtless refocused that plan. "Yeah? What?"

"I need to use your phone," I sputtered.

"No," he said. That surprised me.

Waters pushed forward and pleaded. "Roddy's been murdered."

His brow furled, the man stuck his head out the door, peered in the direction of Roddy's apartment, and then frowned. "Yeah?"

"Phone," I insisted.

But he wouldn't let us in, though I tried to step around him. He'd place the call, he said. We were to wait in the hallway. The door slammed shut. "Good God," I roared. "Is the man crazy?"

A few minutes later he opened the door and announced the cops were coming. Then, like that, he slammed the door shut again.

Waters whispered, "That's Mr. Porter. He doesn't like people." As if that explained his bizarre behavior.

"But murder…" I shook my head.

◇◇◇

Minutes passed. We stood in that awful gray and green hallway, my eyes shifting between the oppressive battleship walls and the depths-of-hell linoleum.

"What are we gonna do?" Waters asked. He'd cradled his arms around his chest and was bouncing back and forth against the wall.

"We wait."

The front door opened. Lawson strolled in, yawning. When he spotted Waters and me standing beneath the dim hall light, he looked baffled, as if he'd entered the wrong house, but then he smiled. "Are we up to something today?" Light-hearted, bantering. But there was something wrong with his speech, his words slurred, a hesitant drawl. In the faint hallway lighting I thought his eyes looked bloodshot. Could he have been drinking so early in the morning? My Lord, was the lad staggering home from a night at a speakeasy? Dressed in a spiffy charcoal gray suit, the pants wrinkled and the shirt pulled out of his pants, he carried his overcoat slung over his arm. He looked like he'd just tumbled out of bed. Which, no doubt, he had.

"We all going out?" He had trouble saying the line.

"Lawson," I began. "There's trouble. Roddy is dead…"

He actually grinned, though his eyes closed dreamily.

"No, Lawson…"

He shuffled by me, a drunk's lazy walk, though I put out my hand to hold him back. Waters and I followed him into the apartment. He stopped in the kitchen, reached for a glass, and glanced back over his shoulders at the sideboard drawer on the floor, its contents scattered. "What the hell?" Puzzled, he looked at me as though I were the culprit. Then he headed into the small hallway and, though Waters called out his name, he reached the entrance of Roddy's bedroom. I saw his back stiffen, the muscles in his neck jut out. He turned, tottered against the doorjamb, ready to faint. But still that line of a smile, plastered on now, frozen. "I don't understand," he said. He glanced back into the room and from where I stood Roddy's grotesque corpse stared back, ghoulish now, frightful.

Then Lawson moved to his own room, and the first words out of his mouth startled me. "Who opened my damn door? No one is supposed…"

Inside, he paced across the mess of typed sheets covering the floor. Staring down at his feet, he seemed suddenly to wake up. "Goddamn it." He swung his body in circles, taking in the chaos. Frantic, he rushed to a bureau and yelled something about a ring. "Money." Then, as Waters and I watched, stupefied, he crumbled to the floor, his face trembling with fury, as he grabbed the typed sheets. Some were ripped, crumpled, smudged. Insanely, he cried, "One hundred one, one hundred three. Where, Christ, is one hundred two? I can't find it." He started gathering the sheets to his chest.

He had to stop when the cops rushed in and, surprising us in Lawson's bedroom, demanded that we leave immediately, wait in the hallway until summoned. "What are you doing in here?" one cop yelled. "Get the hell out of here."

So we stood in the hallway by the front door, waiting for the police detective to call us. I was trying to memorize the details of the apartment. The chaos, the knife, the body. Waters, the tears dry on his flushed cheeks, leaned against the wall with his eyes closed.

Lawson was sitting on the floor next to Waters, his knees up against his chest, his head rocking back and forth. He was sobbing loudly now, little-boy breathless gulps. He kept looking at his hands, as though missing the typed sheets. The police had refused to let him carry them out of the apartment. He wailed so loudly that the super cracked the door and grumbled, though he quickly slammed the door shut. And I didn't know, as I watched the crazed young man, whether he was sobbing for the dead Roddy or for the destroyed manuscript covering the floor of his bedroom.

Chapter Six

The next morning, battling a headache that crowded my sleep with nightmares, I skipped my usual brisk one-mile walk. Instead, achy with fatigue, I lingered over two cups of hot coffee and buttered toast, then canceled appointments with both my hairdresser and my dressmaker—and ignored a call from Ziegfeld's office about rescheduling yesterday's missed meeting. I'd promised Detective Carl Manus that I'd appear at his precinct in Harlem to give my valueless but necessary statement. I had no idea when Waters was expected, though I hoped we'd meet there. I needed a comforting face inside those stark, regimented police walls.

Detective Manus was a gruff, slovenly man, big-bellied and cigar smoking, with a wide moon face, babyish, that belied the penetrating no-nonsense deep blue eyes. He reeked of drugstore cologne, some obnoxious sandalwood confection best left to Arabian deserts and Valentino movies, and what little hair he possessed, once gloriously blond and wavy, now consisted of a few vagrant strands that he looped, embroidery fashion, across his gleaming red cranium. He looked, if you squinted, like a circus clown, but those piercing eyes—did the man ever blink? I wondered—suggested a sheriff who always got his man. A tough cookie, I thought, and totally impressive.

Squiring me graciously into his small, cigar-noxious cubicle, he fawned and flattered and circled around me, and I didn't trust a bit of it. He knew who I was, he assured me; and, honestly, *So Big* tugged at his heartstrings. "Really it did." His wife wept.

His ex-wife, actually, though they still talked. And obviously, I thought to myself, discussed current literature. His daughter read it twice. She wept—"What's that word? Copious, yeah, that's it"—copious tears. Then a sudden clearing of his throat, and it was down to business. "And why were you *there*?" He threw out the line so quickly I had to breathe in.

I explained the scheduled lunch date, my casual work with some young Negro writers I'd met through Waters. He was dismissive. "Oh yeah, that squirrelly Negro boy." As I went on, his face suggested I would better spend my leisure hours volunteering for a Salvation Army soup kitchen or as a pillow-stuffed Santa ringing a brass bell in front of Gimbel's.

"And you were going to lunch for what reason?"

I sucked in my cheek. I was about to say *Because I like to eat at noon* but seemed to make it worse with: "The pleasure of that young man's company."

He ran his tongue over his lips. "You're a famous lady."

"That I am. But what is your point?"

"Traipsing in Harlem can't help your reputation, ma'am. You did notice you were mentioned in this morning's *News* and *Mirror*."

"I can't be concerned with tabloid nonsense."

"Hey, I make a living off it."

"Sir," I broke in, "what are we talking about?"

He ignored me. "Why do you think this Roddy fellow was murdered?"

"I have no idea. Like my young friend Waters, I am stunned."

"Yes, your young friend Waters. The seventeen-year-old boy."

I was going to reiterate that Waters, the son of my housekeeper, was a particularly bright though too serious young man, but I decided I'd wasted enough time with this line of chatter.

"You gotta admit it's bizarre for a middle-aged white lady to be hopping cabs in Harlem with all these Negroes."

"All these Negroes?" I echoed. "Are you keeping count?"

"You get my point, no?"

"I wasn't crammed into the back seat with the entire cast of *Shuffle Along*, sir." My tone was as biting as possible.

But he ignored me. He looked down at some papers, pushed them aside, and I sensed him closing up. "We'll have the murderer by tonight."

Now I was intrigued. "And who will it be?"

His burst of laughter degenerated into a rheumy cigarette rasp. "Let me do my job, ma'am."

"I have no intention of usurping your detective skills, sir." A pause. "Of which, I gather, there are many."

A puzzled look on his face. "And I ain't gonna write a novel."

I smiled. "Burton Rascoe of the *Herald Tribune*, the Book Review Editor there, just breathed a sigh of relief."

"Whatever." He stood up and scratched his generous belly.

I wasn't through, and stayed seated. "You will be arresting someone?"

"We got evidence from the scene."

"Like what?"

"Good day, Miss Ferber. You'll read about it in the *News* and the *Mirror*. Doubtless. I don't expect to see your face on a wanted poster."

I stood. "Not yet, at least. I've decided to let my sister Fannie live a few more torturous years."

He shook his head. Before I left, he handed me a card and told me if I remembered anything else—anything trivial might be of value—to call him. Any time. He even wrote his home phone number on the bottom of the card.

I turned in the doorway. "But why do you need anything more from me…if you've solved the crime?"

He snickered. "Maybe I just wanna tell my friends the *So Big* lady rang me up at home."

I took a step out of the small office. "Don't sit by the phone, Detective Manus."

He chuckled as I closed the door.

I had little interest in the dinner Rebecca served me on a tray. Anxiety lacing her gentle features, she served the meal but then left me alone. I craved silence, darkness, the blinds drawn and only a small nightstand lamp switched on. Slowly, methodically, I reviewed the long, unpleasant day, but, of course, my brief hour at the precinct dominated, intruded. I glanced at the clock: early, just seven. The night stretched ahead of me. Lying in my bed with a Joseph Hergesheimer novel unopened in my lap made me seem too much the Victorian invalid—smelling salts and bromides and Japanese lace fans be damned. I needed to act…to locate answers. But how? What could I possibly do?

I carried my tray into the kitchen where Rebecca was sitting with the morning *News*. Doubtless she'd been reading over and over the small account of Roddy Parsons, "a Negro," aged twenty, murdered in his own bed up on 138th Street…and the curious and unnerving coda: "The body was discovered by best-selling author Edna Ferber, whose *Show Boat* and *The Royal Family* are scheduled to open on Broadway right after Christmas." A cryptic line, that, and one most likely calculated to get idle and possibly malicious tongues wagging. I wondered whether the short paragraph, buried inside the paper, would have even been there ("a Negro") had I not stumbled onto the murder. A black man murdered in Harlem did not warrant generous copy. Yes, the phone rang throughout the day, ignored by Rebecca and me; and yes, perversely, my publisher Nelson Doubleday sent a wire because he knew I wouldn't answer the phone. He asked me, point blankly, if I knew what I was doing.

I always knew what I was doing. And Doubleday knew that. A lapse of judgment and character on *his* part, this nincompoopish telegram. Also ignored.

Rebecca looked up. "Waters told me the superintendent, Mr. Porter, Harriet's father no less, refused to talk to the police. When he did talk to them, the cops told Waters, he suggested that Roddy was alive minutes before Waters walked in." She bit her lip, nervous.

"That's foolishness." I felt hollowness in my chest.

"I'm worried. Miss Edna. You don't think…"

I looked into her troubled face. "No."

"But young Negro boys…"

"No," I insisted. "Rebecca, don't worry. Harriet's father is a mean-spirited man, hardly believable. A drunk no less."

I could see my words gave her no comfort. *But young Negro boys...*

In my workroom I picked up the card Detective Manus had given me, and dialed the precinct number. As I expected, he was off duty. "No, I have business with him," I informed the operator. No, I didn't need to speak to anyone else. Instead, I dialed his home number, scribbled on the card. He answered on the second ring.

"Yeah?" His gentlemanly opening.

"This is Edna Ferber."

A deep intake of breath, a slight hint of a cough from an inhaled cigarette. "You remembered something?"

"I remember a lot of things, but nothing that you want to hear."

"So, you're calling me because..."

"Because I'm concerned for my young friend, Waters Turpin."

"Your sidekick?" I could detect the tickle in his voice.

"You've watched too many Tom Mix one-reel Westerns, Detective Manus."

Again, the cigarette rattle. "'Cause the good guy always wins in the movies. It gives me something to believe in, Miss Ferber." He waited a second. "Nobody is accusing the boy."

"Mr. Porter, the super..."

"Is a foul-mouthed, lousy drunk with a rap sheet from here to Detroit, where I wish he'd move to, in fact. With that Bible that he uses as a weapon. He tried to smack an officer with it. Praise Jesus he missed, or he'd be in jail right now. Divine intervention, I guess. Getting info from him was like striking up a conversation with a mongrel dog—the breath will kill you if the fangs don't get there first, and in the end you got nothing."

"Be that as it may," I broke in.

"Look, lady. The fool said he heard music from Roddy's apartment early that morning, thought Roddy walked up front to check for mail, and says he thought Roddy was alone when young Turpin came looking for him, with you keeping the old motor running. The getaway car. But the medical examiner says *rigor mortus* was setting in long before noon, frankly, and he suggests the murder happened at two or three in the morning."

"So Waters…"

"Is clear. Unless he was in on the planning stages…"

"Absurd."

"Most things are."

"Well, It seems we've found an issue we can agree on, Detective Manus."

"Hey, I'm an easy person to get along with."

"I'm not. Purposely. Less wear and tear on the soul."

Noise in the background: I could hear a toddler whimpering, crying out. He spoke louder. "Since I got you on the phone, I might as well make your day. We pulled in a suspect a few hours back. You'll read about it in the morning, and probably see a mug shot, front and sideways, as well as the gentleman, cuffed and cursing, being put into a squad car."

I held my breath. "Is it someone I know?" Stupid, those words, but they simply escaped my mouth.

"Given your recreational companions, I'll hazard a guess—yes. But it's a gent named Harold Scott, a.k.a. Skidder Scott, aged forty-nine, these days a familiar homeless derelict who sets up shop in an alley off 134th Street and Seventh Avenue, in an abandoned building, keeping out of the cold. A squatter. In fact, Mr. Scott is well known to the police, a colorful figure, given his occasional drunken tirades delivered at subway stops, his crazy and non-stop protests against the invention of the automobile. He's been known to stand in the street and…"

I was impatient. "How do you know he…"

"Well, he made it easy for us. I should send him a thank-you card. First, he's a documented felon, having a prior for armed robbery when he was a young man, spending a bunch of years upstate. Second, he's been known to frequent Roddy's neighborhood, simple breaking and entering, petty thievery, pawnshop stuff. A break-in next door, in fact. This seems to be one break-in that went way off-track. Maybe it was the cocaine dripping from his red, red nose, or the bottle of bootleg whiskey in his hip pocket. Clever enough not to leave fingerprints—winter gives folks an excuse to wear gloves, lucky us—but somehow he dropped a battered pack of cigarettes, Chesterfields no less, by the bed, probably tumbling out of a breast pocket as he plunged a knife into Roddy, who probably woke to find the scum pocketing his bureau change. And there's the issue of some cheap gold ring, property of Lawson Hicks, as well as some cuff links that were once owned by Mr. Roddy Parsons himself, found wrapped in rags in a corner of the decayed building Mr. Skidder Scott calls home sweet home."

"So that's it."

"Strings tied. I can sleep well tonight."

"I wish I could." I breathed in. "I know Roddy Parsons as a decent, talented young man who…"

He cut me off. "Miss Ferber, he *was* a decent, talented young man." He hung up the phone.

Restless, I tottered about my apartment, debated calling George Kaufman or Aleck Woollcott, but my mind kept ricocheting back to Jed Harris, that imp of the perverse. *Call him*, I thought. I needed to talk to someone. He'd seen Roddy at my apartment. He sat at the same table with him at that chop suey joint up in Harlem. Images of Bella and Lawson and Roddy and Ellie intermingled with quick snapshots of Jed in my living room and uptown. His feigned indifference to Bella. His hostility… His contemptuous attitude that afternoon in my apartment. So what? Like Ellie and Bella and Lawson, even Freddy and Harriet, Roddy was *there*, the tall lad with the grin and the baby cheeks. There, then not there. Yet Jed's darkswept look annoyed me. It made me think of Roddy, the grotesque, bug-eyed corpse, that dagger in the pale chest.

Rebecca fixed me a bootleg martini. She was always good at reading my mind.

Later in my workroom, I fiddled with letters I had no intention of answering and was relieved to hear two low-rumble voices coming from the kitchen. Waters and Lawson had stopped in. Though Rebecca knew I didn't welcome impromptu visits to the apartment, especially socializing in the evening, I bustled into the kitchen, almost frenzied, in need of conversation.

"I'm sorry, Miss Edna," Waters began, "but we won't stay. Mom just wanted me to let her know I was all right, and Lawson…"

I cut him off. "Stay a while. Sit down. Please."

"I told my cousin Mary I'd be back right away. She's worried about me." When Waters visited his mother in the city, he stayed with relatives in an apartment in New Jersey, an old couple distantly related to his mother's second cousin.

So we sat in my living room, behaving as though nothing had changed in our lives, Roddy not cruelly butchered in his peaceful bed. Rebecca served us hot cocoa and crispy soda biscuits, turned to leave, but I insisted she sit with us, a shifting of household protocol she always had trouble with, this unorthodox blurring of lines. No matter. I'd come to relish the brief, sensible talks the two of us had, often late at night when neither of us could sleep. Or restless early mornings when the fireball sun over the East River pierced the shadows of the living room.

Staring at both young men, I was intrigued by the overnight transformation. Waters, the overly serious, indeed, often ponderous, young boy, so earnest and yet always incredibly boyish, seemed now older than Lawson, as he assumed the role of comfort giver. He kept glancing at his friend, his eyes old with compassion. Lawson, that fashion-plate hero with that matinee-idol affect, looked crushed, rattled, slumped in a chair with his shoulders drawn forward and hunched up; his face, light-complected to begin with, now seemed delicate parchment, breakable. As he leaned forward into the lamplight, I noticed small flecks of white, bits and pieces of tissue, perhaps, or lint. A disheveled young man, wholly consumed by a confused and insidious grief. I had trouble looking at him.

But I needed to. "Lawson, how are you?"

He looked up, smiled thinly. "I'm all right, Miss Ferber."
Clearly he wasn't.

"What's going on at the apartment?"

Waters answered for him. "Lawson hasn't gone back. He *won't*
go back there now. I picked up some clothes and things for him.
He's staying with an uncle in Queens. Temporarily."

Lawson muttered, "Better."

"What?"

"Better that way." A heartbeat. "I had to deal with Roddy's
father, who is, you know, somehow related to my father." He
sucked in his breath. "He wanted nothing to do with it. Arrange-
ments and all. He didn't even want to show up. Just…indifferent.
The cops told me he walked out on them. Like…Roddy was
dead…years before." Lawson stared into my face now, the eyes
wide. "He was horrible."

"You're not doing well, Lawson," I offered.

A wispy smile. "Big surprise, no?" He looked at Waters. "I'm
sorry about the way I acted yesterday morning. I'm sorry, Miss
Ferber. I don't know why I was so out of it, dizzy and all. I felt
like I was walking in a fog or something."

"I noticed that."

"Well, Bella and I…the night before. You know, we drank
too much, got into a fight, but, I don't know, I've passed out lots
of times before, but this time I woke up so groggy, like I didn't
know where I was. I sort of stumbled home." A pause. "Home."

Waters commented, "You're gonna die from that bootleg
gin you drink."

Another slight smile. "That's what's for sale in Harlem."

Waters frowned. "Another fight with Bella?" He shook his
head.

"She told me it was over. We're done. Like I didn't know
that. But she was serious this time. So we drank and we fought
and…well…"

"The police kept asking me why I was there with you, Miss
Edna," Waters suddenly said.

"I know. They're baffled by all human behavior that doesn't fit onto an index card."

"I talked to Harriet when I went to pick up some of Lawson's things," Waters began. "The cops interviewed her and I guess she was belligerent."

"But why?"

"She doesn't trust them."

"Surely she wants Roddy's murderer caught?"

"I guess so, but…it's hard to explain, Miss Edna."

I grumbled. "I don't get it."

"She told me that her father, Mr. Porter, gave the cops a hard time. Just like the way he treated us, you know. He wouldn't open the door at first, then fought against giving an interview. He told different stories—claimed he heard music in the apartment just before I went in. Then he changed his mind. What's clear is that he didn't like Roddy. He doesn't *care* that he's dead."

I narrowed my eyes. "But why?"

A shrug of the shoulders. "Who knows?"

"Well, there has to be a reason." I looked at Lawson. "Any ideas?"

He shrugged his shoulders. "They argued over things."

"Like what?"

"I dunno. The rent was late. Often. Roddy mocked Mr. Porter—the way he never lets go of that Bible."

"Roddy didn't believe…"

"Roddy said Mr. Porter is an old-fashioned Negro, the kind who thinks everything is copasetic, you know. Swell. Don't rattle the chains."

"Did Harriet say anything else?" I asked Waters.

"Strangely, she seemed, well, happy when she told me about her father, who is a man she fights with and ignores. But I guess his belligerent attitude with Detective Manus made her look at him differently."

"This is making little sense." I bit my lip. "I can't imagine that gentle boy arguing with anyone."

Lawson looked up, startled. "Roddy could be gentle, yes, but he could be real stubborn, too. Ornery. He liked things a certain way. The fact is he always thought the super was a fool and was always ready to tell him so."

"Well, I think he is a fool, and I scarcely know the man, but…"

"You know, I didn't see much of Roddy lately because I stayed at Bella's." He looked into my face. "I mean, I sleep on the couch there…late at night. Most times Roddy was at work. But he did tell me that Mr. Porter was on his case."

Waters got up, stretched, and began walking around the room. His mother, who had been silent, watched him, her eyes wary. He stood by the dark window and stared down into the city streets. Then, suddenly, his shoulders convulsed and he started sobbing.

"Waters," his mother called out. "What, honey?"

He faced us. "Harriet told me something else. Roddy was stabbed with his own knife. I didn't know he kept a knife on his nightstand. He was *afraid* of something."

"Lawson?" I asked.

He nodded. "There've been break-ins on the street. A month back, a prowler came in through the back window, which Roddy'd forgot to lock. It looks out on the alley. He took some cash. I guess twenty dollars. Some junk stuff. Since then Roddy kept the knife there. I joked that he'd never use it. I mean— Roddy? Can you imagine Roddy fighting off someone with a knife? But he felt safer, I guess. Especially since I started spending my nights at Bella's. He was alone."

"He didn't manage to fight off his murderer," I commented. "From what I saw, there didn't seem to be any signs of struggle. He was asleep, I guess, and woke to find a knife plunged into his heart."

Slumping back into his seat, Lawson moaned. Immediately I regretted my words. I wasn't painting a pretty picture. "I'm sorry, Lawson."

"They'll get him," Rebecca announced. "They *have* to." She motioned to Waters, who sat down next to her. She leaned into him, affectionately.

At that moment I realized I'd not mentioned Detective Manus' conversation with me earlier. Quietly, I summarized: the arrest of the homeless felon named Harold Skidder Scott, the discarded cigarette pack, Lawson's gold ring and Roddy's cuff links, hidden in the bundle of rags. I sat back, satisfied. But if I expected both young men to look relieved or gratified, I was wrong because both wore quizzical expressions, dumbfounded.

"What, for heaven's sake? I would have thought this news would please both of you."

Waters muttered, "Him?"

Lawson scoffed. "Skidder Scott?"

I gasped. "You know him?"

"Everybody knows him. I didn't know his name was Harold. He's one of those guys who are always around the neighborhood. You know he's up to no good. A junkie, drunk, you know. Begs for money, food. He stands outside the Catagonia Club when people are going in or out. He crashes rent parties. Steals small stuff."

"Well, the police found his fingerprints…and your ring, Lawson."

"I don't see it," Lawson said. "My ring was worthless. Not gold. I wouldn't leave something good out like that." A pause. "I just don't see him *hurting* Roddy."

Waters was nodding his head up and down. "Skidder Scott. God, even I know that man. He's, well, harmless. A local character. He stands and yells at the cars going by. He hates…cars. Roddy even said he'd put him into a short story someday. A Harlem drunk in an alley…or something. A big bushel of a man, but harmless."

I bristled. "Apparently not."

The two young men glanced at each other, Lawson still looking puzzled. "Skidder always runs from a fight. Yeah, he takes stuff but not when someone is home…sleeping. I suspected he was the one who broke into our apartment and took the money Roddy had on the bureau. But the cops wouldn't even come out when we called them."

Waters added, "He's a big beefy man, true, but he looks kind of weak. You know, a soft sponge of a guy. Roddy, waking up, could fight him."

"Not if he's startled when he's been sleeping."

Suddenly Waters jumped up, nervous, and looked at his mother. "I wonder if there's more to the story, Ma." Then he looked at me. "Miss Edna, Skidder Scott did things for money, but if he broke in that door, Roddy would have heard him, no? He would have yelled out. And Skidder would beat it out of there." Waters circled the room, frenzied, his mind clicking away. "Skidder wouldn't come into the apartment like that—rush at Roddy. He shuffles along. You know, I think somebody else planned this." He turned to Lawson. "That's it, Lawson. Think of the Skidder we know. Lord, people make *fun* of him. This is…"

I interrupted. "Lawson. Waters. Come on, let's be realistic. A felon, notorious for breaking and entering. It's inevitable his luck would turn and he'd find someone home…"

"Lawson, tell her," Waters pleaded.

"What?" Lawson asked.

"Do *you* think it's Skidder?"

Lawson stood up and stared out the dark window. For the first time since he'd arrived he acted…alive. He swung his arms crazily, and his dark eyes, wide now, were lit by fire. "Listen to Waters, Miss Ferber."

"Somebody killed Roddy," Waters stated dramatically. The words hung in the air, choice and rich. "Somebody *else*."

"Waters…"

"Help us, Miss Edna."

"For Lord's sake, Waters…"

"You know people," Waters said. "Lots of people. People will listen to you. No one will listen to us. To me and Lawson. You can talk to people. Someone has to talk to Skidder. There's a story behind this."

"Someone had it in for Roddy." Lawson's voice was quiet and low.

Waters was nodding.

Grimly, I thought: the Negro Hardy Boys, young men in a hurry, driven, excited, an adventure now, something to distance themselves from the awful grief and the nagging horror. Boys at their games, macabre though they were.

"No."

"Miss Edna, please." Waters' eyes looked into mine.

Lawson was nodding in counterpoint to Waters' pleas.

"No," I repeated. "No."

Chapter Seven

No, of course not.

As Rebecca leaned into the breakfast table the next morning, pouring my hot coffee, with a generous wash of whipped farm cream, she whispered, "Now, Miss Edna, don't pay those boys any mind."

I smiled as I reached for the cinnamon toast. "Your son is such a serious lad, Rebecca. And he does have a winning way about him."

"The murder has thrown him off balance, I guess. And with Lawson playing Greek chorus to his pleadings, well, it could be a little intimidating."

I munched on savory toast and reached for the *New York Times*. "Never mind, Rebecca. I don't think Detective Manus, all that male braggadocio and burst blood vessel, wants the *Show Boat* lady tagging after him, especially now that the police have put a *finis* to the case." I paused. "Though Waters and Lawson did get me thinking. With the apartment door wrenched open, splintered, would Roddy still have been in bed? Was he that sound a sleeper? It puzzles me, really. People don't shift character so casually, like this Skidder Scott character." I shook my head. "What grown man calls himself Skidder?"

She laughed. "I suppose the nickname was given to him. No idea what it means."

"It means I'm minding my own business. I have a long day ahead of me."

Show Boat and *The Royal Family*:—my one-two punch on Broadway. That should be my concern, not brutal murder up in Harlem. At mid-morning someone from Oscar Hammerstein's office phoned to apologize for the missed meetings at the theater. No matter, I told the caller, but I noticed that he didn't suggest rescheduling. Later, reviewing Jed Harris' last minute changes to the dialogue in *The Royal Family*, I decided the man liked to tinker with dialogue simply because—he could. His maniacal hand excised some of the flavor and verve George Kaufman and I put into our dialogue. But at this late date I'd lapsed into utter resignation because, truthfully, my protestations, wily or innocuous, brought me nothing but indigestion and sleepless nights.

When I arrived at the Selwyn Theater, I watched the players wilt under Jed's surprise noontime visit. "Do you really think you will be ready on December 28?" he screamed at them. Then, blithely, a mischievous smile on his unshaven face and a hum in his voice, he grasped my elbow and said, simply, "Lunch, Edna?"

I had little choice.

We settled into a booth at the Double R, a Brazilian coffee shop on West 44th and Sixth Avenue, a chaotic eatery I knew he favored, largely because the I'm-an-actor staff tripped over themselves serving him. It was always packed with theater folks. We sat at the back of the restaurant, with Jed insisting he face the front door.

"You afraid of armed theater critics?"

He smirked. "All critics, including your buddy George Kaufman, are congenital sissies. I might get an hysterical slap from Brooks Atkinson, but I don't think he could even lift a gun without trembling."

"You underestimate your foes."

"When you only have foes, life is amazingly predictable."

"And am I a foe?"

"No, you're a maiden lady, twice my age, who'd love a romp in the hay with me."

I bristled. "You're a presumptuous cad, Jed Harris."

He grinned. "I am that. But you like me."

"I appreciate talent."

"That's an evasive answer."

"It's the only one you'll get from me." I sipped my coffee and gingerly picked at my tuna salad. Purposely, I avoided eye contact. I barely listened as he prattled on about a new car he'd just bought—a Marmon, whatever that was, a "nifty" car, he intoned, not some "tin lizzie flivver like you see *everywhere.*"

I stared at him.

A man notorious for his brusqueness and his cruelty, Jed had a keen sense of popular theater that was unrivaled. Yet, sitting there facing him, I suddenly believed his career would be short-lived—he'd burn out from self-congratulation and the ready availability of easy cash. Already he'd bought a yacht he didn't need. A yacht, mind you. Moored at City Island, it cruised the placid waters of the Rivers East and Hudson. Still, I had to admit—and didn't he read me well?—that this dark, menacing young man with the beard stubble and wolf's hooded eyes, with the doomsday East European complexion and slender waist—well, he made my heart jump a bit. Few men did that—and lived to talk about it. But this dapper swell of the theater, so nasty and viral, fluttered my Victorian pulse. He'd be an easy man for me to hate— eventually I would, of course, I *planned* on it—simply because he was, for me, one of the few men I could actually love.

But now he was yammering on about *The Royal Family* and the empty threat of a lawsuit from Ethel Barrymore. Suddenly, he stopped, held his hand suspended in the air—so that I could appreciate his manicured nails, I supposed—and said with a grim voice, "So you begin the Ferber season!" It came out almost a threat, though I don't know why I thought that. "Two Broadway openings, a day apart, right after Christmas. You will be wined and dined, feted, and will doubtless have more ego than is humanly bearable. This may be the last lunch we share where we can still talk as equals."

I smiled sweetly. "Jed, you still have some reach before you're close to being my equal."

He roared. "You do like yourself a bit."

"This is foolish talk, all of it. I'm a writer. That's what I do."

"Oh, come off it, Edna. Humility is not a cloak you don well."

I'd had enough. "Tell me about Bella Davenport, Jed."

My words slammed him back against the booth. He struggled to find a response, weighing, deliberating, and manipulating some elaborate lie he knew instinctively I wouldn't buy. Finally, he leaned forward, ran his tongue over his lips, and actually winked. An unpleasant gesture that seemed girlish, high school antics. "A beautiful girl, no? Stunning, in fact."

"She is that."

"She is that," he echoed.

"What's the story, Jed?"

A sly grin. "I figured you'd bring it up. You've been *itching* to interrogate me. I must say, I was surprised to see that dicty crowd assembled in your living room. Flaming youth in black face. Edna Ferber's Underground Railroad."

"We're talking about Bella Davenport."

"If you're probing into my sex life, Edna—very unseemly of you, by the way, and I doubt if any of your romantic characters would do so, since your heroines believe in Immaculate Conception—well, yes, love, I've seen her. I *did* see her."

"Why?"

Now he laughed, loud and hearty, and heads swiveled. "I was sitting in on auditions for Lew Leslie's *Blackbirds*, watching the young Negro performers stroll in and out, hungry for any part, and there she was, an ambitious young lady, that girl, driven, ready to flatter and preen and beg. She just assumed she'd get the part, even cozying up to the likes of Mr. Bojangles."

"For Lord's sake, Jed."

"Well, she's not a nice person, Edna. A liar, dissembler, manipulator, fabricator. Shall I go on?"

"But she knew who you were?"

"Who doesn't in the world of theater?" A sigh. "She batted those eyelashes and cooed at me. You can't trust her, by the way. She didn't get the part because Florence Mills was a softer, less ferocious performer, and more talented, but she agreed to let me take her to Johnny Jackson's restaurant up on 135th Street. Not surprisingly, she'd written a play."

"Which you'll not produce."

"Of course not. I deal with quality plays, the likes of Kaufman and Ferber."

I harrumphed, which tickled him. "She didn't seem happy to see you in my doorway or in that chop suey joint."

"I don't suppose she wanted to advertise that she's been keeping company with the plantation owner."

"That's crass, Jed."

"Come off it, Edna. White or black, these actresses know the game."

"Why keep your mouth shut about it? That awful silence that night in Harlem."

"Well, I *did* see her. Past tense. No more. We ended on a sour note."

"What happened?"

"I dumped her."

"Why?"

He shrugged. "None of your business."

I went on. "Did you know the young man who died? Roddy?"

"No." Said too quickly, I thought, so I didn't know whether I believed him. Then after a while, "I didn't *know* him. Yeah, I saw him at your apartment and then uptown at the eatery. Elsewhere. Once or twice. In Harlem. An insolent, dreadful boy. Bella talked of him too much. Lately she became obsessed with him. I guess he—spurned her." He smiled, sickeningly. "For a girl as stunning as Bella, no man is allowed to refuse her. I believe some other girl likes him, someone she has contempt for."

"Ellie."

"Ah, yes, the young torch singer at Small's Paradise."

"Yes, that Ellie. As I suspect you already know. But you do know that Bella was seeing a young man named Lawson, right?"

"Of course, Edna. I have more of a history with these folks than you do. To tell you the truth. Bella talked nonstop about

Lawson and how she was going to dump him. She rattled on to the point of utter boredom. And about her anger toward Roddy, who didn't love her back. I don't know why she thought I was interested in the messing around that Negroes do. So, yes, I'd already been through the theatrical wars with young Lawson. He came to some audition for a revival of *The Chocolate Dandies*. Cocky, too good-looking for his own good. He was perfect for the part because he *lived* the part. They didn't hire him. Bella's lover. Whatever that means. Two people using each other, a symbiotic organism that festers and bleeds. Pus and blood, the two of them. Bella actually arranged for me to read his full-length play, which I read. He's hoping for Broadway. Downtown. A talented boy, but I'll have nothing to do with him."

"But why?" Exasperated.

"Ambition in a young actress is good, Edna. It hones the edges of their beauty. Ambition in a young man, especially a handsome Negro like Lawson Hicks, is unnerving and intrusive. Young Lawson has a lean and hungry look—such men are…annoying."

"I like him."

"Of course you do. He's one of your romantic heroes, though unfortunately Negro."

Jed reached for the check and stood up. Sitting there, my meal half eaten, I sneered, "So lunch is over?" He slapped some dollar bills on the table.

As he walked away, he looked back at me. "I knew there was a reason I never read any of your novels, Edna."

I sat there, steaming.

The next afternoon I rode uptown in a cab with Rebecca and Waters, the three of us headed to a memorial service for Roddy at St. Mark's A.M.E. Church on 138th Street and St. Nicholas. I hadn't intended on going, though I grieved for his short, aborted life. Waters, phoning in the morning, had such a plaintive, wistful tone as he spoke of the service he and Lawson had organized that I found myself saying yes, of course I would go.

When I hung up the phone, I realized he hadn't asked me to go—I simply found myself saying yes.

Lamentably, I was the only white person among a smattering of local souls who knew Roddy. The emptiness of the church saddened me. Young people, dying young, usually had hordes of friends attending church—but not Roddy. Bella and Ellie, both dressed in black chemises and weeping, sat apart from each other. Bella wore a dramatic turquoise cloche, which made her stand out. Surprisingly, Lawson wore an old-fashioned black suit that looked like something he'd got from a thrift store. That intrigued me, especially considering he always looked spiffy, polished, the man-about-town from *The Smart Set*. He sat bent over in a pew, his head buried in his lap. There were a few relatives, I assumed, though Lawson whispered early on that he didn't know these distant members of his own family.

"And his father's not here." Lawson was furious. "They didn't talk after he left home, Roddy and his dad."

Harriet and Freddy were conspicuously not there. The minister sermonized, though no one eulogized the sad young man. I was tempted to rise and say a few celebratory words, but I rejected the inclination as inappropriate. Bidden by the minister who said twice he didn't know Roddy, as though to explain the impersonality of the service, Ellie finally walked to the altar, turned to face us, and sang "We Will Meet Him in the Sweet By and By," her sweet, soprano voice clear and full, only breaking at the end, the last words lost in her swallowed grief. An organ echoed her lovely voice. Sitting on my right, Rebecca was weeping. And then, the minister blessing us, folks filed out.

Rebecca was in a somber mood. Tearful most of the short service, she kept brushing up protectively against her only son, as though to ensure he was safe, secure. A couple of times, straining against his mother's smothering hold, Waters pulled away, but only slightly; the bond between the two of them—they only had each other—was too important to violate. I thought of my own mother, currently my housemate and my constant disapproving and censorious eye, luckily now spending the holidays with family visiting from Chicago. She trucked no such physical intimacy; her grip was patently psychological, and thus more destructive.

As I stepped onto the sidewalk and surveyed the street for a downtown cab, Rebecca was calling out to Bella and Lawson, both walking away, far apart from each other. Neither had said goodbye to us. Then she called out to Ellie, who was also bustling away from us, headed uptown. I thought the behavior unseemly and impolite. Reluctantly, the trio stumbled back to us.

"After a service," Rebecca insisted, "it's only right and proper to celebrate life." They glared at her as if she'd announced an alien invasion. "We'll have a bite to eat." She looked around. "There."

She'd spotted a small eatery tucked into the crumbling façade of an old brownstone, a hole-in-the-wall that looked, to me at least, dangerously prone to health code violation. "Hot soup and smothered pork chops." She smiled. "And sweet potato pie. Not as good as mine, surely, but…" She tucked her hand into Waters' elbow and moved us all toward the restaurant.

"I can't," Lawson mumbled. "I'm already late to my job. I can't."

Everyone nodded as he scurried off, waving at us in a feeble valedictory, a bittersweet smile on his face.

"Liar," Bella muttered.

Bella seemed ready to leave, taking a few steps away, but Rebecca had already taken her arm. "An hour of your time, Bella."

Bella had no choice, though I noticed she cast a furtive side-long glance at Ellie, who, to my annoyance, was looking over our heads into the sky, as if checking for signs of impending blizzard—grasping for a meteorological excuse for hasty flight.

Inside the empty restaurant, the fat proprietor, wearing a food-stained apron and an incongruous chef's hat, nodded toward the window table. Rebecca ignored him and led us to a back round table by the kitchen, a corner of the restaurant lost in shadows. Served bubbly lemon phosphates and root beer and, for me and Rebecca, steaming coffee, we raised our cups and glasses to Roddy's memory, though Rebecca's heartfelt toast seemed absurd in the dim, light-speckled room.

As we munched on surprisingly savory smothered chicken and pork chops, with paprika-laced roast potatoes slathered in gravy, Waters repeatedly caught my eye, and once, without a trace of subtlety, he nodded toward Bella, then noisily drained the last of a root beer through a bent straw. His steely look demanded, emphatically: Talk to her, Miss Edna. Ask her questions.

Ignoring him, I did remark, "I was surprised that Harriet and Freddy weren't at the service."

Ellie looked up and actually smiled. "Well, Freddy never cared for Roddy and made no apologies for it, the way he is about everything. So it didn't surprise me, him not coming. But a little tasteless, no? And Harriet, well, I think she has to do a double shift at Clark's Restaurant. You can't say no to the bosses there. She would have come."

"Why would Freddy not like such an innocent like Roddy?" I wondered.

Bella laughed. "Just because he comes off as shy and boyish with you—*was* shy and boyish, I mean—doesn't translate into innocence, Miss Ferber."

"What does that mean?"

Ellie thundered, "Bella, stop this nonsense. To speak ill of the dead. Poor Roddy. He *was* innocent. A harmless boy who stayed in his room when everyone else was whooping it up at rent parties and speakeasies, just scribbling on his pad all night long."

Snidely, "All night long? How would *you* know?"

The words stung Ellie and she sucked in her breath, turned away, and looked ready to cry. "I believe what people tell me."

"Even the lies?"

"I leave *that* to you, Bella."

"Roddy liked to lie to us."

Ellie fumed. "How dare…"

"Stop it, the two of you," Rebecca pleaded. "What's the matter with you?"

"I *know* things," Bella sputtered.

"What?" Waters leaned into her, his eyes wide.

She shrugged. "Nothing. Nothing at all."

Ellie summed up, looking at me, her lips trembling. "Roddy liked to be left alone." Then she turned to Bella, her voice low. "He told me how you'd chosen him as...as the lunch special of the month. You, stringing along Lawson and casting mooncalf eyes at Roddy."

"Frankly, Roddy is more interesting than Lawson," Bella said in a flat voice, weary, her eyebrows raised.

"Ridiculous," seethed Ellie.

"Well, *you* chased him, too," Bella said.

"Ridiculous," Ellie repeated. "Roddy and I went to clubs. We *talked*. We were close..."

"*Were* close." Bella's words were biting.

I sat back, listening to this give-and-take nastiness, the gnawing bitterness, all over a dead man who, from all reports, seemed to have no interest in either woman, these two niggling warriors on the battlefield of love. It was interesting how much Roddy's death had opened the valves of bile. Dead, Roddy exerted a curious power over them, an energy that brought out the worst in both. What was going on here? I caught Waters' eye. He was blinking furiously, looking from one woman to the other.

Ellie withered under Bella's relentless disregard of Rebecca's pleading, finally tucking her head into her neck, a frightened sparrow, becoming still, though I could see the tension in her neck muscles.

Waters, confused by the sudden vitriol, started to babble, deadly serious, about Lawson and his refusal to return to his old apartment. "I make so many trips, you know." We all stared at him. "I have to get personal toiletries and clothing, a typewriter." His voice trailed off. But when he sensed Bella about to begin a fresh assault, he said, "I even had to face Mr. Porter in the hallway. The man, I swear he was drunk, demanded the rent that was due the first of the coming year. From *me*. It's overdue."

"You don't pay rent to the super," his mother said, a practical remark that seemed to skirt the real issue here.

Waters nodded. "I guess he collects it for the owner, some white guy downtown. And I guess the back rent is overdue."

"How will Lawson pay his share by himself?" I wondered.

"Well, he's not moving in with me," Bella declared. "I told him we were through the night that Roddy died. Over. Simple as that. Finally. My brother already can't stand him and is tired of Lawson sleeping on his couch every night. A slobbering drunk. He's gonna have to move to some hovel…maybe." Bella withdrew a mirror from her purse, foraged for her lipstick, and, while we watched, meticulously painted smudged lips. I caught Rebecca's eye. Not happy, the woman.

Ellie stood up, her face flushed. "Roddy is rolling over in his grave. This conversation is…sickening, Bella." She threw her cloth coat over her shoulders, gathered her scarf and gloves from the ledge nearby, and, nodding at Rebecca and me, spun around and left the eatery.

Bella didn't wait until Ellie closed the door behind her. "Did she really think she had a chance with Roddy?" She slipped the lipstick and mirror back into her purse and snapped it shut.

Waters squirmed. "Does it matter now, Bella? It seems stupid to talk about it."

She interrupted him. "I'll talk about what I want to, Waters."

His mother bristled and seemed ready to defend her son, but Waters, clearing his throat, said, "There's something called poor taste, Bella."

Inwardly I smiled.

"I've never been accused of phony sentimentality," she said.

"All sentimentality is phony," I told her.

She said nothing, showing at least a modicum of good sense, and collected her things. "All Ellie has going for her is a good voice. I will say that."

"Such a generous spirit." Rebecca's tone bit in a way I'd never heard her use before.

"I'll tell you a secret," Bella confided. "Lawson told me that Ellie had told him she was gonna surprise Roddy the night he died."

I sat up, alert. "So?"

A casual flip of her head backwards. "She was angry at Roddy because they were supposed to check out a new jazz club where she hoped to sing, but he backed out, said he had other plans that night. He *told* her *not* to stop in. Ellie told Lawson she suspected him of being up to no good. She was going to surprise him. She thought he'd sneaked some girl into the apartment by the back door, defying Mr. Porter's Bible-thumping no-girls rule. Of course, she feared it was me—which is why she told Lawson."

"You're…making that up," Waters boomed, angry.

"Am I? Ask Lawson. Maybe she'll deny it, but that night she might have actually been there the same time that Skidder was lurking around."

I broke in. "Bella, you have such a good-looking boyfriend. Or *had*. Lawson is…"

"Is like an old dog, affectionate but requiring too much attention. I called it quits that night. For good. He holds no… fascination for me."

"Like Roddy did?" Rebecca asked.

"Of course."

"But Roddy spurned you, too, Bella," Waters added.

Bella was reaching for her coat, but she slipped back into her chair. "End of story."

"Tell me about Jed Harris," I said quickly.

My abrupt question didn't seem to take her off-guard. A lazy smiled covered her face. "Nothing to say."

Waters waited a second. "Lawson hates him, Miss Edna. Mr. Harris mocked his acting and ignored his play. All because he knew Lawson was going out with Bella and Jed didn't…"

"Will you be quiet, Waters," Bella sniped.

Waters looked at me. "Miss Edna, we all agreed *not* to mention it to you…because you…know him. Like your friend. But it seems to me…"

Bella broke in. "Change the subject, Waters. The only career I care about is mine."

"But Lawson is a great playwright," Waters said.

"Enough about Lawson. I don't care. I told Lawson to get lost last Saturday. We'd been out dancing, drinking. We got into our usual shouting match. It got real nasty, both of us tipsy, and he passed out on me. As is his usual amorous behavior. In the morning I had to shove him out the door but he kept walking in circles, claiming he couldn't find his shoes. Lord, schoolboy delaying tactics, trying to make up with me. Goodbye, Lawson. As I said, enough about Lawson."

At that moment, I suddenly pictured Julie LaVerne in *Show Boat*, the mulatto ingénue who passed for white, the beautiful young woman who fashioned a life singing on the Mississippi. A woman whose marriage to a white man leads to her expulsion from the showboat—and the beginning of a descent into poverty and decay. The price Julie paid to entertain—to use her talent. Here were Bella and Ellie, beautiful, talented…and Negro, hungry for a moment at the downtown strutters' ball—Broadway. Within days the character of Julie would open in a glitzy, romantic musical on Broadway, life on the wicked stage, but would Bella or Ellie ever shine on the Broadway boards? Julie, a creation of my imagination, singing "Can't Help Lovin' Dat Man" while, sitting opposite me in a dingy Harlem eatery, two beautiful women could only dream!

I thought of Jed Harris squiring Bella into clubs. The venal seducer, cynical.

Empty promises and dashed hopes. An awful price, too dear. For Roddy…and Lawson…

I shivered in my seat.

I indicated I was ready to leave, so Rebecca graciously reached for the check. Waters had been fidgeting throughout Bella's recounting of that night with Lawson. Now, with perfect and calculated timing, he cleared his throat. "When I went to get some of Lawson's things, I had a talk with Harriet, who heard me in the back apartment." A pause. "She told me something strange, Bella. Late that night, maybe around midnight, she was coming back from her waitress job and she swears she saw you on her street. A quick glimpse, you hiding in the shadows of the alley next to the building. She swore it was you lurking there as she walked by. The scent of gardenia in the air…"

Bella's face closed up. She sat back in her seat, wrapped her arms around her chest, her body stiffening. Then, forcing herself, she loosened up, and said, too loudly, "That's just absurd. I was *not* there. That inky-dink Harriet is delusional. She had her own fantasies about Roddy. She told me, though grudgingly. She's making it all up. Jealous. Of course she is. And a bold-faced liar." She rose from her seat, clutching her coat. Suddenly, wildly, her hand swept across the table, sending the glasses and dishes flying. A plate smashed into a wall, shattered. "Around that time I was getting furious with Lawson, who was slobbering drunk on my sofa. Around that time, yes, around that time I was slapping him as hard as I could across his pretty face."

Chapter Eight

The following afternoon, tucked into a front row seat during a run-through of *The Royal Family*, with George Kaufman at my side scribbling notes and muttering *sotto voce* observations aimed at the director Burton, I could barely sit still, squirming, jittery, until George grasped my wrist and insisted, "Edna, do you have a bodily function it would be indecorous to discuss?"

Bothered by Roddy's death, I'd found my sleep disturbed, my attention lacking, my dramatic and purposeful sighs ignored by all. No matter the shifting machinations of *Show Boat* and *The Royal Family*: both were entities now beyond my control, creations conceived and now delivered, and it remained for the world—and the *New York Times*—to judge their merit and durability. These days I was just the pensive mother—or *Show Boat's* surrogate mother—who was nervously expectant after the delivery.

Sitting beside George, my mind sailed back to yesterday's lunch in Harlem. The image of Bella sending those dishes flying nagged at me, but, worse, my sudden and unwelcome association of Bella with the doomed mulatto Julie LaVerne in *Show Boat*. I flashed to images of Bella cast as Julie, betrayed, lost, condemned. But I knew no one would entertain Bella as Julie…a Negro couldn't play a…Negro in midtown. Not in such a highly charged, big-budget musical. Or Lawson Hicks playing the dashing and maddening John Barrymore-like Tony Cavendish in *The Royal Family*. Or Ellie as Magnolia Ravenal singing "After the Ball is Over" on the *Cotton Blossom* stage.

The house slaves forbidden to enter the front rooms of the mansion.

And yet, ironically, audiences would applaud those characters onstage.

Finally, spent, George and I stood up, George intending to berate the director while I planned to stumble home for a rare afternoon nap. At that moment Jed Harris strode into the theater, all swagger and excessive cologne and cigarette smoke, galloping down the aisle, his voice stentorian and vicious as he assailed the faltering cast onstage. "Balderdash!" he roared, reminding me of some Victorian villain, mustachioed and dark-complected, perhaps the heavy from *Show Boat* itself. As he neared the aisle where George and I stood, tentatively and unhappily, he turned and eyed us both, a look so baleful and dismissive I fairly caught my breath. His hostile look settled over me, finally, and I swear his lower lip trembled with menace. What in the world? Had the man gone mad? Eccentric certainly, delusional perhaps, but some Broadway folks speculated that the *wunderkind* would invariably sink into utter madness, foam at the mouth, eyes ablaze, tongue flapping in an obscenity-laced mouth. Had that moment arrived? The bus to Bedlam just picked up one more rider?

But Jed narrowed his eyes and strode away.

"Ah," George cried, "fresh as poison ivy." It was a line he often used, and it never wore thin.

"Let's get out of here," I whispered. "I'm not in the mood for juvenile antics."

"If we had a sandbox, we could hide his body."

"The world exiles its pompous short dictators. Why can't we send him to…New Jersey?"

We fled the theater.

Back at my apartment, hanging my coat in the closet by the front door, I heard Rebecca singing softly in the kitchen, a melancholy song, and I realized, sadly, that I'd come back to the world of Roddy's death. Bella, at that awful memorial lunch in Harlem. Ellie, angry, headed that night to Roddy's apartment. Maybe. Bella, already there in the darkness.

Hearing me, Rebecca stopped humming and asked me what was the matter. "Is my face so transparent?" I asked her.

"Miss Edna, you got yourself a poker face about everything but confusion."

"These days it's the only face I seem to have."

"Bella," Rebecca intoned, a declarative word.

"Exactly," I sputtered. "Yesterday stays with me like an old dog."

"Well," Rebecca added, "I can't stop thinking about Bella myself. That thing about her going to Roddy's apartment and hiding in the shadows, watching, waiting. For what?"

"If it's true, Rebecca. We don't know. That's Harriet's take on things. To begin with, it might not have been Bella there. Night shadows, winter chill, fatigue." I grinned. "There must be other beautiful women who bathe in gardenia perfume. And Harriet obviously doesn't like Bella."

"No one likes Bella." Flat out, final.

"I can give you a list of men who do."

"That's not helpful, Miss Edna."

"I know, I know." A pause. "Waters really took me by surprise when he blurted out that remark. He waited, held back the information, perfect timing. For effect, I suppose."

Rebecca chuckled. "The little scamp. You know, Miss Edna, he knew all about Bella and Mr. Harris but never opened his mouth. At least to *us*. But you know people are always confiding in him. Maybe because he looks so proper in those prep school creased trousers and that Harvard College crew neck sweater."

"And because he's so serious all the time."

"Until he starts to wisecrack."

"Well, he's your son." I turned away. "I'll be in my bedroom. I need to nap."

Once in my room, the door closed, I lay wide awake on the bed and gazed around the room, purposely decorated in velvety yellows and greens to relax me, to comfort me. My apple-green bed was supposed to suggest springtime, new-mown lawns, fresh country air. The joy of apple blossom time. Nothing worked now.

Both Waters and Lawson believed that something else happened at Roddy's apartment that night—and that I, for some reason, needed to do something about it. My mind bounced around that foolish, alliterative name: Skidder Scott.

Of course, he was the murderer, a burglary gone wrong.

Yet my gut response to Waters' and Lawson's sketchy scenario and the violent lunch with Bella and Ellie led me to suspect something else happened at Roddy's apartment before—or maybe during the time?—Skidder Scott stabbed Roddy with his own knife.

What did I know about Roddy? He was a charming, good-looking young man, talented, magnetic, someone who seemed soft at the edges, decent and caring. Someone, yes, who drew in, seduced others. Did he have a dark side? Flashes of anger, supposedly. And stubbornness. Did it matter? Roddy was dead. Emphatically. Yes, Bella Davenport had demanded his attention or more, and supposedly he'd rebuffed her. Bella was one hell-bent woman. Or was Bella simply invading territory she wanted to wrest from rival Ellie, that petite girl with the nightingale voice?

What about Ellie? Had she gone to see him that night? Why? Herself rebuffed, and probably not happy. Did she confront Roddy? Women scorned! A familiar and trite tale, though painfully commonplace. Others? Freddy, who disliked Roddy—irrationally. Even Harriet—or her father, that angry man. Lawson, watching his girlfriend make goo-goo eyes—maybe more?—at his cousin. What was there about Roddy—so deferential to me, so decent—that brought out the venom and the obsessiveness in others?

It gave me a migraine, those speculations.

Later, going to get a book from the living room, I heard Rebecca on the kitchen phone talking to her son. "Waters," she kept saying, "I *know* you are bothered. I'll tell Miss Edna. I promise. I know…I know…but…"

"Rebecca," I interrupted, "may I speak with Waters?"

Rebecca gladly handed me the phone, shook her head, and left the room.

"Waters?" I could hear his deep intake of nervous breath. "What did you want to tell me?"

I heard static on the line. Waters cleared his throat. "Miss Edna, Ellie wants to talk to you."

"She's there? Now?"

He rushed his words. "No. I mean, we talked earlier. You know, she heard what Bella said yesterday—about her going to see Roddy that night. About fighting with him. Defiant. Well, I was the one who told her about it because I wanted to hear what she had to say."

I broke in. "Waters, what does this have to do with me? For heaven's sake, why does Ellie want to talk to me?"

"Well, you heard what Bella said and she thinks she has to explain—that's her word—explain this to you." A ripple of soft laughter. "She said that you're Edna Ferber."

"I know who I am, Waters."

"You know what I mean, Miss Edna. You're the only famous person she's met, and you're a writer and she's…"

"No," I said empathically. "I'm sorry, Waters. It's not my place to be involved here. Goodbye."

Hours later, my supper finished and my nose in a short story in *The Saturday Evening Post*, the doorman called to say I had a visitor. I sighed because I knew who it was. Within minutes, Ellie knocked on my door and stood there, dripping with apologies for interrupting my evening but—

I invited her into my living room. Visibly nervous, she avoided eye contact, her face registering emotions from shame to guilt to embarrassment to triumph. She seemed surprised at her own audacity, and though I didn't approve of anyone dropping in on me unheralded, her gumption—the passion that made her act so—somehow impressed me. It was the kind of behavior I'd practiced during my young reporter days in Appleton, Wisconsin.

I told her to stop apologizing.

She was dressed in a drab gray dress, low slung, with a brilliant crimson band of wide ribbon below the hip. Trendy, especially with the wide-buckle shiny silver high heels; but, curiously, she still seemed a country girl, a startled Mary Pickford in crinoline and pleats. She sat demurely, her hands folded in her lap. There was no make-up on her face except for a trace of lipstick. The good girl vamp versus Bella's cat's-meow flapper with bobbed hair and dog-collar choker.

"Tell me," I demanded.

Slowly, her speech building momentum like a prairie wind-storm, she told her story. Waters had convinced her that I now believed the full story of Roddy's murder was not being told. In fact, Waters insisted someone was hiding something—a view, he insisted, both he and I shared. My eyebrows rose at his hyperbole.

Ellie narrowed her eyes. "I resent Bella saying I was at the apartment that night." She stopped, breathed in. "I wasn't."

Lord, I thought, Waters stirred the pot—and now I had to deal with it. "So you knock on my door…"

"I want to explain." I waited while she chose her words carefully. "When I met Lawson heading home from his job, Roddy had just told me he was busy. Well, we had made plans for that night. Suddenly without explanation, he said—Ellie, don't show up. I was singing at a small club near where he lives and I'd be free after eleven to stop by, and we'd talk. Just *talk*." She bit the corner of a nail, stared at it, bothered.

I waited a bit. "Tell me, Ellie. Were you involved with Roddy?"

The question stopped her. After a long pause, she swallowed. "No." But then she held my eye. "I *wanted* to be. But Bella thought I *was*."

"Roddy wasn't interested?"

She shook her head. "He had been, I thought. A little fling. But I thought that, maybe, well…" Her voice trailed off. "Miss Ferber, we had good talks, the two of us. Late at night, after my shows, he'd sneak me in by the back door. We just *talked*." She smiled. "Actually, lately, I was the one who talked. But he always listened to me. He was that kind of guy. I felt he was actually listening to what I was saying. Most guys don't do that." She sighed. "So when he said, no, not tonight…"

"You were angry."

She nodded. "Maybe he thought I was too much trouble. That's why he told me not to come. Maybe he had other plans."

"So late at night?"

A wistful smile. "I think his plan was to sleep in." For a second her eyes closed. "Maybe he didn't want to see the longing in my eyes."

"But you went anyway."

Her voice rose. "Oh, no. I didn't go. Bella was wrong. I mean, when I saw Lawson, I was furious. Kind of like—I'll show that roommate of yours. I'll see what he's up to. But then I calmed down. What was I gonna do? Break in?" Her cheeks flushed as she turned her head away, her voice strained; so I knew, to my soul, that Ellie was lying to me about something. She stammered, "I couldn't bring myself to go there."

"You say you always talked. What did Roddy talk to *you* about?"

She looked back at me, her voice firmer. "Roddy liked his secrets. He liked to be mysterious. But he did tell me a week or so back that he wanted to move away from the apartment. They got this month-to-month lease, and he didn't like it there any more."

"Well, what's the problem? You're unhappy—you leave."

"It's not as easy as that. Lawson is family, sort of. A distant cousin. But it wasn't working out with him. Lawson is a shirker, Miss Ferber. He's been late month after month with his share of the rent because he spends too much at the clubs. Roddy had to pay the difference. Then he'd be late, too. Mr. Porter was on his case." Ellie blushed, which surprised me. "He didn't like Roddy because one time, months ago, I slipped into the apartment from the back and we were just talking. Sometimes Roddy liked to talk the night away…when he was in that sort of mood. You know, talking about dreams…poetry and singing and…our futures. Innocent stuff. I forgot to keep my voice low and Mr. Porter heard me laughing. He raised hell. He's got this rule about girls staying after ten at night—like he's running a monastery. And once before, I guess, he caught Bella back there. She flaunted it, of course. In his face. Arrogant. It drove him wild. So Mr. Porter, I think, sometimes put his ear against the door, if he heard noise. You know, he's crazy. He used to like Lawson because Lawson flattered him, played big man with him, two men of the world. They got drunk together. But lately he wanted both boys out of the building. I know Roddy hated Mr. Porter because he didn't like to be told what to do. So Roddy was delaying telling Lawson about moving."

"Because?"

"I told you. Family. He didn't want to hurt Lawson's feelings."

I'd been nodding to her rambling narrative, but this last line struck me as fanciful. "That's absurd, Ellie. As I said, he's not happy—he moves."

Ellie widened her eyes. "No, no. It's not that easy to do. It wasn't only the rent not being paid. Lawson is like…a gigolo. And Roddy thought he was too ambitious. 'He scares me because he wants to win the moon.' That's how Roddy said it. I guess Lawson's hard to live with—Romeo in the next room, you know. With Bella talking about ending it with Lawson for some time now, that meant Lawson would have to be back in the apartment and not at Bella's brother's place, wooing this one and that, partying all night, getting on Roddy's nerves. Roddy *liked* being alone."

"Did Lawson know Roddy was planning to move?"

"I don't think so. Maybe he suspected, but Roddy kept talking to me about it. What was the best way to do it. 'What do you think, Ellie?' You know, maybe it was a lot of talk. He probably wasn't going anywhere soon."

"Then why talk?"

"Roddy lacked courage, Miss Ferber."

"Bella cheats on Lawson. We know that. So Lawson cheats on Bella?" I waited. "Did he pursue you?"

The question stopped her dead. She began a garbled lie, then began again. "Once. Drunk." She scoffed. "He even made a pass at Harriet, the tribal princess herself. God, she slapped him in the face." She smiled. "Sooner or later, every girl finds an excuse to slap Lawson in the face."

"You don't like Lawson, do you?"

Again the deliberate hesitation, the measured words. "Once, drunk again, Lawson announced he planned to leave us all behind." An exaggerated, phony laugh. "There were people in his future who would be exciting and available and rich and… probably downtown among the white folks."

"He's a cocky lad, this Lawson."

"It doesn't always work and sometimes he miscalculates. Like Bella introduced him to your friend, Jed Harris. She got Mr. Harris to read Lawson's full-length play. But Mr. Harris rebuffed him, and I heard there were nasty words exchanged. Probably because Bella was in the middle of it all. I never got the full story, but Roddy was there when Mr. Harris embarrassed Lawson and hinted it wasn't pretty. Roddy wouldn't tell me the details. It got real ugly. Lawson came crawling back to Harlem with his tail between his legs. He used Bella, and it fizzled out." Her voice was suddenly arch and thin. "Your Mr. Harris can be…vicious."

"He's not *my* Mr. Harris."

"Sorry," A sigh. "So that's why Roddy wanted to move away. In a nutshell. It's hard being in the shadow of a bright sun."

I waited a long time, then asked, "Is all this true, Ellie?"

She hesitated, avoided eye contact. "You mean, *why* was I going there that night?" A sliver of a smile. "I *planned* to go there. Well, I enjoyed our late night talks, mostly in some café or coffee pot after I'm through singing. He waited for me many nights."

"And you fell in love with him."

"Maybe, a little." She pouted, her eyes darkening. "I made the mistake of telling Bella I had a crush on Roddy. Of course, she told Lawson, who found it funny. 'That's a dead-end street,' he told her. She then told me what he said. But Lawson's words were like a challenge to *her*."

"But Bella suspected you and Roddy now, no?"

She nodded. "Jealousy."

"Hence her fury."

"What Bella knew was that Lawson would leave her soon. I don't know if she told us the truth when she said *she* broke up with him that night Roddy died. They're always breaking up."

Ellie reached for her coat, draped over the back of the chair. "I didn't mean to get into all this…this boy-girl nonsense, Miss Ferber. I'm sorry. You can't be interested in the romantic and unromantic lives of a bunch of misguided boys and girls."

I wasn't through. "Roddy's murder changed everything, Ellie. Everything stands out now. A spotlight shines on even the smallest detail."

I could see her struggling for the right words. "You don't think any of this is related to his…murder, do you?" Her hand rose to cover her mouth, but the gesture seemed exaggerated. "God, no! That was Skidder Scott, the derelict." She was buttoning her coat. "It was. It *had* to be." Then, suddenly she sat back down. "You have to believe me when I said I didn't go there that night. I planned… to check up…I didn't want to go. It was cold, chilly, I was tired…"

"Harriet claims she saw Bella lurking in the shadows outside the apartment that night."

"I know. Waters told me. She's a sneak, that Bella. I think she spied on Roddy more than once."

"Harriet didn't see you?"

She looked at me strangely. "Because I wasn't *there*." She caught herself. Then, in a thin, sad voice, she said, "Miss Ferber, Roddy wrote a poem for Bella. A simple little lyric, like an Elizabethan celebration of her beauty. Can you believe it? He actually asked me to read it before he gave it to her." A moment of anger, her eyes blinking wildly. "To Bella. A woman who calculates… evil. I couldn't even comment on it because I was so surprised."

"You still seem angry about it, Ellie."

She made a false laugh, held onto it too long. "Yes, I was. Then. It's okay now." She looked me full in the face. "But I wouldn't kill Roddy because of a mediocre poem."

"I didn't accuse you, Ellie."

Sharp, biting. "Are you sure?" An awkward pause. "I'm sorry. I don't mean to be snide with you, Miss Ferber."

I echoed her own words. "Are you sure?"

◇◇◇

I walked her out, rode with her down the elevator to the lobby, headed as I was to the newsstand on the corner. The *New York Times* morning edition would be out, with a piece on Ann Andrews, the unfortunately wrong actress playing Julie Cavendish in *The Royal Family*. Like Jed, I didn't trust her to do well with the play. The part called for a sophisticated woman born to serve high tea, a woman who put on her gloves in such a way that the act itself defined the word patrician; Ann Andrews was born to play women who sling hash in Jersey shore roadhouses. Ellie tagged along beside me, nervous now, not speaking, looking for the chance to break away and head to the subway. Finally, as I paused at the crosswalk, I waved goodbye, and she scurried up the block.

I stood there watching her, contemplating the gravity and tenor of her words. Had I been duped? Manipulated? My reportorial nose suggested blatant half-truths, perhaps a colossal fabrication. But for what end? Why lie to *me*? Did Waters unduly magnify my concern with Roddy's murder—and the murderer?

The light changed, and I started across the street. I glanced back up the block to see Ellie standing at another crosswalk. She was bent into the slight breeze, head inclined, hands tucked into her pockets.

But in that instant, looking back toward the news kiosk, I saw a dark figure slip quickly behind a parked bus. Standing just a few yards from the murky specter, I realized it was Freddy, that strange and quirky street lad. He hadn't spotted me, I knew, because his body was turned toward Ellie's stationary figure. The streetlight lit his face and, in the moment before he disappeared, I recognized him, remembered him lingering outside Small's Paradise in Harlem, that first night I heard Ellie sing. He'd been watching Ellie that night, not Roddy, not Bella. Ellie. He was following her. And in the fleeting seconds before the bus shielded him, I saw how the tough guy pose was defeated by the abject longing in his face.

Chapter Nine

Two days before Christmas I panicked: presents for my nieces, for Fannie, for my mother who'd persistently hinted at a particular mink wrap at Saks. For a prideful Jewish family, we spent an inordinate amount of time orchestrating a happy Christmas holiday! So the morning was spent shuffling among the maddened shoppers on Madison Avenue, jostled but a little thrilled by the bubbly cheer that would evaporate the day after New Year's. Clerks knew me in the stores, of course; the simple pointing of a finger had a sycophantic clerk scurrying to put aside, wrap, and ultimately deliver the chosen booty.

Done by noon, I met Waters in the entrance of Bloomingdale's where, in response to an earlier plea on the phone, I was to help him choose a fashionable scarf for his mother. The seventeen-year-old, squirreling away part of his allowance, wanted something special, and, clueless, he turned to me. As we rifled through the racks of silk scarves, I found myself enjoying the experience. Waters seemed to be enjoying my company, and I enjoyed his, of course. There was something in those dark, flickering eyes that suggested a real thrill of being with me. I wasn't used to people liking me. Being famous and wealthy, I spent too many hours in the presence of fawners, flatterers, and manipulators, to the point at which I sometimes believed the world was one gigantic Uriah Heep, hunch-backed and whispering buttery blather in my ear.

Waters and I spent most of the hour together laughing.

Back at the apartment, the wrapped scarf hidden in his oversized briefcase, we settled in for a lunch prepared by his mother, who, savvy lady, had intuited the reason for her son's meeting up with me.

Afterwards, sitting with cocoa in the living room, Waters became serious. His spine stiffened and the endless rocking and leg jiggling that adolescent boys seemed to perfect now ceased. Dramatically, he withdrew a thick accordion folder from the same battered briefcase. I could see the jagged edges of typed sheets spilling out, bound by a thick black cord.

"You know, Miss Edna," he began, breathing in deeply, "I've been going back and forth to Lawson's place, bringing a lot of his stuff to Queens. Way out there, an hour by subway. And then an hour back, even longer to where I stay in New Jersey. It's a different world out there." His voice sounded amused. "Anyway, we gotta get everything out because they didn't pay the rent, and Mr. Porter wants to let the place in January." Waters was thumbing the sheets of a manuscript, trying to align the sloppy edges. The ungainly mess seemed ready to slide to the carpet.

I smiled. "You are going to get to the point?"

"Sorry." But I noticed he had no intention of abbreviating his rehearsed story. "I brought over some of his folders of stories and poems, but he never looked at them. He doesn't *care* and I don't understand that. I picked up the pages of Lawson's work that were scattered all over the place, knocked off a desk when it was rifled through. I told Lawson I was doing it but he just shrugged. It didn't matter, he said. Just throw it all in a box. But slowly I found all the sheets—Lord, some had slid under the bed and I swear the corners were nibbled at by a mouse or something—and I put them in order. Sheets were ripped, smudged, bent. I took it home with me. I wasn't supposed to but…"

I interrupted. "I just thought of something, Waters. What about Roddy's writing?"

He seemed flummoxed. "It's there in his room, but I don't know if I can touch it."

"What's there?"

"You know, folders of stuff. Everything in a drawer, organized, neat. Lawson is a slob, but Roddy was, well, the opposite. He told me he'd finished three short stories about Harlem jazz life. And poems, too. I suppose they're all in those folders." He paused. "I won't go into that room."

"They can't be left there."

"No one in his family cares. They didn't come for *him*." Angrily, Waters emphasized the word.

"Then *we* have to."

Wide-eyed: "You think we can publish Roddy's stuff?"

"I don't know if it's any good, but we have to look it over, Waters. We just can't let Mr. Porter throw it all out with the trash."

Waters was waving the manuscript at me, anxious. "That's why I got the rest of Lawson's work, Miss Edna. Even though he doesn't seem to care one way or the other."

I smiled. "I'm sure he'll forgive you. Eventually he'll want to start writing again."

Waters looked impatient, thumbing the loose sheets. "Miss Edna, I stayed up last night and read all of this. I *like* it." He tapped the pile of typescript with his fingers. "I always liked Lawson's plays, but I liked this…novel. I mean, I can tell it's not finished, but there are parts of it, well, I *liked* it."

He pushed the manuscript toward me and I took the stack of sheets from him. The title caught my eye: *Hell Fighters*. He saw my quizzical look because he jumped in, excited, "Ten years ago, during the Great War, Harlem sent a regiment to fight in France. The 15th Infantry Regiment. All Negro volunteers, in fact. Most people don't even know that. His novel is about Negroes eager to fight for America in France in 1917. These groups were recruited from a cigar store on the corner of 132nd Street and Seventh Avenue. They drilled at the Lafayette Dance Hall with broomsticks. With *broomsticks*, Miss Edna. Imagine that? They even dug trenches in tenement alleys. Ask my mother about it. She knows."

"I never knew this, Waters. How many folks do?"

He nodded quickly. "Then they went to France, fought in the trenches even though the regular Marines scorned them. Pershing assigned them to the French 4th Army and called them Hell Fighters because of their bravery. In 1918 they fought at the front for almost two hundred days. Heroes, all of them. Every man. When they got home, they marched proudly up Fifth Avenue, led by a jazz band. When they marched in Harlem, people went nuts. They played 'Here Comes my Daddy Now.'" Waters' voice had been filled with excitement, but now it dropped, somber. "They thought America would be a better place now."

"But everything went back to what it was before."

He nodded. "The KKK is bigger than ever."

"Unfortunately," I added. "So this is the background of the novel?"

"Yes." The enthusiasm appeared again. "Imagine Negroes playing jazz on the streets of France."

I got curious. "Lawson was just a young boy, then, no?"

"But he must have listened to stories. Talked to veterans. He *talked* to people. I remember the time he told me it was a good subject for a novel, but I didn't pay that much attention." He pointed to the manuscript. "The way he wrote war scenes…"

I smiled. "Stephen Crane writing *The Red Badge of Courage*."

"What?" He looked confused.

"A lesson in American literature, Waters. Stephen Crane never experienced the Civil War but he wrote the best novel on that horrid war."

Now Waters smiled. "Lawson does, too."

I didn't know about that, but, at Waters' urging, I agreed to give the novel a glance, though I promised nothing. I slipped off the title page and there, badly typed, was a simple dedication page. Waters noticed me looking at it.

"Read it," he said softly.

I did: "'To cousin Roddy, thanks for telling me about these brave men and for telling me to do this book.'" The dedication was followed by some handwritten lines of poetry in a cramped, chaotic penmanship. The ink had smudged and some words were barely decipherable. In parentheses Lawson had scribbled, "'Harlem,' by Roddy Parsons."

I read the scribbled words:

Saturday morning Harlem says nothing at all
Yet the hum and whisper of night lingers
The echo of a midnight saxophone
The poet sits in shadows
Waiting for Truth.

"Very moving tribute," I told Waters. "What I can make out." I read the lines again, their import now cryptic, revelatory, as if these words by the dead poet possessed a weight I couldn't grasp. That last line: *Waiting for Truth.*

"It's a poem Roddy wrote last year. We all liked it."

I placed the manuscript on the coffee table. "We'll see."

Waters looked disappointed. What did he expect me to say?

◇◇◇

That night, around six, a cab dropped me off at Carl Van Vechten's apartment on West 55th Street. I'd declined Carlo's invitation to his annual pre-Christmas cocktail party, bothered as I was by Roddy's death; but some of my favorite people planned on going, especially Mary and Louis Bromfield, staying in town for Christmas, and Neysa McMein, the illustrator whose covers you saw on *Good Housekeeping* and *Women's Home Companion.* George Kaufman said he'd drop in with his wife Bea. So, dressed in my new black taffeta dress with the cascading sequined fringe, with the rhinestone dog collar I'd bought myself but had never worn, and with my sequined lavender cloche, I hoped I looked like a ravishing flapper, a jazz aficionado, and ten years younger than my forty-one years. Of course, I didn't.

"Edna, you surprise me." He grabbed my hand. "A delight."

"Hello, Carlo." I used the nickname everyone called him.

He always insisted I be at his parties, which flattered me. He adored my novel *The Girls*, he once told me, my nearly forgotten saga of three generations of Chicago women, a piece of fiction I particularly favored and used as a gauge to judge the quality and character of those souls who said they loved my work. Carlo not only read it, but he'd committed some passages to heart, a gesture I found not endearing but curious. A photographer and magazine critic, Carlo threw dazzling parties attended by both exotic and drab celebrities in a scintillating mixture of the *avant-garde* and the mundane. His ballerina wife Fania Marinoff, a delicate eccentric blossom, sat by herself in a chair and looked like a hothouse flower as she watched her husband circulating from one group of men to another.

An aficionado of Harlem life, a man who roamed its streets and clubs, Carlo peopled his gatherings with a mixture of Negroes and whites, something taboo in many quarters. He didn't care and cultivated vigorously the *outré* pleasure. A plumpish man, silver-haired and cherub-looking with prominent buckteeth, prone to flamboyant, wild gestures, he dominated his own parties with his roaring exuberance and his peals of high nervous laughter.

There was always someone new at his side—the young Parisian pianist or the new iconoclastic Negro artist, or, once, an American Indian, a leathery-looking man who wore, at Carlo's insistence, an embarrassing headdress. Carlo loved to celebrate the primitive, and Negroes, I gathered, were his chief affection. Rushing about the living room dressed in a ruffled ivory shirt, his diamond rings catching the overhead light, he was always the darling of any party.

For an hour I hobnobbed with the smart set, exchanged a few words with George Kaufman, who warned me that Jed Harris might show up. Because George had spent the afternoon with him at the theater, he was sharpening his butter knife and his caustic wit for the evening encounter. "Particularly odious, that young man," he hummed in my ear. "Our own Napoleon." Later I saw George and his wife Bea slipping out, doubtless headed home because Bea was never happy at parties, especially glittering soirées. The Bromfields, my good friends, had begged off because Louis had to catch a train to Cleveland. When I realized all of my friends had left, I headed to the guest bedroom to retrieve my fur and purse.

A finger tapped me on the shoulder, and I stopped walking. A rich, velvety voice, tentative, murmured, "Miss Ferber."

I turned and faced the poet Langston Hughes, who was carrying his overcoat over his arm, his fedora cradled against his chest.

"Mr. Hughes," I said, "are you arriving or leaving?"

"If you're leaving, as you seem to be doing, then I suppose I shall be leaving, too. The party's over."

I laughed and he joined in. "Ah yes, I'm the cynosure of all these merry men." For, indeed, there were few women in this male enclave of writers and editors and journalists. "But keep up the flattery, which, you know, never goes out of style."

"Stay a bit," he implored, and I nodded.

He dropped his coat in the guest room, returned, and the two of us sat with cocktails in a corner, our two chairs pulled in close together.

I liked this bright young man, who'd sought me out a few weeks back at a party, and confided his discovery of my working-class short stories when he was in high school in Cleveland. I'd been immensely flattered. Now, leaning into me, he was talking about his new fascination with Theodore Dreiser. I watched him closely, taken with his warm, smiling face.

Here was a man who seemed a tad uncomfortable with his height, with his long, stringy body, a gangly adolescent's body, all jutting limb and angle, constantly readjusting itself into the soft contours of the chair. Dressed in a sharp-pressed gray conservative suit, with a bland gray necktie, he looked the Wall Street up-and-comer, the man ready to take on New York. A handsome face, with a rigid jaw line and a high, sloping forehead, his prominent cheekbones under a rich copper-hued complexion, he appeared a shy man, reserved, deferential. Only when his eyes caught yours, infrequent and sudden, did you notice the wariness in them, a look that suggested a desire to like you that was tempered by suspicion that he was in the wrong place.

"Are you back in the city for the holidays?"

He nodded. "A break from studies. Some poetry readings."

The young poet—what was he? twenty-five?—had gone back to college in Pennsylvania, despite publishing an acclaimed collection of poetry last year. *The Weary Blues*. One of the faces of the Harlem Renaissance, he still struck me as a young lad, thrilled that his verse was now appearing in national magazines. And yet, driven, he went to classes, determined to get his degree.

"I was just talking about you," I began. "About meeting you a few weeks ago."

He raised his eyebrows. "To whom?"

"Some young folks. A group of young Negro…"

But I stopped, struck by the look in his eyes. "I'm sorry," he began, "but your words just reminded me of…Miss Ferber, I have to say that it was strange seeing your name in the *Mirror*. That murder up in Harlem. The young man…"

"Roddy Parsons." I looked around the room and shuddered. "It was so horrible, that."

"The article in the paper, of course, had no details, but I gather he was a singer in the Negro Chorus of *Show Boat*, and a writer…"

"A budding writer."

"Such a sad story."

"Tragic," I added. "I'm still rattled by it."

"Were you his patron?"

"Lord, no." I flashed to an image of some big-bosomed Fifth Avenue matron, awash in barrels of dirty cash and guilt, smiling her *noblesse oblige* superiority on the young struggling Negro lad. "Heavens no!"

Langston smiled. "I'm living in that white shadow now. It's not…ennobling for either party." He nodded toward Carlo, who was recounting some escapade to a small cluster of guests. "Carlo would like to be patron to all of Harlem."

"You don't seem happy with that idea."

He reflected, "Carlo is my good friend."

I told him about Waters, son of my housekeeper, a boy obsessed with becoming a writer—how he'd become part of a group of young Negroes up in Harlem, including Roddy, most in their early twenties, who met in coffee shops, at the YMCA, in church basements. I mentioned how, last summer, intrigued by Waters' description, I'd invited them to my apartment, and I became interested in their work.

"Mentor," he commented.

I smiled. "A better word than patron, certainly." Then I added, "They're not much younger than you. Roddy Parsons was just twenty. I liked him."

At that moment, wildly, my mind tunneled to images of Roddy, Lawson, Bella, Ellie, and even Harriet and Freddy. Somehow, in that second, staring into the serene face of young Langston Hughes, I didn't think of their talent for music, the stage, for literature—or their desire to succeed—instead, I thought of their rivalries, their romances, their fabrications, their—their angers. And at that instant, unwanted, I found the word *murder* echoing in my head.

"Miss Ferber, what?" he asked, nervous.

"What?"

"You look like you've seen a ghost."

"Perhaps I have." I shook my head. "I was thinking of that sad young man, Roddy."

"That must have been horrible—finding the body." He saw the look on my face and immediately stammered, "Sorry."

"It's all right."

But I stood and mentioned leaving. After my thank you to Carlo, I left the apartment, escorted downstairs by the young poet who insisted he hail me a cab. Outside it had started snowing, a light, fluffy mix, pleasant, softening the shrill edges of glittering New York so that the streetlights formed fuzzy halos around the traffic. He shook my hand. Just before I got into the taxi, I asked whether he might meet with Waters and his friends. I mentioned how much they venerated him and how Roddy had considered *The Weary Blues* his Bible.

"I'm too young for sainthood," the poet quipped, to which I replied, "Assume the mantle when you're young, young man; when you're my age the devil lurks around every corner, pitchfork at the ready."

He agreed, yes, after the New Year, he'd love to spend an afternoon at my apartment with them.

I thanked him and as I floated away in the cab, I smiled at the notion of Waters' young face trembling at the delicious Christmas present I'd scheduled in. With echoes of Langston Hughes' honey-toned voice in my ears, I swelled from the pleasure of that man's company.

◇◇◇

That night, sitting up in bed, I reached for a novel on the nightstand. *Elmer Gantry*, an inscribed copy sent to me by my old newsroom buddy, Sinclair Lewis, whom I still affectionately called "Red." But my eye caught the pile of Lawson's manuscript on the bureau. I'd forgotten I'd carried it into my bedroom from the workroom, and now, in the dim light, that pile of poorly typed sheets encased in a torn accordion file beckoned. Let me at least read a chapter or two, hopefully not so soporific I'd drift asleep and scatter the sheets to the floor. Lawson's manuscript did not need a second spilling onto anyone's floor.

I felt a tug at the heart as I read the simple, heartfelt dedication to Roddy, and once again read Roddy's verse. What was there about those simple words that bothered me? I had no idea. *The poet sits in shadows / Waiting for Truth*. I began reading the novel about a happy-go-lucky Harlem boy named Leroy Watkins who is recruited from a cigar store on 132nd Street, joining a revolutionary regiment of idealistic, excited young men. The opening scene, a little sentimental, nevertheless gripped me with its bold, staccato language and its crisp diction. I thought of Langston Hughes' vernacular poetry as I moved through smudged and wrinkled pages. One page was missing its bottom half. At one point I found myself smiling: Lawson had described the handsome young protagonist—an especially talented and personable young man, ambitious and clever—and I realized he was describing himself.

The next thing I knew it was dawn. I had stayed up all night until, weary-eyed and dizzy, I put down the last page. I never stayed up all night, good book or not; but I found myself moving to a boudoir chair, at one point reaching for a forbidden cigarette. The hero drank and smoked too much, and Lawson's description of the intake of cigarette smoke filling his lungs had convinced me I needed one myself. I'd wrapped myself in my flannel robe. The pages piled up next to me. It was, quite frankly, a marvel, this wildly erratic book. It was a war novel with all the obligatory battle scenes, stark and gory, but what propelled the book—indeed, what made its language soar—was the sheer exhilaration behind it.

The Negro soldiers, I learned, were the first Allied unit to reach the storied Rhine. I didn't know that. What white person did? What did we know of Negro life? The prose oozed pride and joy and terror and heartache and despair; it captured the plight of the Negro who excelled on the battlefield, brave to a fault, and then returned home to find, not the equality he'd expected and earned, but a wall of intolerance, discrimination, ignorance. The same old dreadful dismissal as inferior. Lawson had fashioned a gripping scene of the massive company phalanxes marching up Fifth Avenue, led by a jazz band, only to experience jeering and hooting. Yet, in Harlem, they marched under a banner that proclaimed: OUR HEROES WELCOME HOME! The scene tugged at my heart. My eyes teared up.

I thought of Bella and the others, rejected by the downtown producers...groveling for a meager part...mocked by Jed Harris.

I sat back in the chair, exhausted. An unfinished manuscript, I acknowledged, in parts too flowery, other parts sketchy; but mainly an achievement. A loud and vibrant celebration. A roaring hymn to Harlem, writ large. It needed an editor's sure and deliberate hand, but the essence lay on the white pages: majestic, triumphant, splendid. My fingertips tingled on the typed pages. This book needed to be heard. It was a voice that cried out: Listen. I'm here. I'm here. I'm a Negro man. I am a man."

I lost my breath.

I slept for a couple of hours, ignored Rebecca's polite knock on the bedroom door, and rose blurry eyed at ten. I hadn't done that since...well, I never had. Ever. Usually I woke before the sun decided to rise.

Bathed, refreshed, I called Waters, told him I needed to see Lawson.

At four that afternoon, Waters and Lawson strolled into the apartment.

I hadn't seen Lawson since the memorial service for Roddy. Then grief had given him a wasted, lost look. Now, time passing, that grief had made him sickly, his earlier cocksureness and hungry eyes lost to an ashy, drawn face, his eyes sunk deep in their sockets so that he looked famished. Where once he swaggered about, his looks displayed like a birthright, he now slumped in a chair, bent over. He looked, well, exhausted. He'd lost weight, I noticed. Unshaven, in unpressed corduroys and scuffed shoes, he scared me. Here was a young man spiraling downward as though he'd been slammed in the gut.

"Lawson," I exclaimed. He looked up at me. "Are you all right?" A ridiculous question, I knew, but one that needed saying. Waters sat beside him, nodding rapidly, alarm in his face.

"Lawson hasn't been eating."

"But you need to deal with…" I faltered. What? The death of his cousin, grotesque in that final bed?

Lawson tried to smile. "I'll be all right. I just can't seem to get any…steam." For a second he closed his eyes, ready to fall asleep.

"Lawson, I asked you here this afternoon because I read *Hell Fighters*. I know it's not done and perhaps Waters was unwise to put it into my hands." I glanced at Waters, none too happy with my remarks. "But it's done—the deed. You captured something here, something glorious, something…" I paused. "What?"

"It's not ready, Miss Ferber. Next year, maybe. I need to do more research…dealing…"

"Yes, yes," I said in a hurry. "There are holes. Weaknesses. But over all, it's a strong work."

He smiled. "You know, they said that about my play but then no one wanted to produce it—turned it back to me. 'Wonderful job, young man.'"

"But this will be published."

His glance was quizzical, unbelieving. "Not now," he whispered, swallowing his words. Suddenly he glanced at the pile of manuscript I'd foolishly positioned on the coffee table. His eyes narrowed, then widened, as though he were staring into a brilliant sun. "Roddy said it wasn't ready. He was gonna help…"

"I agree, but…"

He stood up and fumbled with his overcoat, then wrapped a scarf around his neck. "Published." Not a question, but hardly an affirmation. Then in a peculiar twist, he recited the lines from Roddy's poem that he'd used in his dedication. "'The poet sits in shadows / Waiting for Truth.'" The same lines that stayed with me, haunted me. "Tell that to Roddy." Without another word, he turned and walked out of the apartment.

Dumbly, I turned to Waters. "Is that a yes or a no?"

Waters shrugged his shoulders. "Dunno."

"He looks ill."

"Miss Edna, I know why he won't go back to that apartment. He *told* me."

"For Lord's sake, why?"

"He's afraid the murderer will come back."

"But why?"

"He thinks someone wants to kill him. They got Roddy. Now him."

"But what proof?"

"He says, well, the way they tore up the rooms—and his room—somebody they know wanted *something*. Somebody wanted them dead. He's afraid to stay there." A pause. "I think he's afraid of Mr. Porter."

"Such a hateful man…"

"But he also mumbled something about his friends."

"You mean, Ellie or Bella or…"

Waters cut me off. "Although he won't say it, I think he's afraid one of them is a murderer."

Chapter Ten

The taxi flew uptown.

My doorman had secured a yellow checkered cab after Waters came back to the apartment and announced that he'd failed to flag down a taxi outside my building, even though, as he cynically termed it, he was dressed like a fugitive white boy from Phillips Exeter in his tan cashmere topcoat, leather gloves, and, horror of horrors, a suede trilby cap he'd inherited from his dead grandfather. Cabbies, I knew, were sometimes loath to squire a young Negro lad up to Harlem. So Joseph the doorman, obsequious to a fault, hailed one, though he couldn't resist frowning at the young Negro boy who blithely and slowly climbed into the back seat of the battered cab, sitting between his mother Rebecca and me. We were going up to Harlem.

After Lawson had vanished from my living room, Waters and I discussed his behavior, befuddled; and Rebecca finally joined us, she conceding, a twinkle in her eye, that "even with the sunken eyes of a cadaver and the haunted look of a dying hero out of a Gothic romance, Lawson looks appealing." She chuckled. "It's hard for Lawson to look bad." Waters groaned and eyed his mother disapprovingly. "But I'm worried about the boy," Rebecca went on. "Worried to death."

Waters was nodding. "You know, I don't think Lawson thought much about cousin Roddy as a friend until he died. Roddy was just the goofy cousin who shared his apartment, who stayed out of his way. I mean, he liked him, pushed him to be a part of the group way back when, but Lawson probably never really thought about him. For a while they were always together, and then…well, they weren't. I think they'd started growing apart from each other." Waters was still tapping his fingers on the manuscript. "When Roddy got murdered, I think Lawson realized he'd lost something. It…you know…*jarred* him. Lawson doesn't have many friends because…well, Lawson likes himself too much. The one guy he'd pal around with was Roddy."

"It's also the way he died," I commented. "The shock."

"To all of us," Rebecca added. "But the body there…*there*… in his apartment." She shuddered. "I'd have trouble sleeping in that place, I have to tell you."

"People die of sadness, you know," Waters went on, a line that sounded melodramatic coming from the skinny boy. His mother raised her eyebrows and looked long at him.

Then Waters, glancing toward the window where the disappearing afternoon sun was painting the Manhattan sky a swirl of orangy red and shrill yellow, told us that Harriet had mentioned that Skidder Scott was arraigned yesterday. "Funny thing is, I asked her how she'd heard about it, and she never answered me. Like she regretted saying anything at all." Then, Waters said, he saw the front page of the *Amsterdam News*. There was a photograph of Scott being led out to a sheriff's van, with stragglers bunched on a sidewalk. And there, bundled against the cold day, stood Harriet, a grainy shot but definitely her, watching.

"Why in the world would she go to the arraignment?" I wondered.

Rebecca echoed my thoughts. "Last place I'd want to be."

Waters had a reason. "Well, the man killed someone in *her* building, you know."

"What did Harriet tell you?" I asked.

"Well, before she clammed up, she said that Skidder Scott has been close-mouthed, only saying that he had nothing to do with it. He's got this public defender who spoke for him in court, but all of a sudden Skidder came out of some haze and began yelling. They had to restrain him."

"Haze?" I asked.

"Like in a fog. Like he hadn't known where he was. It was the old Skidder Scott. He used to get drunk and stand on Seventh Avenue and scream at cars passing by. I used to stand and watch him. But in court he yelled about being set up for the fall, that people *lied* to him. The judge tried to shut him up, but once he started going on and on, there was no stopping him." Waters bit his lower lip. "Just as we suspected, Lawson and me, if you remember. Sounds like someone *told* him to do it." A pause. "Except for one thing."

His mother twisted her head around to look into her son's face. "What's that?"

Waters smiled. "He started saying that the devil must have made him do it. The devil always gets him into trouble, he shouted."

"Well," I said, "that's probably true, but it doesn't help us at all."

"I told Harriet that I believed Skidder," Waters went on. "I said I didn't know if he was innocent but Lawson and me, we think someone who *knew* Roddy was behind the killing. There had to be a reason for it. That startled her."

"What do you mean?" From his mother.

Waters drew in his cheeks. "She got real mad. She told me to stay out of it. It was all nonsense, but it was over now. Just don't get the police back into it. It was bad enough that they were crawling all over the place when it happened. I guess her father did some time and, like Harriet, doesn't trust the cops, afraid they'd railroad someone for something they didn't do. Anyway, she got a little nuts, and finally warned me."

I stiffened. "Warned you?"

He tried to make light of it. "She said someone could get hurt."

"That's unacceptable." I raised my voice, angry.

Rebecca was bristling. "We'll see about that."

Waters insisted, "No, no. Forget it. It didn't mean anything. You know how people talk."

"Waters," I announced, "people I know do not threaten others with harm." I thought a second. "Well, that might not always be true. I did hear Dottie Parker threaten to strangle Aleck Woollcott. And we all begged her to do it." I shook my head. "But I'm making light of a serious threat."

"Let's just forget it, okay? I shouldn't have told you *that*."

Then he began talking about Roddy's papers, his notebooks, his cardboard folders of stories and poems. "Harriet told me her father is going to throw it all into the trash bin. All of Roddy's writing is there, and no one cares."

I sat up. "I care. We care. That man is dangerous, and I don't trust him. Something of Roddy must be rescued…"

"There is only one solution," Rebecca remarked.

She suggested we take a cab to Roddy's apartment and retrieve his writing. That made sense, and foolishly, caught in the moment, I agreed to go with her and Waters.

Which was why, as darkness fell on the city and everything looked bitter and icy and desolate, we three huddled in the back seat of a yellow checkered cab that dropped us off on 138th Street. On the corner at Seventh Avenue a Negro Santa clanged a bell for the Salvation Army and was singing "Jingle Bells" in a deep gravelly voice. I'd never seen a Negro Santa before and it jarred me, momentarily, before I smiled. Merry Christmas to all.

Waters used Lawson's key to open the apartment door, which the super had obviously repaired because a short strip of unstained wood was nailed where the jamb had been splintered. No one was around, the long hallway eerily quiet and dimly lit. I thought I heard the hum of music from the super's apartment, but I wasn't sure. Inside the apartment, as Waters switched on the overhead light, Rebecca and I stopped short, both seized by squeamishness. A violation, this visit. Yet Waters, who'd been methodically emptying out Lawson's possessions and trekking them off to Queens, seemed at home, the absent tenant returning to a place he knew well.

"There's nothing left to take from Lawson's room," Waters noted. "Except for the stuff he's leaving behind. The old bed and bureau. Some chairs. Junk."

Rebecca and I peered through the open door of Lawson's room: we saw a single bed stripped of linens, a stained and ripped mattress, a chipped headboard, a bureau with the drawers halfway pulled out with ragtag unwanted clothing spilling out, a small threadbare wool carpet, a pinewood plank desk. A closet door, ajar, revealed a few items of clothing, neatly arranged on hangers. A stripped-down room. Waters frowned and pointed to the bureau. "Someone's been rifling through the stuff left here. I leave things neat. I didn't leave the drawers out like this."

The faint patina of pale fingerprint dust covered everything.

I supposed we lingered there because Roddy's room felt lit by fire, a telltale heart, something forbidden behind that closed door. Yet we had no choice. The last time I was here my mind was riveted to the dead boy in the bed. Now, surveying Roddy's room, I saw a bed hidden under a drab patchwork coverlet, a shabby bureau identical to Lawson's, a blackened hardwood floor with no carpet, and clothing scattered everywhere, as though Roddy had just left and planned on returning shortly. A flannel shirt was draped over a chair, pants crumpled on the floor, socks tucked into shoes in a corner.

"I don't want to be here," Rebecca whispered.

Glancing at his mother, Waters bustled about, moving to the old oak desk, which, incongruously, someone long ago had painted a hideous deck green. Chunks of the awful paint had chipped away, giving the desk a mottled look.

"I haven't been back in this room," Waters told us. "I mean, I stood in the doorway and looked in. It's not the way the cops left it." He pointed to the pulled out drawers of the bureau and the desk. "Yes, the drawers were pulled-out and stuff scattered, but someone has been in here since. Things have been moved around. I can tell."

Someone—the murderer?—had hurriedly searched the bureaus. A few dimes and nickels were scattered from an overturned jar, suggesting that Roddy's amassed subway and bus change had been pocketed. What else had the intruder looked for? On most surfaces there was that awful patina of white, which gave the room a ghostly reflection, as though a fog had settled into the space.

Quickly, sensing our discomfort, Waters moved through the contents of the desk and finally lifted out a cardboard box. Roddy had been a meticulous young man, organizing his writing, because the box contained a sheaf of poems bound with clips, a folder of one-act plays, and a few short stories, each one labeled "Harlem Jazz," number one, two, three. Here was Roddy's life as a writer. In another desk drawer he located Roddy's scribbled notes, some earlier drafts, bits and pieces, notebooks, all tucked into cardboard cartons. Each drawer was inspected, and Rebecca assembled the pile on top. "Do we take it all?" Waters wondered.

"Of course," I said. "If there is something to publish, we may need the background notes."

"What about his typewriter?" Waters pointed.

All three of us stared at the ancient Remington pushed into a corner of the desk. It struck me as some awesome talisman, some instrument that bore Roddy's precious imprint, his life's breath.

"No," Rebecca said. "We have enough to carry."

So we divided the pile into three, each of us carrying a section of Roddy's brief, aborted literary dream life. My bundle of sheets seemed weighed with a power I truly hoped was really there; otherwise, this was vain pursuit, an exercise of feeble eulogy.

"We need to leave." Rebecca looked toward the doorway.

As we lumbered through the shadowy hallway, folders cradled in our arms and against our chests, the super's door opened suddenly and Harriet stood there, hands on hips, faced flushed with anger. "I thought I heard you rustling back there," she said to Waters. "I didn't know you brought the posse."

"Hello, Harriet," Rebecca said.

Harriet's gaze took us all in. "You're lucky my father isn't here."

"And why is that?" I asked.

"He's not too fond of intruders in his hallway."

I used my pleasantest voice. "Then the police spending hours in Roddy's room must have sent him into a frenzy."

"He's not fond of the police."

Waters looked puzzled. "Harriet, why are you so…angry?"

Surprisingly, she smiled. "I'm not angry, Waters. I'm just… surprised, that's all. It's just that when cops are around—or when other authority figures stop in"—here she eyed me suspiciously— "well, things fall apart." She shrugged her shoulders. "The police make frequent stops here anyway because Pop did ten years upstate, and they assume he's ready for his next batch of years behind bars. Pop and I battle each other and most times we don't even speak to each other, but I've inherited his healthy—or maybe it's actually unhealthy—dislike of the white men in blue who rat-a-tat-tat on our door late at night." She actually rapped her knuckles against the open door.

"No one is accusing your father of anything," Rebecca said to her.

"Really?" A broad smile. "Before they rounded up old Skidder Scott, they were dusting my father's soul for prints." She turned to Waters. "Waters, are you still insisting Roddy's murder was some conspiracy, some hired-gun episode, some…revenge against the hapless Roddy?"

"Lawson and I believe…" he began, defensively.

Her voice boomed in the hallway. "Based on nothing but wild imagination and folly."

Rebecca leaned into her. "Harriet, why did you warn my son…say that someone would get hurt?"

For a moment she stared at us, as if trying to recall her own words. Then she laughed, a phony sound leaking some fear and panic. "I didn't *mean* that, Waters. For God's sake, a little hyperbole and the battalion of women come charging from the Upper East Side to lambaste the little pickanniny Harriet in her shanty."

Rebecca fumed. "It *was* a threat."

"As I said, I didn't want the police back here." She shrugged.

I was frustrated. "Why not? Especially if you—or your father—have nothing to hide."

Now she scoffed. "So, Miss Ferber, you believe there's more to the story of Roddy's murder than a simple burglary gone really bad?"

I paused, reflected. "I don't know what happened here that awful night."

"Roddy got a knife plunged into his chest. That's what happened."

"That's no reason to threaten Waters," I told her.

Waters wore a look that suggested he could defend himself, but he kept silent.

Now Harriet smiled at Waters. "Come on. Think of it. This little boy questioning me? Running off half-cocked, like a darker shade of Sherlock Holmes, strutting his stuff through Harlem dressed like a prep school lad in sweater vest and two-tone shoes."

Waters grunted.

"Just what do you know?" I cut into a speech she obviously found a pleasure to deliver.

For a moment she swung away, her face closing up. Then, "Nothing."

"You think Skidder was involved?"

"That's what *all* the evidence and *all* the police have concluded. The rest is aimless imagination on your parts."

A tenant from the second floor bounded down the stairs, stopped short when he saw us gathered in the hallway. He eyed us warily as he buttoned his overcoat and slipped out the front door.

"Good," Harriet announced loudly. "We're providing entertainment for the winos that occupy the upper floors." She motioned behind her. "You might as well come in. Pop won't be back for an hour, if then, so there's no chance he'll go into shock at discovering all of you, especially the famous novelist, huddled on his old sofa." She stood aside and shooed us in, our arms bearing the piles of manuscript.

I took in the apartment: stark white plaster walls cluttered with gaudy knickknacks bunched onto makeshift shelves, so many that the ceramic ivy planters and orange carnival vases and plaster-of-Paris figurines seemed on the verge of crashing to the floor. It was a hoarder's dreary paradise, a world in which the smallest object that catches the eye, be it a shiny glass snow globe or a tin ashtray stamped Atlantic City Boardwalk, was pocketed, and then duly displayed. Shelf after shelf of tchotchkes, sagging under the burden of utter kitsch. Harriet spotted me surveying the mad bazaar and said out of the side of her mouth, "My mother, when she was alive, couldn't pass a church rummage sale without adopting the most hideous items offered. And," she summed up, "my father assumes it is some kind of shrine to her, seven years after her death."

A quick rapping on the door, and she jumped. Freddy walked in, brown bag in hand and a cloth satchel over his shoulder. He strode in but stopped short, faced us, some fierce judge and jury lined up on the sofa. "What?" he stammered.

"The Inquisition," Harriet told him. "Come in. You're a half-hour late."

"Really, Harriet," Rebecca admonished.

"Sometimes Freddy surprises me with food. I suspect he works in a restaurant, but he's taken a vow of silence." She pointed to the brown bag. "I smell a ham sandwich perhaps."

He slid into a chair, mouth shut, but his eyes danced about the room. I caught him glancing furtively at Harriet, but then he lowered his eyes, avoiding us.

For the longest time we sat there in awkward silence. I kept adjusting the stack of folders in my lap.

Finally Waters, nervous, spoke. "Guess what, Harriet? Miss Ferber spoke with Langston Hughes at a party and he said he'd meet with us after New Year's."

He had barely got out the excited words when Harriet broke in. "Good Lord, Waters. Listen to you. Langston Hughes is not a god. He's a young guy. What is he? Twenty-five or -six, maybe. So he's published. So people know who he is. He's a Negro like the rest of us, a guy who writes poetry while bumming around Harlem."

"He's successful, that's why," Waters answered.

She drummed her fingers on the table. "And so will we be… without his connections. Think about it, Waters. How did he make it? Didn't he go to Columbia, a white man's school? And, like Zora Neale Hurston, he's got this white woman supporting him, a few dollars here and there, a smile, a biscuit, clothes, some bus fare. Please write me a nice little poem about Uncle Tom and Little Eva. Yes, Massa. Everyone knows about Mrs. Mason, that rich dowager in her Fifth Avenue penthouse. Langston, do this. Zora, do that. Ridiculous." She turned to me. "Is she your friend, Miss Ferber?"

I stared into a hostile face, the petulant child, confused and bursting. "No, Harriet, I've never met the woman. And I'm certainly no one's patron."

Harriet ignored me. "Freddy and I are different from you, Waters. And from Lawson and Bella and…" She stopped when she heard Freddy grunt. He wanted no part of this. "I grew up here. I look out my window and see an alley. You look out and see a prep school."

Waters sputtered, but his mother laid a gentle hand on his wrist.

"The new generation," Harriet went on, "has to have a *Negro* voice. Everything else is dead now."

Silence in the room: the kitchen clock ticked too loudly.

"Well," I said, "we have to be going." I nodded at Rebecca.

Then Harriet thundered, "Freddy, these people think somebody else killed Roddy. Or helped Skidder. Or paid him. Or…I don't know."

Freddy sat straight up and the brown bag of sandwiches slid off his lap to the floor. "So what?"

Harriet laughed. "Do they know something?"

Freddy now looked directly at me. "Forget it. Yeah, Harriet and I talked about it. I mean, the nonsense Waters has been mouthing off about. Just because everybody showed up that night and now lies about it." He stopped, uncertain of his own words.

"Everyone?" I asked.

He backtracked. "I didn't mean 'everyone.'"

I followed up. "So far we've only heard about Bella hiding in the shadows, which she denies. And Ellie, who says she never got here."

Harriet grumbled. "Of course, Bella denies it. It makes her look bad, sneaking and spying on Roddy, hiding like that. But I know Bella—I told you I could even smell the gardenia perfume she slathers on. I caught a glance of her shadow. She was here. Maybe midnight or so."

"But she says…" Waters began.

"I *know* what she says, Waters. Bella can never be trusted, folks. This here is an evil woman, out for number one. Her looks are her curse. Like Lawson. Good looks stop the growth of character in children." She grinned. "Write that down. Words of wisdom. She and Lawson with their ofay skin think they can be honorary white folks. But it doesn't work that way. Dark black folks like me"—and she pointed at Freddy—"and him, well, we're the lampblacks and we learn the truth early on."

"What is the truth?"

"Miss Ferber," she responded, her voice softening, "you're a nice lady and all. I'm sure of it. I *know* that. The fact that you're sitting up here now in Harlem—and I don't mean listening to jazz at Connie's Inn—says something good about you. But you'll never understand *this*." She waved her hand around the room. "That afternoon when I was in your apartment—the grand piano and the thick carpets…the…eighteenth century writing desk you're proud of…and the view of the treetops of Central Park. Your living room is longer than my life. I felt…lost there."

"You can't let a grand piano intimidate you, Harriet."

"It's worth more than I am…in some eyes." She breathed in. "So, yes, Bella is a liar who *was* outside the apartment that night. But, as much as I dislike her, I'm not calling her a killer. She was hiding in the shadows here because she's jealous of Ellie, not because she was waiting to kill Roddy. That makes no sense."

"But Roddy had rejected Bella," Waters said.

She laughed. "Roddy rejected everyone."

"You, too?" Waters asked.

"He had no interest in me. One time a drunken flirtation. Men get drunk and they gotta flirt. I'm the super's rebellious daughter. Roddy was all soft edges; I'm hard as glass. And I like it that way. He's...he was..."

"What?" From Waters.

"Nothing. I don't know."

"Freddy," I asked, "So you didn't mean that everyone was here that night. But I suspect you were."

Harriet laughed derisively. "Of course he was. Maybe Freddy's right. Everyone was here that night."

Freddy squirmed. "Shut up, Harriet."

"Come off it, Freddy. The Upper East Side Detective Agency will find out sooner or later. Tell them why." Freddy bit his lip while Harriet settled back in her seat. "It's because Ellie was here that night. Supposedly. Even though she *denies* it now. She told everybody, it seems, that she was going to see Roddy, no matter what. She was an angry woman."

I tried to recall Ellie's exact words. "But Ellie swore to me that her plans changed, that she never came here after she finished at the club."

Again Harriet scoffed. "Poor little Freddy," she began, though there was some affection in her voice, "has an unrequited crush on Miss Ellie Nightclub, and, though she looks right through him because she's part of the high-yeller club herself and he's inky-dink, the boy can't help himself. No lie. He follows her everywhere, supposedly to 'protect' her from evil, but, more likely, to catch a view of her as she moves through the street."

"Shut up, Harriet," Freddy muttered.

"I think it's kind of charming," she added.

"What about Ellie?" I asked. "Did she lie to me? Was she here?" Silence.

Harriet waited, and then looked at Freddy. "Tell her, for God's sake. You spend enough time looking at Ellie with mooncalf eyes, Freddy. Tell her."

Freddy was fidgeting in his seat, his foot kicking the dropped paper bag.

I spoke up. "Freddy, I saw you outside my building the day Ellie visited me—when she swore to me that she went home after singing that night. You were by the bus shelter."

Freddy looked embarrassed but he nodded. "That was stupid of me. Yes, I was there—to see what she was up to. She was supposed to meet me for coffee, but broke it off. I saw her on the subway platform, so I trailed her. Yeah, I was there. Real stupid. Not good, let me tell you. You don't get a lot of Negro boys hanging out at bus stops in your neighborhood. I didn't look right. I had to deal with a cop for an hour before he let me wander off."

"Tell her," Harriet said again, irritated.

Freddy sighed. "I saw Ellie that afternoon. I stopped in at my sister's for a bite and Ellie lives next door with her grandfather. She was coming out of a grocery as I left my sister's apartment. She called me over, which surprised me. Lots of times she saw me on the block and looked away. She was in a real crazy mood because, I guess, she had made plans with Roddy but he broke them at the last minute. I guess he'd done it to her before. She was yelling she'd show up at his place after her club act, just see what he was up to. She was boiling. She'd already told Lawson she was going. I guess he told Bella. You know, she suspected Bella was gonna be there. Then she said she was going home after the club. That it wasn't worth it. I think Lawson told her the same thing. So that night I was hanging out with some buddies, nothing to do, hanging outside a coffee pot a block away from the 135th Street subway. Hanging out on the cold street. I was smoking a cigarette and then, out of the corner of my eye, I see Ellie walking up the stairs from the platform."

"What time?" I asked.

"After midnight." He waited a bit. "She was coming from the club. I suspected she was headed to Roddy's after all. Okay, so I was jealous, surprised, but by the time I started after her, she was gone, lost in the crowd that turned the corner."

"What did you do?"

"I went past Roddy's, but everything looked quiet. But I knew Roddy would sneak Ellie in by the back door so Harriet's father couldn't hear. So I went down the alleyway to the back, but nothing. Roddy was home—the lights were on, I could see—but everything was quiet. So I figured…well, I don't know what I figured. I went home."

"Where is that, Freddy?" Rebecca asked.

He didn't answer her.

Harriet was smiling. "So everyone *was* here that night. Including me, sleeping in my lowly bed."

Freddy spoke through clenched teeth. "It doesn't mean she killed Roddy, Harriet. It doesn't even mean she came here. You know that. We talked about it already. I didn't say anything because Ellie *wasn't* here. I was."

"At midnight," Waters mumbled.

Freddy went on. "She was probably going to one of the clubs. Not to Roddy's."

"But she was angry with Roddy," I said.

"Yeah, so what? We all get mad at each other."

Harriet grumbled. "Maybe she was meeting Bella in the shadows. A meeting of the Roddy Veneration Society, Harlem chapter."

"She wouldn't kill Roddy," Freddy insisted. "She loved him."

"All the more reason to kill him. He didn't love her back." But she paused, drew in her breath. "I'm not serious. None of us killed Roddy, Miss Ferber. Skidder Scott did it for a few pieces of silver on Roddy's bureau."

"You didn't like Roddy," I said to Harriet.

She pursed her lips and looked toward the street window. "I don't suppose I did."

"Why?"

She rolled her tongue into the corner of her mouth. "Well, if you gotta know, he thought he was better than us. I mean, Lawson *acted* that way, Mr. I'm-Gonna-Make-It-Big, but Lawson would knock on my door, we'd go to a rent party together, dance. He may have been bored, but he could be *nice*. He'd even read my poetry—seriously read it."

"And Roddy didn't?

"Roddy lived in his own world, and you had to pick a number to come into it."

"What about you, Freddy? Did you like him?"

Freddy fidgeted. "He was all right."

"Tell her!" Harriet screamed.

"Christ, Harriet," Freddy said. "What's with you?" He swore under his breath. "I didn't get along with him, okay? One time, you know, he sort of made a…pass at me." Harriet burst out laughing. "I think it was, but it was hard to read, and he, well…"

Harriet roared. "My God, Freddy, you were furious at the time. Right outside in the hallway, and my father watched it all. He saw Freddy shove Roddy into the wall. And Pop told me to stay away from him—and even Lawson—and when Pop told Roddy he didn't want him in the building, Roddy shoved him." It was a furious rush of high-pitched words, and Harriet, her head bobbing nervously, finally stopped.

"I don't like this conversation," Rebecca murmured.

"Well, I'm sorry," Harriet said. "You know why Pop didn't want the cops crawling around here any more? Yeah, his prison record, sure thing. But when Roddy hit him, Pop yelled that he was gonna kill Roddy, so loud that one of the tenants upstairs, drugged out though he was, came running down the staircase."

"If he's innocent, what does…" I began.

She held up her hand, a traffic-cop stop. "You know, Miss Ferber, I hate Pop but I still don't want to see him strapped to an electric chair."

Chapter Eleven

"Love and jealousy," I remarked as Rebecca, Waters, and I walked back into my apartment.

Rebecca smiled. "It never changes, does it?"

"I don't get it," Waters said.

"Well," I noted, "those young friends of yours, Waters, are filled with rivalries, fierce and potent."

"Roddy was like a lightning rod," Rebecca suggested. "A gentle boy, though I guess he could get angry and strike out at folks. Those spurts of violence. But pushing folks away did nothing more than attract folks to him. Ellie with her late night talks with him, though she wanted more. Bella, the *femme fatale* who probably never looked at Roddy until Ellie shared her infatuation. Even Harriet, so intense in her dislike. Her father…"

"And then the murder that same night when things were coming to a head," Waters said. "Maybe."

Rebecca was nodding her head. "Everyone lingering around the building while Roddy slept alone in his bed."

"I don't know if any of this intrigue has to do with murder, Waters." I added, "But there *was* a lot of activity at the apartment the night he died. Ellie, maybe. Bella in the shadows, maybe. Freddy lurking in the back alley. And no one was there during the murder."

"Do you think Ellie lied to you?" Rebecca asked me.

"Yes, but why come to my apartment and fashion such an elaborate lie? Maybe she's being truthful that she wasn't at

Roddy's, but Freddy saw her in the neighborhood, so clearly she was nearby. But was she in his apartment? Was she sneaked in through the back? Who knows?"

"The killer came through the front door," Waters said. "The broken lock."

"Did you look closely at that?" I said. "A simple screwdriver could snap that old lock and splinter the wood. The killer still could have come in through the back. The broken lock could be a deception."

Waters smiled. "So I've convinced you, Miss Edna, that something else is going on."

I smiled back. "I don't know that, Waters. But something else happened there. What reason does Ellie have to lie? Her visit to me bothers me. It seems so…unnecessary. And what about Bella hiding in the shadows, even though she says she wasn't there."

"Love and jealousy," his mother repeated my words.

"How's Lawson doing now?" I asked Waters.

"Better, I think. Living way out in Queens isn't helping his spirits, though. He misses the excitement of Harlem."

"He travels to his job there every day? It's quite a trek by subway."

Waters grimaced. "He's been missing quite a few days. But he's getting better. In fact, I got him to go to a poetry reading at the Hobby Store later tonight. It took a little arm-twisting but he agreed." Waters looked at the clock. "I'm meeting him in two hours at Columbus Circle."

"Tell him to meet you here," I said suddenly. "I'd like to talk to him."

Waters grinned. "The detective."

"Well, maybe," I acknowledged, "but I'd like to get the events of that night clear in my head. We'll give him supper." I looked at Rebecca. "Possible?"

"Of course."

"I'll phone." Waters went into the kitchen and I could hear him talking to someone. Then I heard him dialing another number and reaching Lawson. When he returned, he looked content. "Yeah, he's coming. I called his work first, but he was home, getting ready to get on a subway. Some errands. I promised him food."

Rebecca stood up. "He's getting back to normal. Lawson always was a big eater."

Lawson sat in my living room, pensive, shoulders hunched, his eyes darting around the room, at times narrowing and staring toward the window, as though searching for something out there. He may have been getting better, if I believed Waters, but he still looked like a bony cadaver with those huge sunken eyes and that ashy parchment skin. That Broadway smile now was wan and melancholic.

"Love and jealousy," Waters said out loud, and Lawson shot him a quizzical glance.

"We think Ellie and Bella were both at your apartment that night," I started. "This is none of my business, Lawson, but ever since Ellie made a point of visiting me and proclaiming what now seems to be a lie, I've become curious. Why involve me?"

Lawson locked eyes with me. "Maybe Ellie was there that night, but not Bella. She was with me."

"Well, tell us what you remember about that night."

He hesitated, squinted. Silence in the room. All of us zeroed in on that stark, unreal scene, the body in the bed, the contorted face, that knife thrust into the chest. I swear Lawson shivered.

Gently, I said, "Just tell me *your* story. I'm trying to place people…"

"No," he answered too quickly, "you're trying to catch either Ellie or Bella in a lie."

"Neither one seems to need my help, Lawson. They both rattle off comfortable stories that are immediately countered by eye witnesses."

"These are my friends, Miss Ferber."

"I know," I told him. "I'm sorry, but we have to have this conversation."

He spoke in a rush of words. "This is all about the killing. I know that, no matter what you say. I just don't see Ellie or Bella hurting Roddy. Yeah, we all get angry at each other. We got arty temperaments, we flare up, we argue, we stop talking to each other for months; but the bottom line is that we *like* one another. That's why we get together as a group. Look someplace else."

Waters jumped in. "Lawson thinks it was Mr. Porter. That's one reason he won't go back to the apartment."

Lawson shot him a harsh look. "For God's sake, Waters, isn't any of my conversation private?" For a second he closed his eyes and seemed to drift off.

I repeated myself. "Tell me what happened that night. To you."

He settled back into the cushions of the sofa, breathed in. His head shook, and I thought I saw tears seep out from the corners. His stare was vacant, faraway.

"Well, it was our usual Saturday night." A pause. "Except it was different. You know, I've been thinking about this a lot lately. I'm not sure what I mean by that, except…well, Bella seemed real edgy, like she was ready to pick a fight. We fight all the time, of course—it was what held us together—but the way she was curt with me told me she was angry from the start. She'd been sniping at me ever since I got back from my job and told her I'd bumped into Ellie—and Ellie was going to see Roddy. Earlier her brother hinted that she was leaving me for good. I knew he was tired of me sleeping on his sofa." He smiled. "Bella had left me many times before, but I'd seen this coming. Bella was getting into new people."

"New people?" I broke in.

"She saw herself moving up and out of…her old world. And I was the old world. She was socializing with…with more white folks. Downtown." He shook his head. "Anyway, I thought we'd make it one last fling. One more big night on the town. I got a little depressed because I figured I'd be forced to come back to my apartment."

"You didn't want to live there? With Roddy?" Rebecca asked.

"Well," he stretched out his words, "I knew Roddy wasn't happy with me. Not that we argued or anything, but I didn't pay my share of the rent. I don't make much as a janitor, and I go out to the clubs. Sometimes Bella requires good bootleg gin." He grinned. "So do I."

"Did you know Roddy was thinking of leaving the apartment?" I asked.

He stared into my face. "I had a suspicion. When I came to get a change of clothes or whatever, sometimes to get a bite to eat with him, his talk was strained. But I didn't think he'd thought it through. Where would he go?"

"But you didn't pay your own way," I emphasized.

He frowned and dipped his head. "I thought I'd catch up."

"He told Ellie he was going to move."

That surprised him. "You sure?" He waited. "Well, I didn't think he had the nerve to go."

"He was afraid to tell you."

His eyes moistened. "That sounds like Roddy."

"Then what happened?" I went on.

"Nothing much. Bella and I got all dressed up. She wanted to hear Kid Chocolate's early show at the Spider Web, then go dancing. She insisted we go."

Waters wandered to the window, staring down into the street. For a moment, Lawson paused, watching him.

"Go on," Rebecca said.

He furrowed his brow. "She loves to dance. So do I." He grinned. "The turkey trot. Everyone wants to dance."

"I don't," I spoke up. "If I did the Charleston, I'd gather a crowd."

He looked at me strangely, but went on. "We got drunk, the two of us. Real drunk. We knew people at the club, so it was easy." Doubt suddenly swept across his face. "But, you know, even though I was pretty loaded and Bella got wild and funny, I felt that she wasn't nearly as drunk as I was."

"What do you mean?" Waters walked away from the window to stand next to Lawson's chair.

"I'm not really sure. When you get drunk with a woman lots of times, well, you sort of know how they act—the silliness, the foolishness. Well, Bella was out of it. I can't really put my finger on it, but it was the little things. The way I caught her watching me when she thought I didn't notice. The way she staggered too much, grabbed onto me. Of course, it may just have been the fact that when we got back to her place—early, too, just after eleven because she said she was tired—she picked the fight she'd been leading up to all night long."

"And she told you it was over?" I asked.

He nodded. "And she told me it was over."

"Yet you stayed."

"I was drunk. It was late. And she told me to stay. That's what I thought was strange. Get out of my life, but stay over tonight. On the sofa. I didn't plan to go home anyway. We ended up drinking some more, and I got real dizzy. I fell asleep on her sofa. I don't remember much after that." A pause. "I do remember reaching out to her, you know, to fool around, but she brushed me off."

"That's it?" Waters asked.

He bunched up his face. "Oh, I remember something we fought about. Earlier. On the way back from the club, she talked a blue streak about Ellie and Roddy—how Ellie was making believe she was Roddy's friend for late night talks, but really she was trying to seduce him." He got quiet.

"And?"

"Well, as I said before, I'd met Ellie just that afternoon—she was walking by the building where I work and I was leaving—and she told me about going to Roddy's that night. Bella brought that subject up again—like she couldn't leave it alone. We were walking back to her apartment."

"And?" Waters prodded.

"I thought it was funny. But that news drove her crazy. She kept saying that she was much more beautiful than Ellie. I asked her— what does that have to do with Roddy?"

I was flummoxed. "But Roddy never showed any interest in Bella, right?"

"She was *my* girl," Lawson insisted. "Why would he?"

"But Bella flirted with him," Waters added.

Lawson sighed. "Bella flirted with everyone." He swallowed. "And Roddy *teased* her—and Ellie. He flirted, he flattered. It was all an act. Not because he was cruel but because he didn't know how else to be."

"He was playing with fire," I noted. "Bella and Ellie, eyeing each other across a table. Weapons drawn—sharpened."

"Anyway, walking back that night, drunk, she brought it up again. Leave Roddy and Ellie alone, I told her. It made her furious. 'You don't know your own cousin!' she screamed. We were walking on the sidewalk in front of her apartment. And she turned and slapped me hard in the face. It surprised me. We went inside and she said she was leaving me. Next thing I knew it was morning."

"You woke up before her?"

"No, she was banging around the apartment, trying to get me on my feet. I had to get to work and I overslept. I had a wicked hangover. It felt like my head was cotton. I kept staggering around, couldn't find my shoes. She stood there, laughing. 'What's the matter with you? Can't you hold your whiskey?' But I'd never felt like that before. So when I got to my apartment and you all were there and then there was Roddy, it was like I was not even awake yet."

I changed the subject. "You said Bella was socializing with new folks…white folks. I think you mean a particular white man, no?"

"Oh my God. That's another thing we fought about that night." He spat out the words. "Jed Harris."

"Jed Harris," I echoed.

"Your friend. " The name hung in the air like a foul curse.

"Well, hardly," I insisted. "A business acquaintance."

"Not to hear him tell it." He smiled. "We knew he was the producer of *The Royal Family*. We all talked about it. It was a little awkward, meeting last summer in your living room. It's a very small world. Everyone knows he is the man who can make or break a career."

"Why didn't you say something to me?"

"What could we say?" He shrugged his shoulders. "You can imagine how surprised we were when he showed up at your apartment last week, standing there, staring from Bella to me... and the others."

"But why?" I looked at Waters.

Sheepish, Waters answered, "I guess because of his relationship with Bella. It was...a touchy subject."

"And what was that about?" Rebecca wondered.

"Mr. Harris likes the Harlem jazz clubs and spends time there. He's got a weakness for beautiful women. Even Negroes. Some folks do. Especially when they look like Bella, light-skinned, gorgeous, sexy, flirtatious...ambitious. Somehow Jed met Bella— uptown at a club, I figure, or at an audition. Bella wouldn't tell me. I'm not sure where. Maybe even at some speakeasy where the races mingle. He seduced her. It was an opportunity for her—maybe, and she saw a rosy future downtown. The fact that she was seeing *me* didn't amount to much." The last words, spoken bitterly, hung in the air.

"It must have bothered you."

"Well, yeah. Sure. But nothing surprised me with Bella. She loves money more than men." He closed his eyes a moment. When he opened them, I saw hurt. "They used each other. I knew she'd mentioned me to him— to make him jealous, but I don't think Mr. Harris gets jealous. She told him about my play. I *asked* her to. I was drunk with the possibility of success, and he said to go ahead, send it to him. He'd read it. He'd meet with me. Now I don't believe he was serious, he was playing games, but I sent the play and a month or so later I called at his office. He hadn't returned my calls." He stopped and bit at the corner of a nail.

"It's all right," I prodded.

"So I stopped in one afternoon, bold as can be. He was in, but irritated, snapping at me. I sat in his office, and he pushed the play back at me. 'It's real good. It needs work but you got a story here. I can see this working on Broadway.' So I got a little intoxicated, but then he stood up and said, 'But I have no interest in helping you.' I didn't know if I heard him right, so I sat there, dumb. Then he said, 'Why would I help Bella's pretty Negro boy?' Just like that."

"Jed," I sighed, almost to myself.

"So I stood up, flustered, nuts, and yelled, 'Maybe you should stay away from Bella! She's mine, not your plaything. You rich white guys come to Harlem and take our jazz and women and…' I went on and on, everything spewing out of me, and Mr. Harris got real still. Then he said, 'You arrogant buck. Get the hell out of my office.'"

"My God," I breathed in.

"But I couldn't move. I realized I'd made a stupid mistake—and then made it worse by yelling at him. He came around to the front of his desk and flicked his finger against my chest. It stung. And I swear he whispered in my ear, 'No Broadway, no acting, no writing, no career. Your career is over. You just lost your chance for success. You'll be a…what did you say you were? A janitor? You'll be a janitor for the rest of your life. No one will ever touch your stuff.' I stumbled to the door. He followed me into the anteroom. He was sputtering, livid."

"Then what happened?" Waters was stunned.

Lawson stopped. "Roddy was waiting for me. I just remembered that. He came with me. And he'd heard the exchange between us. I must have been pale and barely moving because he rushed over to me."

"What did Jed do?"

I was flabbergasted by Lawson's story, though not surprised. I'd witnessed other episodes of Jed's irrational and random cruelty to those he deemed inferior—easy fodder for his venom.

"Mr. Harris looked from me to Roddy. 'And who is this boy? Another failed playwright?' He *sneered* at him. Roddy was always so quiet, but the guy had flashes of rage in him. So he said to Mr. Harris, 'You don't deserve your success.' 'Who are you?' Mr. Harris asked. 'I'm Lawson's cousin, Roddy Parsons. Remember that name. In a year you'll be hearing about me.'

Mr. Harris laughed. 'Christ, more stupid vanity at work. From the looks of you, I'd say you'd do fine as a busboy in a Harlem eatery. Now get out, the two of you.' But Roddy wasn't ready to leave, and I had to push him out. The last thing Mr. Harris yelled at me was, 'Your career is over!'"

"Then?"

Lawson shrugged his shoulders. "Then nothing. I walked out of the building."

"What did you think?" I asked.

"I believed him. I had an enemy now in Jed Harris. And that, I knew, wasn't good."

Chapter Twelve

Jed Harris glared back at me with those cold eyes, the pupils pinpoints of cut diamond, and as hard. We'd been sitting across from each other at Sardi's, a lunch he'd requested; but as the minutes passed, Jed simply stared at me with those icy eyes, and he said perhaps ten coherent words, whispering in that annoying, purring voice. Dressed in a splashy pinstripe suit, with his signature fedora with the red feather, and the cigarette glued to the side of his thin lips, he struck me as some stage door Johnny with too much money and too few marbles, an unrepentant *yeshiva* boy drunk with Broadway chorus girls and blazing footlights. The staff at Sardi's, used to Broadway royalty, bowed and scraped—and generally irked me.

"Well," I said for the fifth or sixth time, "you demanded lunch, and yet you avoid my questions. Am I missing something, Jed?"

Again, the silence. He turned to the waitress and complained about the tepid coffee. She scurried away, tripping over herself.

"Last night," I snarled, "you woke me at midnight and babbled nonsense about your yacht in the Hudson. Not, as I assumed when I answered the phone, some crisis with *The Royal Family* that couldn't wait, but a yacht I never was on, nor intend ever to be on."

"Nor will you ever be invited, Edna."

The waitress, her fingers trembling, refilled his cup.

I smarted. "A yacht moored in the Hudson is like a canoe drifting down the Nile. Or an elephant squatting in an English garden. Something is wrong with the picture."

He studied me long and hard. Then, blowing a circle of blue smoke in my direction, he sputtered, "Boys like to play with boats."

"About *The Royal Family...*" I began.

I'd had a busy morning at the Selwyn Theater where George Kaufman and I watched the director Burton doing a run-through. Around noon, still rattled by that mercurial phone call at midnight, I watched Jed Harris stroll jauntily into the theater just as the cast was taking a break, and he frowned and stomped his feet as he approached the stage. Beside me, George rose, grunted, and walked out of the theater. I sat there, third row center, and caught Jed's eye as he shambled by. This was not going to be good. I felt bile rise in my throat, a boulder thrust into my gut. Nothing pleased him, and the director stormed off, leaving Jed standing there, upstage, cool, nonplused. No one looked at him. His quixotic personality and the volcanic bursts made me believe the success of the play was iffy. Maybe *doomed* was the word I really meant.

Now, sitting opposite him at the lunch he demanded, he leaned in. "It's all wrong." He inhaled his cigarette.

"No," I insisted, "it isn't." A pause. "I suppose we're talking about the play?"

He ignored me. "I'm firing the whole cast. This isn't worth it."

"No, you're not." I tapped a spoon on the table. "No."

He smiled. "Edna, Edna, you'll never understand the machinations of New York theater."

I bit my lip. "And you'll never understand the workings of the human heart."

He snickered. "Low blow, Edna dear."

"I figured I'd descend to your level for the moment."

He looked away toward the entrance, annoyed by the sudden ripple of laughter coming from two young women. "Enough talk of this play. We've exhausted the topic." He leaned into me, his eyes dancing. "Helen Hayes is trying to seduce me."

"Good Lord, Jed!" I roared. "Do I really need to know this?"

"Though she failed, she's been more effective at the attempt than you've been…" He was enjoying himself, watching me squirm.

"Stop…" I interrupted.

He went on. "But then you've had so little practice in the art of love."

I half-rose. "So you invite me for lunch with the goal of spouting nonsense about stuff you know nothing about."

"Sit down, Edna. People are staring."

He smirked and took a sip of coffee, seemed not to relish it, and replaced the cup in the saucer. "Women love me."

I sneered as I settled back into my seat. "For some women, money is the only aphrodisiac."

He grinned. "We weren't allowed to use that word at Yale."

"What? Money?"

He laughed. "Edna, Edna."

"Jed, are we going somewhere with this conversation?"

He ignored me. "Do you know why I call myself 'Jed'? I made up the name, you know. God told the prophet Nathan…anyway, it's from Jedidiah. Beloved of God. My family still doesn't know. They're hidden on the Lower East Side wondering where smart little Jacob Horowitz has gone off to." He burst out laughing. "I invented myself, Edna."

I'd had enough.

"That's all very nice, Jedidiah, but…tell me about Bella."

He narrowed his eyes. "You've been waiting to ask me that."

"I think…"

"Don't think, dear Edna." He rolled his eyeballs. "Nosiness is the first word a child learns in the great, unwashed Midwest, the place of your nineteenth century birth, right?"

"Perhaps. But I prefer the word…curious."

"Edna, Edna. Dear, sweet Edna. My non-involvement with that voluptuous Negress seems to keep you awake nights."

"No, but murder gives me insomnia."

That stopped him. He sat up. "What?"

"You heard me."

"Edna, what?"

"Another question, Jedidiah. Why are you so hostile to Lawson Hicks, her boyfriend…or former boyfriend? Whatever he is."

He stared at me, his lips drawn into a thin, bloodless line. Finally, glaring, he spat out the words. "If you must know, and clearly you must, Bella was a fling, Edna. A diversion from my wonderful marriage. People seem to forget I'm married…with a wife living…somewhere in this vast metropolis. I forget where exactly. Keep that in mind, dear Edna, whenever you choose to beguile me with your charms. But Bella was a…lark. A lark who willingly and gladly lighted on my bough, Edna. If you know what I mean. Sadly, she believes there's always a reward for licentious acts. She's already a chapter in my history."

"So you used her."

"I use everyone. We all do. That's the way the world spins." He sat back against the chair, folded his arms around his chest, and rocked his body. "She's an incredibly beautiful girl who is taboo. Cleopatra on the Harlem Nile."

"Folderol," I said, though I regretted the word.

He burst out laughing. "You're showing your age, Edna. You sometimes sound like a villainess in a Victorian revival of *The Drunkard*."

"Yet the word somehow works with you."

His voice became a dangerous whisper. "Edna, this is none of your business…what I do. All over town there are chorus girls. I share them with your randy, homely buddy, Georgie Kaufman. You know that. And, frankly, I'm finding your chatter a tad annoying because you, though a captivating woman in your oh-you-kid dress, you insist on posing as a prudish frump, a starved old maid…"

I slammed down my coffee cup. "Enough." But I wasn't through. "I was told about the way you treated Lawson in your office. Praise, then outright rejection of his play. Such a cruel dismissal, Jed. Why?"

His voice was clipped. "Ah, a simple answer. If you must know, I enjoy fooling with him. Because he's Bella's beau. Here you have this handsome young buck, all swagger and bravado, cocksure, sitting there waiting for me to make him the first major Negro playwright. A talented lad, truly reminding me of myself, though I'm barely a whiter version, and a lot shorter, of course."

"But you enjoyed being cruel to him. You told him he'd have no career in New York."

"Yes, I did."

"But why torture him?"

He shrugged. "Because I can."

"He's done nothing to you."

"Oh, but he has. He made demands on me." A pause. "I just don't like him."

"Because he's with Bella." A statement.

"That, and he's too tall."

"No, he's too black."

"Maybe he's not black enough." Another pause. "This is not worth talking about, Edna. He's…nothing." Suddenly he stressed the word, loud, high. "*Nothing!*"

The waitress, approaching our table, instantly swiveled and walked away. I noticed other irritated diners glancing at us.

"Jed," I began, "your voice."

He didn't care. "Edna, let me tell you a story. You like stories, I know. You steal them from others and then publish them in the *Saturday Evening Post*. What did F. Scott Fitzgerald call you in *This Side of Paradise*? The Yiddish descendant of O. Henry? He lumped you with Zane Grey, no? How that must have got under your skin." Grinning, Jed made a clownish face, exaggerated, grotesque. "Anyway, one afternoon I was sitting in on auditions for *The Chocolate Dandies*. It's an inept plagiarism of *Shuffle Along*, a cast of hoofers and singers. Bored, I sat there as the performers went through their paces…."

"What are we talking about?" I broke in, annoyed.

"Well, Bella's beau actually showed up to audition. He was completely right for the part, of course. A young, good-looking Negro, good to look at from the orchestra. Good rich voice. So Lawson read for the part—which takes place, if I remember correctly, in a Harlem jazz club. Or am I thinking of another travesty? The author and the director, I could see, were taken with him. My God, Lawson could have written the scene about himself, so perfect he seemed to us. And they made it clear to Lawson that they liked what he had done. God, the way he beamed."

I pulled in my cheeks. "But you sabotaged it."

"Very easy to do, in fact. After he left the room I whispered that I *knew* his work. I'd seen him act at the Lafayette, a minor role. I told them that he was a shirker, a shuffling and lazy sort, all teeth and brio and no energy to show up on time."

I was shaking my head. "And Lawson probably knew you did this."

"Well, he saw me sitting there. Actually he stared directly at me at one point."

"This was right after you rejected his play?"

"Yes."

"So he probably suspected."

"I hope so." A wolfish smile.

"You blackballed him."

"Exactly."

"Jed, this is maniacal…and…"

"Oh, who cares, Edna dear? The life span of a Negro actor in New York is calculated in seconds. A role here, a role there, and next year they're back to hauling ashes in a basement on St. Nicholas Avenue."

I gathered my scarf and gloves. "Iago had nothing on you, Jed Harris."

"Ah, another Negro-and-white melodrama."

"That one ends in murder, too."

"Are you expecting a murder, Edna. Perhaps of me?"

"Jed, you've forgotten that Roddy Parsons was murdered in his bed."

"Yes, I know all about it. And your excursions into darkest Harlem, as chronicled in the papers."

I'd been reaching for my overcoat, but I slipped back into my seat. "You do remember Roddy, don't you? I don't mean in my apartment or uptown at the chop suey place. I've heard stories already, Jed. You met him before."

"Why is this important?"

"It's considered impolite to answer a question with another question, Jed."

He chuckled. "My, my, Edna, the schoolmarm with verbal stick and lace-collar oxbow."

"An innocent question."

"I rather doubt that, Edna. But yes, in fact, I do recall encountering that offensive, brash boy."

"So you do remember him?"

"I don't forget things, Edna. That's why I'm rich."

"Tell me."

He snickered. "But I'll come across as a hero in this little anecdote."

"I'll be the judge of your heroism."

He rattled his coffee cup, and the waitress, hovering, rushed to refill it. He poured so much cream into the brew that it turned murky white, cloying, sickening. "Actually two other times. The first time was when I kicked Lawson out of my office. I suspect you've been told about that encounter. He was there, introduced himself, and was snotty. But that's not the most interesting encounter with the dead lad. One night in Harlem not so long ago." A pause. "No. Once upon a time in Harlem…"

"Get on with it, Jed."

"Story telling is the art of selection of detail."

"Jed!"

"All right. I doubt you'll hear this version from Bella or Lawson. One night in Harlem I was with Bella at one of those black-and-white clubs and we'd just left and were strolling on the sidewalk. Lawson spotted us. I guess he was coming home from his job because he was wearing that dumb janitor's uniform.

At first I didn't even recognize him. Christ, he was one more Negro traveling the midnight sidewalks up there—but Bella stared, seemed embarrassed and confused. Like she wanted to be elsewhere. Lawson, of course, was not in a good mood. Well, neither was I. Once before I'd met him uptown, and the three of us actually drank the night away in a club. At least Bella tells me it was Lawson there—I don't remember. Bella had been pleading for something—some introduction or connection. Lord, the girl is cutthroat. Well, just days before, I'd told this Lawson his career was over—and there he was, pouting, as I strolled by with his girlfriend. He yelled at me, which, I gather, Negroes don't do to white men down South, so be it. I pushed him."

"Jed, should you be jostling on the streets?"

"Jostling. Edna, Edna." Suddenly Jed's eyes got that steely, cold look, the diamond pinpoints. "You know what he did? He hit me, Edna. He swung and hit me here." He placed his hand on his left bicep. "Here."

"Jed, what?"

"That was it, that one moment. But ugly. He hit me. Bella was screaming, crying. And she seemed ready to go to *him*. Him! There she was, dressed in a sequined flapper outfit I bought. So I stood there, massaging my shoulder, and said, calmly, 'Bella, choose him or me.' She got quiet but I repeated my demands. Lawson, mean-eyed, watched. Finally, looking apologetically at Lawson, as though sending him a secret message, she took a step. She came to stand at my side. Lawson fumed."

"Now I see," I told him.

Peevish: "No, you don't."

"Jed, Lawson never told me this. He just told me about the scene in your office."

He chuckled. "Would you tell anybody such a story? The black boy losing his girl on a Harlem street corner."

"But Jed, what does this have to do with Roddy? That was my question to you."

He stopped laughing. "Oh, that's right. I get so excited recounting my heroism that I forgot your question."

"No, you didn't."

"True, I didn't. Well, I neglected to mention that this Roddy fellow was with Lawson when he approached me and Bella."

"And you knew it was Roddy because you had that scene outside your office?"

"Yes. He stood there, a dumb ass grin on his face, when Lawson and I started spouting nonsense to each other. But the foolish grin dropped when Lawson hit me. He yelled out 'Whoa' as if he were writing titles for a William S. Hart cowboy serial, and I pointed at him. I taunted him, deliberately. 'Ah, yes, so you're the other failed writer. Failed actor. Lord, it's a lethal combination…writer and actor. Two sides of a worn-out coin. The dueling second from my office.' I went on and on like that. I could see I was getting to him. Lawson had pulled back, licking his wounds, as it were; but this Roddy became enraged. Bella, babbling, kept saying, let's go, let's go, come on now, stop. As if that was supposed to make me leave him alone."

"Why didn't you?"

"I don't like to be challenged."

"For God's sake, Jed, they're just young lads."

"They're men. But Roddy did the unforgivable." A pause, as he licked his lower lip. "He made an obscene gesture at me, and he called me a bully. 'You're a bully who enjoys beating down those who have no power.'"

"Well, it's true."

He ignored that. "No one talks to me like that."

I drew my lips into a thin line. "But everyone thinks it about you, Jed."

He was shaking his head, and I doubted whether he heard me. "No one."

"A street brawl, Jed. Think of it."

"Then they stormed away, leaving Bella clutching to my side as though I were a piece of driftwood."

I was shaking my head. "Unpleasant, Jed."

Jed stood, reached for the check, and he looked directly into my face, smiling. "No one insults me like that, least of all a Negro. I called after this Roddy fellow, 'I'll remember your face.' He turned back to me and bellowed, 'Probably long after I've forgotten yours!'" Jed was reaching into his wallet for cash. "So he got himself murdered one night." Jed was counting out some dollar bills. "A pity. Really."

Chapter Thirteen

On Christmas I hosted a brunch for family visiting from Chicago, though no one seemed happy to be in my apartment on the cold, windy day. My sister Fannie kept glancing out the window at the swirling snowflakes and muttering about a cold she was getting. My nieces nodded at their generous holiday checks and talked of ski weekends in Vermont. My mother protested that the mink jacket I'd bought her was too short. Furthermore, she'd clearly recalled suggesting the sable with the red velvet lining. Hadn't I listened? I had little patience with them all, loved as they were.

Merry Christmas, Edna.

The brunch was superb but untouched by me. Rebecca and Waters were spending the afternoon and evening with relatives, though she'd left a magnificent buffet of cold duck salad, scalloped potatoes, green beans with almond slices, fresh cornbread buttery to the touch, and a rip-roaring chocolate cake so dark and high it seemed some mountainous creation. I put nothing on my plate.

"Edna," my mother began as she sliced into the cake, her thumb smeared with velvety frosting, "tell us about the murder. I never tire…"

Fannie was frowning. "Mother, we've heard it before. I'm not sure why everyone is thrilled that Edna found her name in the tabloids, slinking into squalid tenements to find dead young Negroes."

I stood. "Have a wonderful Christmas."

I headed to my workroom.

For a while I lost myself in my mail, but that quickly paled. Through the door I'd slammed, I could hear rustling and whispering as my family left the apartment, though my mother punctuated the blissful quiet with phlegmatic outbursts, which suggested she was dying. I ignored it all, and eventually she left the apartment, going to spend the next few days in Connecticut.

I sat in my workroom, quiet, quiet.

The phone rang once or twice. I didn't move.

I was thinking of Roddy assailing Jed Harris, that hapless, doomed young man sputtering his rage in defense of his cousin; but, sadly, against a cruel and vengeful man. I wanted to think of *Show Boat* and *The Royal Family*; wanted thunderous echoes of "Ol' Man River" sung from the apron of the stage; of Helen Morgan warbling the melancholic "Bill" while she perched on a piano; of the redoubtable matriarch Fanny Cavendish emoting onstage, a triumphant moment. But I couldn't. Outside the wind beat the windows and the afternoon winter streetlights shimmered through the naked tops of the forest in Central Park. I shivered.

At five, insane with the quiet, I dressed in a voguish pale-blue chemise accented with the batik scarf I'd gotten as a Christmas gift, and, wrapped in my fur coat, I caught a cab to George and Bea Kaufman's apartment. He'd proffered an invitation for a Christmas cocktail party, though I'd hedged about going. Now, driven to the edge of madness, I had little choice: two hours of bootleg hooch and doubtless some Broadway trouper embarrassing herself by singing "I wish I could shimmy like my sister Kate," with piano accompaniment. There'd be scintillating, if frenzied, conversation with George and his tribe of friends. And me: the peripatetic romantic novelist, fashionable now because of *So Big*...*Show Boat*...*The Royal Family*. Me: the dutiful middle-class daughter of the Midwest provinces, transformed into Manhattan's trendy flapper and drinker of bathtub gin. I smiled as I got out of the cab. Thank God I'd bobbed my hair last summer and had my nose done. I no longer looked like a Semitic Pollyanna.

George Kaufman seemed surprised that I'd come. Tall, gawky, eyeglasses slipping off his nose, his hair a jumble of electric current, he stood there, puzzled. "I thought you said that…" He smiled. "Come in."

But the party was a mistake, I immediately realized, because there was nowhere to hide. Jammed with frisky, tipsy men and women, all bubbly with holiday zest and bonhomie, they jostled and backslapped and humored. I recognized faces: Marc Connelly, Peggy Wood, Neysa McMein. But I wanted to talk to no one. Dorothy Parker was on her soapbox, and rightly so, about the Sacco and Vanzetti miscarriage of justice, and Aleck Woollcott, who avoided me, was praising Charles Lindbergh, whom he'd just lunched with. George himself, dressed in a foppish tuxedo and holding a champagne glass at a dangerous angle, kept dragging a slender, emaciated young man to each pocket of guests, declaring the skittish young man a rising star in the world of art. I never caught his name—perhaps George forgot it himself—but I overheard snatches of chatter that suggested he'd returned from France where he knew Picasso and had cheese and wine with Natalia Goncharova and Mikhail Larionov. I had no idea who they were, but supposed them exiled Russians who painted oils of dark windswept steppes with borzois and white birch forests. The young man did nothing but grin and scratch an unkempt beard unfortunately speckled with bits of caviar, and I defined him an idiot. George kept leaning into the shorter man's neck, as though to whisper a forbidden tidbit; but then, throwing back his head, bursting into artificial laughter.

A voice spoke from behind me. "We have to stop meeting like this." Hearing the slight laughter, I turned. "I've been moving across two rooms to get to you. I meet you twice in a couple days, Miss Ferber."

I faced Langston Hughes, and smiled. "I'm bored here."

"But this is the most exciting party in Manhattan." A voice soft and low. "I've just started getting invited to such…events."

Then he leaned in, confidentially. "I'm still visiting from Pennsylvania. I'm forced to wear the same suit to them all. I hope no one notices."

"They won't. Then you'd better keep the secret to yourself."

He laughed. "I'm happy to be invited." He pointed to the crowd. "Famous people here. It's exciting."

"This? Exciting? Then we are indeed at the end of American civilization."

"I hadn't known it had arrived yet."

"Clever."

"Not my line. I stole it from someone."

"Then you must be a successful writer."

Another chuckle. "There I go again, confessing my secrets."

I turned away. "But I need to leave. This"—I waved my hand across the room, filled with laughter and the tinkle of glass—"this is not good for me today."

He held up a hand, his look anxious. Suddenly, unexpectedly, he recited verbatim a paragraph from my short story "Blue Blood," which took place in the Chicago stockyards. It had been published in *Cosmopolitan* just months earlier. He recited in an assured, dreamy voice meant for me alone: "'You saw a giant Negro, a magnificent ebony creature with great prehensile arms, and a round head, a flat stomach, flat hips, an amazing breadth between his shoulders. From chest to ankles he narrowed down like an inverted pyramid. He raised those arms that were like flexible bronze, and effortlessly, almost languidly, as you would cut through a pat of soft butter, they descended in a splendid arc.'" When he was finished, a little out of breath, he half-bowed.

I breathed in, thrilled. "You are amazing, Mr. Hughes."

But now he looked embarrassed, as if he'd violated some moment, overstepped a line into indiscretion. But that hesitancy passed, and his eyes twinkled. "I've been savoring that passage, which I love. And I wanted to impress…"

"Which you do anyway," I broke in. "But," I grinned, "such theatrics, while touching, shall not keep me from my own quiet apartment this Christmas night."

Again, the hand in the air. "You sent me some chapters of Lawson Hicks' novel *Hell Fighters*."

The smile disappeared from my face. "And?"

Perhaps unwisely, I'd sent him the first few chapters by messenger, addressed to him at his publisher's office. Afterwards I'd thought my action rash and probably a little unethical. After all, Lawson had told me he was not interested in publishing, and then he'd walked out. "It's not ready." That's what he said— emphatic. And I'd violated those words. Yet I had such faith in the novel, and I thought that Langston Hughes was the person to look at the chapters.

"I read the pages you sent me," he began, "and they are a marvel. If he can keep up the tempo—the power—beyond what I've read, then, well, it needs to be out there." A pause. "Thank you for sending it. Young Negro writers, you know…" His voice trailed off. "But I was caught by something else. I wanted to ask you about the murdered boy, Roddy. Lawson, I noticed, dedicated his novel to that sad young man and quoted a few lines of his verse, after the dedication. I got to wondering about *his* unpublished work. What was left behind?"

I described the stack of typed sheets and the notebooks sitting on a side table in my workroom. "His friends want some posthumous publication."

"I'll tell you, Miss Ferber, I felt some…pulse, in the Lawson quote of Roddy's verse. Just a few lines, out of context." And then he quoted them from memory:

"*Saturday morning Harlem says nothing at all*
Yet the hum and whisper of night lingers
The echo of a midnight saxophone
The jazz poet sits in shadows
And waits for Truth…'"He stopped. "Are there more like this?"

I was nodding furiously. "I've been meaning to…"

"Perhaps we can work together. After New Year's, maybe."

He walked me to the door and we shook hands. "You are a Christmas surprise." I held his hand in both of mine.

My remark obviously amused him because he stepped back, threw back his head and laughed, choking out, "The surprise is that you and I find ourselves chatting together in this doorway."

"Is it untoward?"

"It would have been impossible just decades ago."

"Perhaps the world is finally changing."

"So slowly, Miss Ferber. So slowly."

Back home, content now to sit in the quiet rooms, I found myself pleased at Langston Hughes' reaction to Lawson's novel, but more so to his eagerness to review Roddy's untouched work. Those few lines of poetry, quoted by Lawson, seemed a gateway into Roddy's imagination. Something good had to come from this nightmare—for Lawson *and* Roddy. I played the lines over and over in my head until, perforce, the words became a melody that seemed set against a jazz piano.

I remembered the night Jerome Kern stopped at my apartment, the newly penned score of *Show Boat* in hand, and quietly, with his usual humility, he played his music. Despite his toneless voice, the words soared. "Ol' Man River" and "Only Make Believe" and "Can't Help Lovin' Dat Man" filled the room. My spine tingled, and I wept. Now, repeating Roddy's few lines of verse—that I paid little mind to until Langston Hughes quoted them to me against a backdrop of tinkling champagne glasses and cigarette smoke—I fairly lost my breath. I lamented the loss of that young talent.

The words filled my apartment. I *felt* Harlem, still the outsider perhaps but somehow, through Langston Hughes' smooth and rich recitation, I became privy to a world I never understood... nor could, really. I walked to my windows, the huge eight windows that gave me a breathtaking panorama of Central Park and the taxi-jammed streets below. There was a different rhythm here than that of Harlem, this rich man's elegant stomping ground. What music was here? I wondered. I thought of Browning: *What of soul was left, I wonder, when the kissing had to stop?*

In the kitchen I brewed a pot of strong tea and then sat by the windows, my mind drifting. I thought of Rebecca, away for the evening, celebrating the holiday with her family, and with my family gone, I was glad to have the place to myself. I changed into my robe and slippers and then tucked myself into bed, but not before I'd carried the ungainly mass of Roddy's work to the nightstand. I contemplated the shifting heap of manuscript, previously so uninviting, but now, as though by magic, illuminated by a magician's powerful wand. Reaching into the nightstand, I withdrew a pack of cigarettes, a forbidden and infrequent pleasure. Now, inhaling the slightly stale Camel, I felt a little dizzy, suppressed a cough, but watched, enthralled, as the wisp of blue-gray smoke drifted upward. It took me, that image, to Small's Paradise where the blue velvety clouds hovered over the packed tables.

I started reading the folder of poems Roddy had organized, caught now by Langston Hughes' contagion, moving through the twenty or so poems, a tapestry of Harlem vignettes. A *Spoon River Anthology* for Harlem, miniature portraits of life: street vendors hawking peanuts, nightclubs decorated in jungle or plantation motifs, street crooners raggin', folks at rent parties dancing to the Texas Tommy, crapshooters at the subway stops, Madame Rosa's brothel, a pimp crowing from a cruising Duesenberg, an ode to Florence Mills, imagined afternoons with the writers at the Niggerati Manor on 136th Street, echoes of an Old South he didn't know but had heard so much about, a bitter lyric about a lynching in Tennessee. Each poem moved seamlessly into the next, a weaving in and out of mood, emotion, color. A glimpse of a corner cigar store moved quickly into a night poem—a jazz club. A run of jazz lyrics, fragmented lines, broken images, wailing words that dipped and shimmered on the page. When he described a young Negro flapper reaching for a cigarette, her red-painted lips quivering, I found myself doing the same, so appealing was his imagery, so authentic the moment.

Roddy had obviously culled the poems from his writings, for the larger stack of notes consisted of crude earlier versions of the poetry, jottings, scribblings. But there was also a folder of first drafts, tentative poems or paragraphs, wide-ranging in theme. He'd jotted down notes about the history of the Negro, some lines about slavery, about the power of Negro spirituals. A number of lines dealt with the Civil War and the idea that the horrific war had stunned the black man forever—and, he noted, the white man, as well. Tucked into the paper was his library card for the Harlem branch of the New York Public Library on Lenox Avenue, frayed and bent and obviously much used. Some lines caught my eye: *They gave us a violent past, so the modern Negro expects violence. Our father…give us our daily violence.*

What did these words mean?

But I immediately discovered the reason. Roddy had been working on an essay in the form of a letter: "A Letter to Mr. P." Sketchy, with many cross-outs and marginal insertions, the piece posited the view that people like "Mr. P.," an earlier generation of Negro, inhibited the vision of the young Negro American of the post-Great War era. It talked, vaguely and superficially, to Mr. P. about the older generation's simmering anger and hatred of authority, particularly of white culture, and its distrust of Negro achievement, a resignation to a life of second-class citizenship. Roddy then expanded on W. E. B. Du bois' notion of the "Talented Tenth," that percentage of the Negro world born with singular gifts and voice. Mr. P., it turns out, mocked this generation of Negroes, deriding a society that "sissified" the artist. He mentioned exile in France. Josephine Baker. "Glory in France, isolation at home." "You can exile yourself, but you come back to find yourself a ghost." "You die and they still won't bury you." On and on, bits of thought and heart. "Oh, the sad parade past the white folks who smirk and spit…home to Mr. P's world, where the old Negro kneels before the white man, then stabs him in an alley. The blame is on the uppity Negro… the young writer, the artist…." The essay talked of psychological violence—the crushing of the artist who dared defy custom. The essay then petered off, unfinished.

Was "Mr. P" the superintendent of his building? Mr. Porter? Harriet's curmudgeon father, and Roddy's enemy?

It made little sense to me, this random scribbling. Roddy was clearly trying to fashion some treatise on the difficulties facing the young renaissance writer, dealing with white indifference and old-Negro derision. A penciled-in note: "Pick up *Fire!!* Langston. Zora."

Then: a few lines I recognized from an old eighteenth century Phillis Wheatley poem:

> *'Twas mercy brought me from my pagan land,*
> *Taught my beknighted soul to understand*
> *That there's a God, that there's a Savior too:*
> *Once I redemption neither sought nor knew.*
> *Some view our sable race with scornful eye,*
> *"Their color is a diabolic dye."*

And the notation: "Ha! God had nothing to do with it. Maybe the devil…"

Then, a line in French, a quotation from La Fontaine: *"Rien ne pèse tant qu'un secret."*

I translated it in my head: *Nothing weighs more than a secret.* Then random words: "Exile." "Violence."

Perhaps none of it made sense, just late-night scribbling of a troubled young man.

But at the bottom of the heap was a small spiral notebook, pocket-sized; and inside Roddy had penned a few lines in thick black ink, blotted and filmy, as though he were in a rush. Only three pages had words, all underlined. The first page had one line: *It was not a good idea talking about it…coveting is a sin against a God that doesn't exist.*

Page two had the notation: *I don't trust him.*

Page three amplified the idea, filling the entire page: *I think Mr. Porter comes into the apartment when we're not here. What shall I do? My stuff is touched, moved, searched. I watch…will watch.* He wrote the date: *December 10, 1927. The first day I noticed.* Then a couple of blank lines later: *I caught Mr. Porter standing by my door, guilty looking, probably having just left. When I asked him why he was rifling through my stuff, he flew into a rage. 'You and Lawson are leeches.' But that can't be the reason, can it? Why?* Then a series of words: *why? why? why? why?*

A last line: *He threatened me. I've never been threatened like that before.*

I placed the notepad on the pile, stared at it. When I reached for my cup of tea, it was cold. I'd forgotten to drink it.

My mind reeled, but one persistent thought rankled: Waters and Lawson were right. Skidder Scott, now languishing in jail and still protesting his innocence, was not involved—or, at least, was just a pawn—in the murder of Roddy. Perhaps I was being irrational, making too gigantic a leap here. But evident in Roddy's scribblings was fear, distrust, anger. Something was going on. This was not simply a burglary gone wrong: this was premeditated murder. Someone planned his death. I *sensed* it to my soul.

Mr. P? Mr. Porter?

Night wind slapped my bedroom window, and I stared out into the dark winter night. In the elegant cocoon of my apartment, I shivered. Murder. I felt it to my marrow. Someone I'd talked with had stabbed the doomed Roddy.

Chapter Fourteen

Rebecca, Waters, and I sat in the back seat of a yellow cab, headed uptown.

Earlier that afternoon, munching on reheated leftovers Rebecca placed before me, I reread the aborted "Letter to Mr. P.," as well as the personal entries in the small notepad. From the grave, Roddy was telling me something. But what? In the morning I fielded calls from Hammerstein's publicist about tomorrow's *Show Boat* opening; I took calls from Jed Harris' office about *The Royal Family*. Yet, though I chatted about *Show Boat* and *The Royal Family* throughout the morning, it was as though I remained removed from them. I was the stranger from out of town, maybe Keokuk, Iowa, someone mildly interested in both highly-touted openings. Instead, I ran my fingers over Roddy's papers, and one awful word echoed in my head like a refrain from Edgar Allan Poe: *murder murder murder*. I closed my eyes, saw flashes of lightning, blood red and dark blue and sunburst yellow. Blackness.

When Waters stopped to drop off something for his mother, I caught him as he readied to leave. "Waters," I insisted, "help me understand this." I spread the papers before him, and he read them, his face screwed up and his tongue licking his lips.

"I don't understand," he muttered. "Mr. Porter?"

"Well, we do know that Harriet's father had a problem with Roddy."

Rebecca sat down next to her son. "I've always thought it odd that Harriet badmouths her father so much, yet she stays in his apartment."

"Well, according to this, Roddy was a little frightened. He didn't trust him. Why would Mr. Porter go through Roddy's things?"

"Looking for money?" Waters wondered. "Or evidence?"

"Evidence of what?"

Waters shrugged his shoulders. "I never liked him. I only met him a couple times when I went to visit Harriet. Freddy was there, those times. He's always there. And the old man made a lot of noise about rabble invading his apartment. We thought we'd hold our writing meetings there—or in Lawson and Roddy's apartment. But one time we asked him—I was there—and the old man said no. He didn't trust what we were up to, he said. Harriet told us to ignore him, and, a little tipsy, he disappeared into his bedroom. We heard him snoring so loud, a drunkard's bad sleep, and Harriet made fun of him."

At that moment Rebecca suggested a cab ride to Harlem. "Answers," she stressed. "Maybe it's about time."

But we were thwarted in our attempt to talk with Mr. Porter. When his apartment door opened, Harriet stood there, clad in her waitress uniform, and the look on her face was a mixture of surprise, anger, and annoyance. The three of us were shivering from the ride up in an unheated cab. Harriet's eyes took in Rebecca who was dabbing her tearing eyes with a handkerchief; Waters, rubbing his cold cheeks with the palm of his hand; and me, the novelist, undoing her scarf and adjusting her fashionable Marie Perelli hat. We stared back, as though Harriet were the unwanted visitor, the interloper.

"Am I missing something?" she asked in an icy tone. She glanced behind her into the apartment, and I heard the tap-tap-tap of hurried steps. Suddenly Freddy stood beside her. Freddy, so often there. Freddy, who had no address—or any he'd gladly share. A mysterious lad about whom I knew so little, other than his fiery racial proclamations.

"Is your father home?"

She glanced at Freddy. "No." A long pause. "Why?"

"We have some questions. Going through Roddy's notes, I found…well…" I faltered.

Harriet looked ready to slam the door because she stepped back and raised her arm; but, in a curiously submissive gesture, she half-bowed and stepped aside. "I suppose you gotta do this. Ask your questions. It must make you feel good to crucify a man whose only pleasure—or is it a vice?—is a hip flask of bad gin and the word of God. So, come on in. Ask *me*. Pop's not here."

"Don't let them in, Harriet." Freddy's voice was fierce, and she turned to face him.

"What?"

"Why let them accuse your Pop of murder?"

I shot back, "We are not doing any such thing. Roddy mentioned problems with your father and mentioned that he rifled through Roddy's possessions."

Harriet bit her lip. "Is this Lawson's idea, this interrogation?"

"No," Waters spoke up. "It's ours."

"I don't buy that. Lawson never liked my father, even though he played nice with him, sat on the stoop with him, friendly, unlike Roddy, who was always sarcastic and miserable to him. Lawson is a phony, a charming boy who wants"—she hesitated— "that Roddy's murder be *more* than a random blunder by a homeless man. He wants it to make some sense. You all do. And Pop is a convenient target."

Rebecca interrupted. "Lawson has nothing to do with our visit."

Freddy spoke up. "If he won't step back into this building, I just assumed he sent his Bwana missionary and the house slaves."

Rebecca froze, and Waters sputtered.

Harriet giggled, but she also stepped toward the door. "Freddy's right. Pop's a fool but not grist for your assassin's mill."

With that, she stepped back and slammed the door shut in our faces. We stood there in the hallway. Rebecca fumed, Waters grumbled, and I was simply amazed. I had little patience with such puerile behavior; but in this case, given the reason for our unannounced visit, I had the feeling this was more than a young woman's rude shenanigans. From behind the closed door, Harriet and Freddy's hysterical laughter swelled, as though they'd executed a delicious prank on some attendant fools: Harriet's laugh was shrill, while Freddy's was raspy and broken, the roar of a man not used to indulging in hilarity.

"Well," I announced in my Jack Benny vaudeville voice. But neither mother nor son laughed.

We stood on the front stoop, and I questioned my rash decision to hop into that uptown cab. The door swung open behind us, and we stepped aside as a sloppily dressed man, fortyish and stringy with a gaunt, hollowed-out face, pushed past us, brushing my sleeve unapologetically. If he seemed surprised to see a middle-aged white woman perched on that crumbling stoop, he displayed no reaction. With his unbuttoned overcoat and a scarf slipping off his neck, he looked as if he'd just tumbled, willy-nilly, out of an odorous bed. He stepped onto the sidewalk and fiddled in his pockets. I heard the jingle of loose coins.

"Wait," Waters suddenly called out to him, and the man swiveled, his eyes wary. He said nothing. "You live upstairs, right?"

The man nodded, but I noticed he was looking at me, as though seeing me for the first time. "Yeah?"

"Could we talk to you?"

Hesitant, the man stared up the block, his feet shuffling as if ready to move. He stiffened, danced around. But he stayed there, pulling his tongue into the corner of his mouth. "Yeah?"

"We were friends of Roddy Parsons, the guy who was murdered."

Again, the furtive look, the glance up the street. A battered delivery truck lumbered by, choked out black fumes, and the man jingled the coins in his pocket. "Yeah?"

"Did you know him?" Waters asked. All three of us moved onto the sidewalk now, approaching the man, who moved back a step.

"I seen him, sure. Never spoke a word." I noticed his face twitched, nervous, and the cavernous eyes, deep-sunk, glazed over. This, I told myself, was not going to be good. "A couple times I spoke to his roommate, the Romeo guy, I guess, but I ain't know him either. A rude bastard."

"Lawson?" I asked.

"Looked through me like I was nothing. Couple times he shoved me out of the way, always rushing in and out."

"But you didn't talk to Roddy?" Rebecca asked.

"No reason to." He smiled and I saw missing teeth, blackened teeth. "Place like this you best hide away and not make nice with the pretty boys in the back apartment."

"Have you had any break-ins?" Rebecca asked.

He shook his head. "Nah." A pause. "Ain't got a dime to steal."

"What do you remember about the night he was murdered?" I asked.

A long silence, then a quick intake of breath. "Who are you again?"

I pointed at Waters and his mother. "Friends. Seeking justice."

He chortled at that. "Police done talked to me already. I tole them the little I knows."

"And that is?" I persisted.

"Not much."

"Could you tell *us*?" Rebecca asked, politely. And he smiled at her. She was smiling back at him.

"Most times the house is real quiet, you know," he began, still looking at Rebecca, who kept her beatific smile plastered on, her eyes warm. "But I stepped out a few times that night, it being Saturday night, come back for cash, left, you know, back and forth."

"And?" I probed, impatient.

He didn't look at me, his eyes now cast downward. "First time I left, I was coming down the stairs and someone had just rushed by, headed down the hallway. I didn't pay no mind, and don't know if she went to Roddy's apartment, 'cause it happened so fast. I figured it was one of the tenants in the apartment across from Roddy's. They got a girl living there. Paid it no mind, but she was *running*."

"She?" Waters asked. "You sure it was a girl?"

"Yeah, a girl." He bit his lip. "But don't ask me to describe her. As I tole the police, I just sensed it was a girl, you know, rushing back there." He looked up the street, his feet moving. "Up to the club, but I come back fifteen minutes after, forgot my cash, and I seen someone move in the shadows. There." He pointed to a narrow alley, dark even in broad daylight. "Like someone just stepped then and there into the alley like they seen me stepping out of the house."

"Some girl?"

He fidgeted. "I tole you, I barely *sensed* the first and the second, well, maybe it ain't even a girl. I paid it no mind but the police sat me down and made me go over and over it. What can I say?"

I smiled at Waters. "Bella in the bushes." I pointed at the narrow alley, hugging the building, filled with litter, scraps of blown paper, an icy canyon. Waters nodded. "So you were out all night?"

"No, I tole you I was back and forth. The club I go to is one block over. Most times I come back, get me more cash, you know, hallway is quiet like a graveyard. Except the last time. Sometimes some Victrola gospel coming from Mamie Johnson's in the apartment next to me, old lady can't sleep at night and Sundays she just play the phonograph when she ain't in church..."

"Except what last time?" I asked.

Well"—he enunciated the words—"as I tol' the police, I come home dog-tired after two or so, dunno the exact time, and I'm ready to climb the stairs when I think I hear rustling back down the hall. A noise I can't make no sense of. So I step back there, real dumb of me, you know, peek around the corner, and it's real dark, but I seed their door a little bit open, just a foot or so, and I pay it no mind, one of the boys coming or going. After all, it's Saturday night"—a thin smile, the broken teeth dull in the daylight—"but I realize later, talking to the cops, that there ain't no light on from inside the apartment. Nobody there, door open, but no light shining in the hallway, like you'd expect. So I figure it ain't my business and start to walk up the stairs, a little woozy, you know, and then I hear—I think I hear—this rattling around back there."

"Like?" From Waters, eager.

"Like someone bumping around in the dark, crashing into chairs. Then it stopped. Or—I don't know—maybe it went on, but I was upstairs in the hallway then, and stumbling to my bed."

"And that's it?" I asked.

He ran his tongue over his lower lip. "Ain't much, but more'n most folks would tell the police."

"Do you know Skidder Scott?" I asked.

"Everyone round here knows Skidder. Fact is, he was up on the corner begging that night. I seed him, clear as day."

"What time?" I asked.

"When I come back the last time, when I see the door is cracked open."

"So he wasn't down here then?" I asked.

"Not unless he flew."

"You don't think that Skidder Scott killed Roddy?" Rebecca wondered.

The man shook his head. "Skidder scared of his own shadow, that one. He was working the crowd coming out of Mambo's. No time to murder nobody in their bed. I tole that to the police but they don't count my words."

With that, his antsy feet shuffled, and the man, bending into the cool breeze, moved away, his hand touching the brim of his fedora.

"What have we learned?" I stared at the departing back.

Waters smiled. "Bella in the bushes and, maybe, inside."

"Or Ellie actually making it inside," Rebecca offered.

"Then why didn't Bella see her?" Waters asked.

"Because, if we can believe the man's story, the person entered the shadowy alley minutes *after* he sensed the woman in the hallway."

Someone was crossing the street, weaving between parked cars, and I heard grunting, a slurred curse. "Well, well." Mr. Porter was returning home, a well-worn Bible cradled under his arm. "My, my, the kind of folks daylight brings to Harlem."

"Mr. Porter," I started, "we wanted to talk to you about…"

"Ah, a trio of vigilantes."

"Hardly," I said. "Roddy was writing an essay addressed to a 'Mr. P.' Perhaps it was you, a piece about the conflict of generations among Negroes and…"

His hand flew up into my face. I sputtered, but stopped. "It ain't got nothing to do with me."

"But," Waters added, "Roddy made notes about not trusting you…about how you went into his apartment…"

"I'm the super and I gotta do things." A pause. "I check on things."

"Does that mean rifling through his possessions?" Waters asked.

He looked toward the entrance to his building. "You people are bothering me. I didn't do nothing. I go to church and I pray for the likes of Lawson and Roddy. Especially Roddy."

"Why Roddy in particular?" I asked.

He sucked in his cheeks. "Two lost boys, them two. Lawson is a liar and a cocky boy, a boy who hides from me 'cause he won't pay his rent. In my house. And Roddy. That sick Roddy. Well, Freddy could tell you some things about him. It was my Christian charity that kept forgiving and forgetting. But even God gets impatient."

"But you fought with Roddy."

"Yeah, he attacked me, fact is."

"You fought with him."

"He was a wise guy, sarcastic, thought he was better'n me. He even mocked *this*." He held up the Bible. "No one does that to me. Fancy pants phony. Smug."

"So you went into his apartment? Looked around. For what?"

He snickered. "I don't know what you're talking about. All I know is that boy ain't belong among decent people, and I told him so. He even shoved me, can you believe it? That fool. I know how to take care of myself."

"He hit you?"

"No, you ain't listening. He shoved me when he tried to get past me in the hallway. Like a week before he got murdered. I told him he ain't welcome in this building."

"And what did you do?" Waters asked.

"I punched him in the face."

I started. "You hit him? What did he do?"

The old face moved, the eyes hard and cold. "He said he could kill me with no regrets—that my phony God couldn't protect me. Jesus be a coward like me." Now he chuckled. "Hey, I been in jail. I know what's what. Prison and God temper a man to face anything. I told him he better watch his step." He started to push through us. "I told him I could kill him if I chose, but God got better punishments waiting for him. So I didn't kill him, ma'am. Not worth burning in hell for the likes of him. I just punched him one good one, and he squawked liked a headless chicken." He walked up the steps and opened the front door. "Don't bother me no more, folks, with your little crusade."

"But a boy has been murdered!" I yelled out.

"Well, ma'am, seems to me God calls the shots. And some folks are better off dead."

Chapter Fifteen

Bella was not happy and made certain we knew it, clicking her tongue and biting the broken nail of her index finger. She sat facing me at a round table in Maynard's, a small grubby diner on 145th and Broadway. Flanked on her left by Waters and on her right by his mother, she hunched her shoulders like a scared and trapped animal. Her chin dipped into her chest protectively, a woman ready to be executed—or, at least, mildly interrogated.

"I think this is unnecessary," she said, still staring into my face.

I kept my mouth shut, but nodded at Rebecca, then playing with the handle of the coffee cup. Suddenly she reached over and placed one of her hands on Bella's wrist. Bella stopped fidgeting. "There's a chance an innocent man is unjustly accused of murder, Bella."

Her brow furrowed. "Skidder Scott? I just assumed…"

"Well," I added, "the police have closed the book on it, but Roddy's notes that were left behind, and the…the activity centering on the apartment that night…and…"

"And the contradictory stories," Waters threw in, bluntly. "The *lies*." He stressed the word.

Bella blushed. "No one believes that I *wasn't* there."

I drew my tongue into my cheek. "True, Bella, no one does. You and Ellie seem to invent at will." She frowned and continued to pick at the broken nail. Crimson nail polish flaked off. "But," I went on, "we're talking about a night when someone was murdered."

Venom in her voice: "Well, talk to Ellie. Her life is one big lie."

"Just what does that mean?" Rebecca asked.

Bella shrugged. "Nothing." A sliver of a smile. "Ellie doesn't like me and she's not my favorite person."

"Why?" Though I knew the answer.

But Bella closed up. She sipped her coffee and stared out the plate-glass front window.

"Somehow," I began again, "Jed Harris—a man who should have nothing to do with any of this, surely—is involved, but I don't know what I mean by that." I waited and watched her face.

She scoffed. "Jed Harris." A name said with bitterness.

"There was a time, and recently, when I gather you'd say his name with a certain relish."

She broke into a laugh that ended in a cigarette smoker's husky cough. "That fool."

"Tell me," I demanded.

"Nothing to tell except that he told me to get lost."

"But you were having an affair?"

Again, the exaggerated laugh. "If that's what you want to call it. He can be a charming man, you know, but underneath it all, there's a cold, cold heart."

"Tell me," I repeated.

She shrugged her shoulders. "He took me places, up in Harlem, of course. Never downtown. A pretty silk scarf from Bonwit Teller but, you know, I could never exchange it in a million years. Not that there's many places we could go except maybe around Sheridan Square in Greenwich Village. But up here, yes, clubs where Negroes can mingle socially with white guys. It's like…a cottage industry up here." A sardonic tenor to her voice now, but raw, pained. "Lawson knew about it, but he had no say. What could he say? He's as fiercely ambitious as me. We sort of found each other that way, the two of us auditioning for the rare part of a Negro on Broadway. So we became a couple, and for a while it worked. Then there was Jed, and Lawson was angry, but there was nothing he could do about it."

"A little unfair, no?"

She shrugged her pretty shoulders. "After the embarrassing fights with Jed on the street, him and Roddy, you know, well, Lawson just assumed a what-the-hell attitude. He was getting on my nerves anyway. It was time to say goodbye. He was like a gnat that keeps buzzing in my ear, annoying, pesky. So I thought I'd hitch my wagon to Jed's Great White Way down Broadway. Ah, foolish me! You know, I sort of realized what kind of man Jed was by the way he treated Lawson."

"I never quite understood that," I whispered.

"Well, it makes no sense. It's like Jed took this real intense hatred to Lawson just because he *could*. You know, it's a power thing. Power to Jed, I learned, is more important than sex. Excuse me, Miss Ferber. I don't mean to…to be indelicate. But Jed…"

I interrupted. "I'm not a child, Bella."

She shrugged those shoulders again. "So when I told Jed in my most girlie voice that his treatment of Lawson was wrong, he scoffed at me. 'You and Lawson just want me to produce your simple plays.' Well, that hurt. I'd *hinted* at him looking at my writing but, yes, I really wanted to *act* in one of his productions." She sighed. "Suddenly I realized what a fool I'd been. A fool."

"But you still kept at him, no?"

"He *played* with us, Miss Ferber. You know what Lawson told me—'Jed Harris took away chance.' You know, maybe we'd make it, maybe not. Broadway. When Jed blackballed us, when he said we'd never work again, he took away the chance that we could make it. Sabotaged, Miss Ferber."

Rebecca spoke up. "Bella, it had to be more than Jed's treatment of Lawson…and you. Why did he end it? You did something…"

Bella waited a long time. "Clever, you are." She leaned back on her chair, tipping it, and I feared she'd topple. "Clever, really. I'm my own worst enemy, though the handwriting was already on the wall. I'd learned, because I rifled through his wallet, conveniently peeking out of a coat pocket, that he was married. That really surprised me. He just never *acted* married, if you know what I mean. It never occurred to me." Again, she bit on the broken nail, contemplated it, and frowned.

That news had surprised me, too. In all Jed's flirtatious moments, in all the chatter about him in the denizens of Schubert Alley and at theatrical parties, nothing had been said about a wife until recently. Her name was Anita, Aleck Woollcott told me, a twinkle in his lascivious eye. A flighty girl who threw Bohemian parties with red light bulbs giving the living room the look of a tawdry brothel, with dripping candles stuck into wine bottles…In fact, Aleck claimed he'd been to one, and Jed sat in a corner doing mindless card tricks and ignoring everyone. I assumed Aleck was making it all up. "Did you confront him?" I asked Bella now.

"Yeah, he admitted it. Says most people don't know, which is the way he likes it. She certainly isn't on his arm as he goes to show openings."

I cringed because suddenly my heart jumped and one of my eyes twitched. I thought of Jed and his anonymous flapper wife. What did it matter? I told myself. But it did—monumentally, devastatingly. "Lord."

"Indeed. Well, I foolishly sort of blackmailed him. I felt he was ready to dump me anyway—what girl can't read those signs?—so I said I'd tell his wife about our…tryst…if, well, he didn't give me a part in something."

I swallowed my words, sarcastic. "And, knowing Jed, that obviously worked like a charm."

Bella snickered. "You said it. He howled, burst out laughing, tears in his eyes, and told me to go ahead. I was one of many cheap and available girls, though I was the first Negro he'd 'entertained'—that was his word—and so, go right ahead, sister. God, he laughed and laughed, drunk with it. And then he got up, cold as ice, those hooded eyes mean and hard, and just walked away from me. I knew it was the end. Which, of course, happened a few days later." She grinned. "No more baubles from Woolworth's for me." She sat forward now. "So here I am. No Jed. No Lawson. No…Roddy."

"Roddy," Waters mumbled. "You weren't seeing Roddy. You only *hoped* to. Because of Ellie."

Bella shook her head patronizingly. "Dear, dear little Waters, the innocent among all of us libertines." She smiled, unfriendly. "As it turns out, Roddy and I did have a brief moment this past summer, right after we all met in Miss Ferber's living room to discuss our great artistic scribbling. So brief sometimes it seemed not to have even happened."

"I don't understand," Waters said.

"Simple. Roddy, despite Freddy's assertions to the contrary, was, in fact, a petty and creepy womanizer. I'll never understand Freddy's nonsense about that episode in the hallway. Maybe I can't. Roddy was cagey. He had a fling with Ellie that she crowed about at one point—to me. Then, briefly, a moment with me, and then goodbye. To us both, I gather. He just stopped, cold. Maybe Freddy was right. Maybe Roddy was confused. Nice word, no?"

"But," Rebecca insisted, "this doesn't sound like Roddy." She genuinely seemed baffled.

Bella smiled. "Ah, gentle Roddy. Polite Roddy. So-nice-to-older-ladies Roddy." A pause. "Nasty Roddy. Playboy Roddy. Sissy Roddy. Roddy liked to be mysterious. Who knows? I think he visited both camps, if you know what I mean. But Freddy exaggerated what Roddy did. Maybe not. Roddy was soft and fun and always so charming to everyone, which made us all beat a path to his shuttered door. But he…anyway, Freddy got all bent out of shape over something and ran to tell Harriet, his partner in crime, and I guess her father was there in the hallway and saw something, though probably spied through drunken eyes, which is why he hated Roddy. Well, he hated him in general because he had this thing about girls being in the apartments late at night. Everyone has heard *that* story. And you know he's crazy religious and that doesn't fly with him in *his* home, which includes all the apartments. Roddy would sneak Ellie in, too, especially when she got off work early. Lately, she told me that they were just talking, as friends. Late at night. Like I *believed* that."

"Maybe they did just talk," Waters insisted.

"Well, that's what Ellie told everyone. But I suspected that Roddy and Ellie were back together again, which was why he stopped seeing *me*."

"But you had Lawson," I insisted.

"Lawson is a leech. No one *has* Lawson. And I told you, it was over because of Jed. Jed told me to get rid of Lawson, and I did. Then Jed got rid of me. Cute, no?"

"What did it matter if Roddy started seeing Ellie again?" Rebecca asked.

The voice hard, flinty. "It *mattered*. Ellie and I have always been rivals. We're performers, and she gets the jobs. We're writers, and people praise her archaic sonnets. Look at her, a little dowdy and birdlike, a twitcher. And me…" Her voice soared, triumphant. "It was driving me crazy, the idea that Roddy would take *her* back. But I felt that Roddy was now sneaking Ellie in again, starting up with her again, after Mr. Porter was sleeping, usually drunk on gin, with a Bible under his head. Roddy once told him there was no God—that he was an atheist who supported the Bolshevists in Russia, and Mr. Porter went nuts. Freddy's nonsense was just the frosting on the cake."

"But would Mr. Porter kill him?" Waters wondered out loud.

Bella ignored him, lost now in her own thoughts.

"So you *did* go there that night?" I ventured.

Quiet, quiet, her fingers sliding over the tabletop. "Well, yes."

Waters exclaimed, "You lied!"

"I didn't want to look…desperate."

"Desperate?" From Rebecca.

"When Lawson told me that Ellie said she was visiting Roddy that night, it drove me crazy. I mean, I figured she told him *purposely*—to get back at me. To be mean. Ellie was angry and she was up to something. She uses her…charms, limited though they are. I had this panic moment—Roddy and Ellie. Impossible. She'd be in the apartment, sneaking in through the back, and we're not talking conversation about the Negro revolution and the legacy of Booker T. Washington. I knew I had to be *there*, to be sure. To *see*. Foolish, jealous, irrational, senseless. Ultimately stupid."

"But you were with Lawson that night," I said.

"Yeah, and I was furious with Lawson. With Roddy. With Jed. My world crashed down around me. I sneaked there around midnight, unfortunately a little too drunk, and, yes, I hung in the shadows but not for long. If Ellie came, she'd walk through the alley to the back of the building at that hour so she could rap on his window, and she'd find me huddled there. Comical, really. I'd not thought of *that* encounter."

"So you left?" I asked.

"After a few minutes. Crazed. Yes." She smirked. "I didn't realize that Harriet had such a good sense of smell. But then... most hunting dogs do, right?"

"Wait." I was confused. "Wasn't Lawson back at your apartment? With *you*?"

"He certainly was, passed out on the sofa."

Rebecca was shaking her head. "So you left the apartment and he was there, drunk on the sofa? That makes little sense, Bella. What if he woke up and spotted you gone? You're telling us that you were at Roddy's place the night he was murdered?"

Fury in her voice. "But I didn't murder him. You don't kill someone because they reject you." A pause. "Well, I guess some women do. Yes, I was angry with him, with everyone, but...that's why I lied. No one could know I was there, though I guess lots of folks routinely checked out the aromatic shadow in the alley."

"What if Lawson woke up?" I persisted. "That's a possibility."

She debated answering me. Then, grimly, "I took care of that. Since I'm blabbing everything here—in defense of my pretty neck—I might as well confess to nefarious conduct unbecoming a damsel in distress."

"What are you talking about?" From Waters, exasperated.

"Lawson wasn't rising from that stupor. I made sure of it." She arched her neck, insolent, and I thought: my Lord, what a manipulative woman, this vixen, a woman fiercely proud of the vein of evil shot through her gorgeous body. "You see, I knew that I'd planned on going the minute Lawson told me of Ellie's plans that night. I wasn't thinking straight—I just wanted to *know*, to *see* for myself. So Lawson and I went to Mambo's, and we drank, as we always did. But Lawson drank a lot more than I did because I held back, made believe, poured out drinks when he was away from me, and we staggered back to my place around eleven. Earlier than usual because I said I was sick. My brother was just leaving for his night job and wasn't happy with the two of us reeling on the stairs. He yelled at Lawson, in fact. So Lawson and I fought—or should I say continued our battle?—and I ended the affair. It just came out. It's over. That much is true. But we had more drinks at my home. At my request." A sly twinkle in her eye. "I slipped some convenient knockout drops into his drink. Within seconds he was snoring on the sofa, a dead weight. Slobbering, drool at the corners of his mouth. Delightful to see, I must tell you. He's not so pretty when he's a puddle of spit. Whatever did I see in him?"

"Knockout drops?" Waters exclaimed.

"Up in Harlem on a Saturday night, you can get you most anything lethal—or temporarily lethal."

"Obviously," I grimaced.

Bella looked at me. "They don't have knockout drops in your world, Miss Ferber?"

"An opening night of an Augustin Daly melodrama has much the same soporific effect, I'm sure." I thought of something and looked toward Waters. "That explains Lawson the next morning, Waters. Remember how groggy, out of focus he was, stumbling in on us and gaping stupidly at Roddy's body. I thought at the time he seemed…well, drugged."

Waters was nodding. "I remember."

Bella smiled and bowed her head. "The wonders of modern science."

Rebecca clicked her tongue. "Hardly nice, Bella."

"I'm not a nice person."

"I'll say," Waters broke in, and Bella frowned at him.

"So," Bella went on, "I was off, a little tipsy, with a mission. But, as I said, I was in that alley a matter of minutes when I realized the folly—the downright stupidity—of it, and I left."

"You didn't see Ellie then?" I asked.

She shook her head. "No." A pause. "Was she there?"

"She says she wasn't, but a tenant saw someone—a girl, he thought—in the hallway."

"It wasn't me."

"He's the one who saw your shadow just a bit earlier."

Bella roared. "So I just missed her. She *was* there. She…" Her face closed up. "She probably saw Roddy just before…" She punched the tabletop. "Damn."

"We don't *know* if it was Ellie. The man *sensed* a woman."

"I don't like to lose to Ellie."

Exasperated, I blurted out, "Lose? Lose what, Bella? For heaven's sake, listen to yourself. The only person who seems to have lost anything is Roddy. His life, Bella."

"And you think that Ellie did it?"

"What?" I cried. "We're talking about *your* visit. How do we know you left within minutes?"

She sat back. "Simple. There was an eyewitness. As I was rushing up toward Seventh Avenue to the bus stop, your Mr. Harris was getting out of a cab in front of Barron's Exclusive Club. He seemed surprised to see me rushing by—I wasn't even looking at the crowd going inside because I wanted to get back home. Remember dear Lawson, comatose on my comfy couch? But Jed called out to me. Keep in mind—this was just hours before he finally and viciously ditched me. I had no choice but to go to him. He was alone, already tipsy, headed for a night of drinking; and he insisted I go with him. I had to go because, well, I had to. The master beckoned. The bastard. I sat with him until maybe three in the morning, marooned among all those white folks from Park Avenue. I kept trying to slip away. But not before he told me we wouldn't be seeing each other any more. Finally, he put me in a cab. Just ask your pal, Jed Harris, Miss Ferber. He's my alibi. When I got back around three or four, Lawson was snoring to beat the band. But I was a nervous wreck."

"I'll talk to Jed," I said.

"Of course." Bella smiled at me. "So I couldn't have murdered dear, cruel Roddy."

"I'm not so sure," I countered. "Perhaps Roddy was killed at midnight. You were there, then."

"But I never went inside."

"But you were there, Bella. And alone."

Her face closed up. "No." When Waters started to say something, she reached over and held her hand against the side of his face. "No," she repeated. "Do you hear me? No."

Chapter Sixteen

That night, restless, I took a cab to Jed's small apartment at West 10th Street.

I'd fretted throughout my half-eaten dinner with George and Bea Kaufman, our superstitious pre-opening ritual, my mind not on the imminent openings of *Show Boat* and *The Royal Family*. George, ever vigilant and caustic, spotted my disregard of the scrumptious food at Lüchow's, and noted my distracted state, my non-sequitors, and my stuttered responses to his chatter. Bea, as usual, simply watched, used to the buzz-saw repartee of our dinner talk, though tonight she seemed confused by my persistent silence.

"I'm sorry. This murder…Bella today." I went on, incoherently recounting my conversation with Bella, and George resisted the sharp retort, instead nodding his head as though in the presence of a simple child who has wandered away from a campsite. Until, that is, I uttered the words "Jed Harris" into the chaotic mix, at which moment George, who roundly and joyously hated the upstart producer who'd mocked him one time too many—and cheated us financially, we finally believed—sat up, brightened.

"That ass!" he blurted out. "I should have known he was somehow connected with your ramblings."

I defended Jed, God knows why. "No, not really, George. It's simply that Jed, somehow, saw fit to step into these young folks' lives, mess with them, hurt one, woo and abandon another, and…and…"

"Say no more," George said in an aggressive vaudevillian voice. "If there is murder, he is behind it."

"Oh, God, no. Not really. It's more his questionable character than his assassin's arm."

"Edna, really. Your girlish infatuation with the boy wonder has lost its novelty."

I fumed. "Lord, George, how tasteless."

"George!" Bea admonished him.

"My apologies," he sputtered, with nothing apologetic about his tone as Bea reached over and touched his wrist. He ignored it.

"I shouldn't even bring him up," I said.

George went on. "I saw him at the theater hours ago, crowing like a barnyard cock. So now I understand his cruel gibe."

"And what was that? At my expense, I suppose?"

"He said that good old Ferb was playing interlocutor in a black-faced minstrel show. For your own amusement. And that Ferb was making a little too much of his own minor-league dalliance with a charming Negress, who would remain nameless." George chuckled. "He added, 'By nameless, I mean you'll never see her name in print or in lights. At least not south of 125th Street.' It didn't make much sense, but…" He paused. "What?"

I was standing, roaring mad, my five-foot-two body erect and attempting to be giant, towering. "You'll pay the check, dear George. You've provided the indigestion for the evening." And I stormed away, so emphatic my stride that the hat check girl saw me hurrying toward her and had my overcoat, scarf, and gloves thrust out, pell mell, into my furious arms. And out the door.

Which was how I found myself in a cab heading to 10th Street, where, I knew, Jed Harris maintained his private *pied-à-terre*, doubtless one of many disreputable hideaways in the bowels of Gotham. And certainly not the abode he maintained if, indeed, he did, with the newly unearthed bride, Anita with the red glow. Probably dancing with a lampshade on her head.

I slammed the cab door shut and heard the departing cabbie curse me. A Russian lad with an impossible accent, he was a character from one of my short stories. I stood in front of Jed's apartment building, surprised that there was no doorman. But most buildings in the city lacked that special luxury. I would have thought Jed Harris might deem one necessary, perhaps some dumb-but-tough Damon Runyon type, a goon with gun and beady eyes and cartoon muscle—certainly there were enough folks in Manhattan who'd relish hearing of Jed's painful and prolonged demise. I, among them.

I rushed up two flights, wary of the rickety stairwell, headed down a corridor. I had the sudden thought that he might not be home—or alone. But my instinct said, yes, ten o'clock, home to dress for night clubbing or a late dinner. And, of course, he was. From behind the door wafted the staticky hum of a radio, a broadcast of classical music. *Brahms*, I thought, though the snatches heard through the oak door were muted and echoey. Music to lambaste a venal producer by.

I rapped on the door and he opened it quickly, as though he expected me. For a second I could see a glimmer of surprise in the eye corner, but Jed was not one to betray surprise. He liked to let the world believe that he was ready for any situation—nothing took him unawares, by chance. Except the furious lady novelist, late at night, rap-rapping on his bachelor flat door. "Edna, do come in, I was expecting you." He swiveled around the tiny, cramped room. "No one has ever come into these rooms." A snicker. "I mean, *your* type of people, Edna. Others…"

"Who follow the stench of your dollar bill perhaps," I broke in, and he laughed.

He was dressed in creased trousers and a white undershirt, suspenders draped over his slim hips. Freshly shaved, he smelled of a European cologne. Not pleasant, this scent of overblooming Mediterranean flowers. Bougainvillea for the bad boy. A formal tux jacket covered the back of a chair, and a white dress shirt hung off a doorknob. "I have an appointment."

"Cancel it."

He laughed. "You seem out of sorts, Edna, dear Edna." He waved me into the room.

I sat on the edge of a blue velvet wing chair and stared around the claustrophobic room at the oversized ornate Victorian furniture stacked against walls. A strange room, unfit for human beings, windows lacking curtains, wallpaper looking freshly but unevenly applied. A transition room: the itinerant drummer stopping overnight. On a small table a half-eaten sandwich that he'd doubtless bought from the Automat. Jed saw me looking around. "It's not where I live. I come here to get away from people. Obviously it's not working."

"Then why'd you write *this* address on a slip of paper for me?"

A sickening smile. "I was hoping you'd show up eventually. It certainly worked."

"Make up your mind. It's working…it's not working."

"What do you want, Edna?" Cold, fierce, unfriendly, the hooded eyes wary.

"Bella," I emphasized the word. "Bella. And the night poor Roddy was murdered."

"We've been through this. I am not—repeat: not—involved…"

"You were with Bella that night, and you never mentioned it to anyone. Never. Certainly not to the police. You are important to the investigation."

"Which, I gather, is over, given the newspaper reports."

"Not so far as I am concerned."

He stood over me, glowering. "Edna, this is none of your business."

"Of course it is. There are people I know…"

"Friends? Young Negroes."

I bit my tongue. "At least I'm not…bedding them down."

He roared. "Only one, Edna. Only one. And that's a thing of the past. Mistresses are liabilities when they're young, beautiful, and ambitious."

"Bella told me she discovered you are married."

"So?"

"You kept it a secret from her."

"It didn't come up in our conversations."

"Your wife…"

He whispered, menacingly, "What are you here for, Edna? A morality play with you as the cruel hand of God?"

"I just resent duplicity, Jed. You don't believe the rules and regulations that grease our society are for you—that you inhabit a world…"

"Edna," he broke in, "I'm not one of the characters you create in your fiction, those destructive romantic ne'er-do-wells that test the mettle of your stalwart and purposeful heroines. I'm not Gaylord Ravenal on the upper deck of the *Cotton Blossom*, wooing the ingénue…"

"Nothing of the kind, sir."

He slid into a chair opposite me, but immediately he popped up. A car backfired in the street under his window, and I started. He didn't. A sadistic smile crossed his lips. "Edna, the problem is that you believe such men only exist in your imagination. Most real men you despise, see as weaklings. Well"—here he did a vaudeville two-step—"here is your hero, flawed and all."

"Not you, Jed!"

"Not many men get the best of you, Edna. I may be the first."

"Jed, I came here for a serious talk. This is frivolous posturing on your part, behavior that you…"

"A drink, Edna? A night cap?"

He didn't wait for my answer but disappeared into a small kitchenette, where I heard the crunch of smashed ice cubes, the fizzle of a mixed drink, the closing of a refrigerator door. He walked back into the room, placed the highball on the table before me, and stood there, his own drink in hand, watching me. I picked up the ice-cold glass and sipped the cold whiskey. I'd not realized how parched my throat was, but the drink burned my throat.

He watched me, waiting, waiting. For a moment he closed his eyes but then, in a quick, jerky twist of his arm, he downed his own cocktail. He started fiddling with the fabric of his undershirt, pulling at it, and, for a second, I panicked. Jed notoriously liked to undress in front of guests, something doubtless he'd learned from that other brazen exhibitionist, Tallulah

Bankhead, who liked to dine *au natural* with horrified guests. Now Jed had never dared disrobe before me—even he would not cross that threshold—but George Kaufman had bandied about a delicious story.

He'd gone to see Jed at the Buckingham Hotel, where Jed was holed up to work on dialogue changes, only to have Jed answer the door stark naked. George didn't miss a beat, ignored the blatant affront, and conducted his business. When he readied to leave, he turned in the doorway, looked back, and said calmly, "Oh, by the way, Jed, your fly is down." How we all chortled over that anecdote, George telling it over and over at dinner parties.

But now, alone with him in this dank, renegade flat, I feared an unwanted reprise of that suspect and bawdy one-act play. But no, Jed slipped into a seat opposite me, wrapped his arms around his bony chest, and said, "Yes, I was with Bella the night Roddy was murdered. It was also the night I told her to get lost. To go away. I bumped into her as she rushed by on the sidewalk. Imagine my surprise, seeing her bustling by like that."

"What time?"

"I dunno. Midnight maybe. I was going to Barron's Exclusive Club by my lonesome. She was…" He stopped.

Suddenly Jed stood up and moved to the small window. He stared, entranced, into the darkness, though I could see his neck muscles tighten, his shoulders hunch up. He swiveled, almost a calculated, rehearsed movement, and through clenched teeth said, "Edna, Bella isn't a murderer."

"I didn't say she was."

"Really? I sensed that was the direction of this conversation."

"Jed, stop this evasion. Right now, for God's sake. A young man is dead. Just tell me about it."

He slipped back into the chair, reached for the empty highball glass, and regarded me coolly. "She didn't want to come with me. To Barron's. I know she didn't like the place because they frown on white men bringing their black girls there. But Bella always agreed with anything I suggested. But not that night, which was unusual. I'd flash wads of cash, and women like Bella who instinctively don't trust the world will follow you to the ends of the globe. But she was anxious to get away. She kept saying she had something to do at her apartment. 'What?' I demanded. I figured she had to meet that lout Lawson, and she didn't want me to know. But she wouldn't answer me. Instead, she was nervous and sweating, even though it was numbing cold outside."

"What did she say?"

"She didn't say much, Edna. She started to annoy me almost immediately with her inattention to me."

"Seven deadly sins rolled into one, I suppose."

He ran his tongue into the corner of his cheek. "If you're with me, you act like you enjoy it."

"I'll remember that."

"I doubt if you forget—or forgive—much, Edna."

"Go on, Jed."

The grin disappeared from his face. "So I took her to the Nest Club, not Barron's Exclusive. Because I'm a kind guy. Some jazz cabaret, whites mainly but Negro guests—that is, girls—barely tolerated."

"Did she mention Roddy?"

"No, but she started to babble on about Lawson. I guess she *had* finally told him to get lost. Ended whatever they had." His smile turned into a frown. "That had been my…well, mandate a while back. You want me, well, you have to lose Lawson, the neophyte actor/playwright/preener/fool." The sickening smile reappeared. "And, I gather, she listened to me."

"Maybe it had nothing to do with you, Jed."

"I told her to shut up about Lawson. So she clammed up. We listened to jazz, drank, and she kept trying to get away."

"How late did you stay?"

"I put her in a cab around three. This was after I told her we would not be seeing each other any more. No calls, no letters, no tears, no boo-hoos, no nothing. Get lost—in other words."

"How did she take that?"

"Stunned at first, I don't think she believed me. She just stared. I had to shove her into the cab."

"So she was with you from about midnight until three in the morning."

A pause. "I guess."

That frustrated me, "What kind of answer is that?"

"I mean, yes, she was. She left to use the toilet somewhere in the street. Negroes aren't allowed to use the facilities at the Nest Club."

"How long was she gone?"

"Half hour, hour. I don't recall. I got to talking with friends. I was surprised she came back, but, of course, I hadn't told her to get lost yet. I saved that wonderful announcement to the end—just as the cab pulled up. Theater is exquisite timing, dear Edna. You should write that down for future reference."

I ignored that. "So she could have slipped back to Roddy's apartment."

"For what? Murder? Edna, Edna, you melodramatic spinner of airy tales. Bella only has sex and money on her pretty brain. If anything, she wanted sex, not death, from this Roddy."

"Women have been known to kill for want of love."

"Listen to you! 'Want of love.' You talk like a starved pullet in a Victorian romance written by The Duchess."

I bristled at that. The Duchess' novels, admittedly gushy with purple prose and preposterous situation, had given me constant comfort when I was a little girl in Appleton, Wisconsin. Instead, I wondered out loud, "And you don't know if the taxi took her home, do you?"

He was shaking his head. "Edna, Edna."

"Tell me, Jed. This is all information that you should have given to the police. You have a duty…"

He held up his hand. For a second anger flashed across his face, replaced at once by a cool, hard countenance. "I choose *not* to. I don't want my name involved with this, much as yours was in the tabloids. It's"—a sheepish grin—"unseemly."

"I'll be responsible for my own reputation, thank you. But the police must investigate…"

"Investigate what? They've arrested the bum, with oodles of evidence. It's over, *finis*, complete. Edna, don't you have enough to do with *Show Boat* and *The Royal Family*? I'm predicting *Show Boat* will sink into the muddy waters of the Mississippi. And as for *The Royal Family*…"

"I have nothing to do with them except watch rehearsals and go to the openings."

"So you play detective?"

This was getting nowhere. I stood. "I'm leaving."

Jed watched me, eyes slatted, a twinkle in them. "It's late, Edna."

"Not for New York. Maybe for Hoboken or wherever you hang your married hat."

He chuckled, long, hard, phony. "Edna, you could stay here." His hand reached out and touched my elbow, an electric shock to the body, a grazing touch that seemed curiously volcanic, riveting. It was a quick, calculated move, his body inclined toward mine, and I stepped back, as though contaminated. Of course, all along, I understood that I had a kind of schoolgirl infatuation with the smoldering, arrogant man, involuntarily so, since I'm usually good at resisting the fools and cads that life puts in my path. Even when whole parts of me despised Jed, his manipulations and cruelties—even though I saw him as a soulless man, a Parisian gigolo with swagger, Iago with a five o'clock shadow, even then—there was often a fluttering in my chest, a hint of perspiration on my brow, ringing in my ears. But now, suddenly, his crude gesture of reaching out to touch my elbow squelched whatever sensation—is that the word I want?—I had for him: killed it, stamped it out, obliterated it. Thank God.

It was, joyously for me, a moment of intoxicating release.

His eyes widened, alarmed, as my hand swung free and slapped him soundly across his rough cheek. He fell back, stumbled, one hand grasping his bruised face, the other flaying wildly as if in search of his bruised ego.

He snarled. "I have my way with any woman I want."

I headed to the door. "Well, after tonight you'll have to amend that declaration. Lower the percentage."

He laughed. "For now." He rocked on his heels. "You have a crush on me."

"Had. Before I saw the darkness in you."

"Some women find the darkness appealing."

I turned and walked out the door. Over my shoulder I said, "Little boys like you are afraid of the dark."

He looked puzzled. "What does that mean?"

I had no idea. I was simply looking for an exit line. I slammed the door.

Chapter Seventeen

Rebecca knocked on my closed workroom door at eleven the next morning, something forbidden when I was working. It was the day before the opening of *Show Boat* and I was vigorously answering letters, penning a short retrospective on the genesis of *Show Boat* that was intended for the *Saturday Review*, a day swamped with catching up. I pecked at the Remington, my one finger flurry of activity, because I wrote nothing in pencil or pen any more, the instruments leaden in my fingers. I typed notes to the hairdresser, the doorman, even to my sister Fannie who found it questionable, though she never returned the check that fluttered out of the folds of my letter. "Miss Edna, a call."

I bristled. "Rebecca."

"Langston Hughes." She swallowed. "I told him you were working but I thought I'd check with you first."

"Of course." I picked up the phone.

I was surprised at the call because, indeed, just yesterday, he'd returned the opening chapters of Lawson's novel by messenger. His brief note had repeated what he'd told me at George Kaufman's Christmas party, and he reiterated that the work needed to be published. He asked that I send him the entire novel after New Year's. He also wanted to talk with Lawson. His note concluded with congratulations on the opening of *Show Boat* and *The Royal Family*. "You're entering a cornucopia of success most of us dream of, but I can imagine the stress."

"Hello, Mr. Hughes."

"Miss Ferber, hello."

"Perhaps Mr. Hughes, we can use our first names. After all, I keep meeting you in town. Call me Edna, please. I'll call you Langston."

I could hear the humor in his voice. "Old habits die hard, Miss...Edna."

"That's better," I said, "though I sound like a hectoring schoolmarm with a hickory stick."

He laughed. "An old custom I recall from my boyhood in the Midwest." The squeak of an opened door, someone whispering behind him. "My apologies for calling, but perhaps I'll distract you from the horrible burden of two back-to-back openings on Broadway."

"Not at all."

"The reason I'm calling now...I'm sitting at the editorial rooms of *Opportunity*, which is edited by my friend, Charles Johnson, who's sitting across from me and smiling. I just told him I was calling Edna Ferber and he didn't believe me." I could hear laughter in the background. "I don't know if you know *Opportunity*."

"I do, in fact." I'd seen copies of the journal, a sensible, earnest periodical devoted to furthering the cause of the Negro writer. Waters faithfully deposited them at my breakfast table. To be sure, I'd first read Langston's poem "The Weary Blues" in its pages. "I know of the magazine," I said into the phone.

"I stopped in to see Charles about an essay I wrote, and we were talking about the literary contests that *Opportunity* runs now and then. It's his way of discovering new talent. He's been clearing out a file cabinet, unwanted correspondence, loose ends, flyers, folders of old submissions to the contest, somehow saved and filed but now being discarded."

I waited. Surely he was not going to inflict a packet of inane juvenilia on my doorstep. "Yes?" Tentative, wary.

He chuckled. "No, no." A pause. "Charles has been going through the files and he found a short story by someone named Roderick Parsons. But a note clipped to it, hand-written, boyish, was signed 'Roddy Parsons.' He realized that the story was submitted by the poor lad who died. He remembered the news accounts of Roddy's murder up here, of course. So he showed it me..."

I breathed in, bothered. "Good Lord."

"He must have sent it some time ago, but Charles and I don't want to throw it out." He said something away from the phone, and I could hear Charles Johnson's whispered voice. "I only read the first pages and skimmed the rest. It does go on a bit, and sadly it's a bit sophomoric and stilted, a young writer's attempt to tell a story. It's historical fiction, taking place in Alabama during the Civil War. Cardboard characters, you know—Mammy, Southern colonels, Yankee invaders, Southern belles with mint juleps and foxhunts. A battle scene in front of the old plantation with the house slaves up in arms. Some surprisingly decent writing but... quaint, failed." I could hear him sigh. "Nothing to be done with it, but it seems a sacrilege to discard it. I was wondering if..."

"Of course," I said. "I want it. I'll put it with his other writings. I don't know what's to be done with them, except for his wonderful poetry, but it's not for me to decide."

"I'll send it by messenger." A deep intake of breath. "It made me melancholy, glancing through it. A boy obviously starting to grow, to find a voice."

We said goodbye, and I sat there, a little teary-eyed, not wanting to move. Then I found myself smiling. Roderick Parsons. The oh-so-serious man. The boy writer.

The afternoon was a blur of meeting, pique, and ego, the first the catalyst for the second two. My publisher Doubleday, without my permission, scheduled a press conference at two o'clock to promote both the book *Show Boat* and the musical. Begrudgingly, I sat with Oscar Hammerstein and Jerome Kern, both men looking like my shady protectors.

I survived the decorous photographic ritual with Hammerstein and Kern, though Jerome sensed I was out of sorts. "What?" he muttered as the photogs snapped.

"Jed Harris," I seethed, and he grinned.

Everyone had heard the stories of the beast. My explosive slap against Jed Harris' rough cheek last night still resounded in my head, a moment that made me proud but also deeply ashamed, like the harried housewife who, driven, speaks her mind at a church meeting and then is bothered by her own ferocity. So be it: Jed Harris was a man born to be slapped…if not hanged in a public square. Jerome Kern, an old-fashioned dapper gentleman, now hummed an off-key bar of "Can't Help Lovin' Dat Man," a joke I found not at all amusing.

But then I skedaddled through Schubert Alley and arrived at the Selwyn Theater to hear Jed's bilious roaring and condemnation. Throughout a disastrous dress rehearsal, Jed, cranky as an old well handle, kept stopping and starting the run-through, nasty, nasty. I bumped into George Kaufman, who told me he'd seen enough hell in one afternoon to last a lifetime. That made me laugh, which caused Jed, up front, to swivel and spot the two of us.

Snarkily, a voice aimed at the players: "Perhaps if the two simpering playwrights had penned better lines, you all wouldn't sound so stale." He turned to look at us.

"Ignore the boor," George whispered.

But I couldn't. "Perhaps if you listened to the play, you might understand where your own humanity has failed."

Ice in the room: tension on the stage. The director, menaced already, shuddered. Not good, my outburst. Not good to rattle the already-harried and abused troupe onstage.

"Leave it," George whispered. So I sat down.

I sat there for a half hour, jotting notes on what was happening, though I knew Jed and the director would toss my advice into a waste bin. Jed, the cocky producer, had his own ideas of how a play is built though he'd never written one…and, I sometimes believed, never really *read* one.

Following the run-through, the cast fled, relieved to be alive, and our short, unhappy meeting was held in the front seats of the orchestra, facing a stage where the curtain had not been dropped, so that, ominous, the elegant East Side apartment of the Cavandish clan kept intruding on our humdrum words about pace, timing, projection.

I smelled disaster, and said it.

Jed ignored me and mumbled something to the director, who nodded and then glanced at me apologetically. Then Jed tucked his tongue into his cheek. "Edna, you seem to cultivate disaster." A pause. "Or is it murder you cultivate?"

"Easy now," George whispered, touching my elbow.

He was baiting me, I knew, this irascible rapscallion. "Jed," I began.

"But you're right. It is a disaster. I'll close it before New Year's."

I stood up and walked out of the theater.

The telephone rang all afternoon and into the evening, but I instructed Rebecca not to answer it. The combative afternoon at *The Royal Family* and the seamy presence of a purposely-snide Jed Harris both conspired to make me headachy and weak, so I shut it all out, so easy to do in a high-floor doorman building with a sky of gray clouds hovering just outside my window. Rebecca, sworn to silence and obedience, was the dedicated sentry. No, I told her, no calls. No family wishing me well, no editors, no publishers, no press. Jed Harris had left a bad taste in my mouth, like the ingestion of a sweet but toxic elixir. So the phone rang, and we let it ring.

Rebecca spent the evening readying my clothing for both openings: the periwinkle blue dress for *Show Boat*, with the ermine wrap and the garish orchid; the pearl-colored dress for *The Royal Family*, with the ruffled silk across the bodice, to be worn under a mink coat with scarlet lining. For both nights I'd bought voguish sequined cloches, one hat gold with a rhinestone band across the front, the other hat black velvet. We'd planned the looks for weeks. I loved the way Rebecca ran her gentle hand across the smooth silk, the sheen catching the overhead light. Her eyes shone: wonderland. Dancing the night away.

Walking through the rooms, watching her careful attention to wrinkles and creases, I suddenly was filled with a marrow-deep despair, my insides hollowed out, a vacant feeling of loss and disaster. What was the matter with me?

Though no orchids or gardenias had been delivered yet, I imagined I could smell the cloying, overly sweet aroma, caught in thoughts of funeral parlors and high-school proms.

Later, lying in bed, listening to the tinkle of radio music drifting in from the kitchen, I ate the meal Rebecca served me on a tray: chicken salad sandwich with diced celery and onion on dark pumpernickel bread, a side of cold potatoes chopped with some ground nuts, string beans I didn't touch, and a slab of German chocolate cake bought at a York Avenue Hungarian pastry shop, so sweet that the first and only bite made my front teeth ache.

Restless, I wandered into the living room and stared, numb, out over the tops of the skeletal winter trees of Central Park. The stark branches were illuminated with spotty halos from the streetlights, eerie and windblown. Down below, in the street, the tops of cabs moved, blotches of dark-lit yellow, a checkerboard that shifted, fragmented, disappeared. I touched the icy windowpane, though a dry hot heat seeped up from the floorboards. Dark night, and lonesome. Lonely. Alone.

Walking back to my bedroom, I glanced at the sideboard by the front door. There was the slim manila envelope that must have been delivered earlier. Roddy's short story. Langston Hughes' name and the word *Opportunity* written in the upper left corner. Rebecca must have placed it there. Idly I picked up the slender envelope and carried it to my room, sliding into bed, pulling up the covers to my chin, and unsealing the flap. A brief note from Langston fell out. "Thank you. Langston." That was all. Thanks for what? I wondered. What was I going to do with all these typed and handwritten pages piling up in my life? Lawson's unfinished—maybe never to be finished—novel. Roddy's poetry and that helter-skelter collection of notes and diary entries. *Mr. Porter is rifling through my stuff. I don't trust him.* Those cryptic jottings that conveyed no real message, lost now with Roddy's death. And now this failed piece of fiction, forgotten in the files of *Opportunity*. Ironic, that name now.

I didn't know why I decided to read it, given my already dour and darkened mood. But I did.

And, surprisingly, I was swept with myriad emotions.

The sloppily typed story, nearly twenty pages long, though unpaged, struck me immediately as a young boy's story, a neophyte writer's attempt at the grand theme. Roddy had called the story "Time to Die," and quoted a few lines from a Negro spiritual I'd never heard before:

Lord, I keep so busy servin' my master
Keep so busy servin' my master
Keep so busy servin' my master
Ain't got time to die.

The first paragraph, overwritten and ponderous, identified the piece as a Civil War story, but it was so classically a familiar scenario, a narrative borne out of too many viewings of *Birth of a Nation* perhaps, though told from a Negro slave's viewpoint. I cringed as I moved through the stereotyped and wooden black characters, little Sambo automatons, crowing and bellowing before the onslaught of Yankee blood and thunder. No wonder Langston had immediately dismissed the story after glancing at the first few pages. This was not a little embarrassing. And yet I read on.

The story charmed me, finally, though the tale was dark and gloomy. It was Roddy's early work, a young writer's grappling with fiction—a boy's venture. I felt my mood rise. There was something sweet and tender about the words, a boy's pleasure at the use of language, albeit trite, the conscious play of sentence against sentence. Removed from its hackneyed story line, the piece hinted at Roddy's evolution as a poet, a fiction writer. Lyrical moments were scattered throughout like isolated shiny quartz stone speckling a prosaic beach. Finally, I sat back, snuggled into my pillow, and found myself grinning. Here, then, was a cheeky freshness, though static—an evident intoxication with words. But I couldn't fault the young voice. Of course, I realized that the young Negro of today would naturally look back to Civil War days, to the Old South, to plantations, the slave huts—all indelible daguerreotypes of the racial tragedy that had become the modern Negro's brand and inheritance. What other story did the budding writer have…that is, the young black writer? Charmed by it, caught by it, I lingered over the paragraphs and for the first time that day I felt a tick of life in me.

But it passed because I remembered, shot to the quick, that Roddy was dead. There'd be no more evolution, no transcending the stale claptrap out of Thomas Dixon's wildly popular romance *The Clansman* or the film epic *The Birth of a Nation,* so that a real voice would emerge, No, Roddy was dead. And so, unrelenting, the dark imagery smacked up against me and I felt my eyes tear up, my smile twisted into pained grimace.

I expected nightmares.

At the hint of daybreak seeping past the drawn curtains, I found myself awake, so suddenly it seemed a brutal slap across the face. I struggled to sit up, pulled my nightclothes tight around me because I was chilled, but then realized the room was hot, clammy. Yet I shook from the cold. My mind rumbled with images. Something had happened. Something lay on the edge of my mind. Waiting, insisting. I knew something now, but what? I knew, as I shivered there in the steam-heated winter room, that it was awful and deadly and…and it had to do with the murderer.

Chapter Eighteen

I left the apartment for my morning walk. One mile or more, though I dragged myself along, dispirited. Once back at the apartment, bathed, dressed, I went into the kitchen.

"So it begins," Rebecca smiled as she put pancakes and blueberry syrup before me at the breakfast table; and I thought, perversely, So it does, this day. But though I knew she was referring to that night's opening of *Show Boat* and tomorrow's opening of *The Royal Family*, my mind riveted, willy-nilly, to the murder of Roddy. Something had happened as I slept. Somehow I knew something. But what?

"Yes," I answered her, a little feebly.

In my workroom I fiddled with unanswered letters. It would be a jittery, vacant day, unproductive and unsettled. I had nothing to do with the night's *Show Boat*, save attend and smile, and tomorrow's *The Royal Family*, save attend and smile. And then, each successive morning, rush for the reviews in the *Times* and the *Telegraph* and the *Herald Tribune*. Other papers. Vague, empty daytimes that were a preamble to illustrious and scintillating evenings, the huzzahs of friends, the nods of strangers sitting across the aisles.

The Ferber season, Jed had called it.

Restless, I made phone calls to Neysa McMein, Dorothy Rodgers, Peggy Wood, anyone who was home to answer. No one was.

Late morning, dressed and ready to haunt both the Selwyn and the Zeigfeld theaters, I heard Waters chatting with his mother in the kitchen. Before he could join what would be a daylong chorus of what-a-day-for-you-Miss-Edna, I mentioned that Langston Hughes had sent me Roddy's failed short story.

"Roddy? An old story? How was it?"

I sighed. "Perfectly awful."

He started. "I'm sorry."

"Waters," I kidded him, "you didn't write it."

He laughed. "I'm headed uptown this afternoon to visit with Ellie. She's rehearsing for a show at the Spider Web." A pause. "Lawson was invited but begged off. He's avoiding Harlem these days."

"You can't run forever," I announced, imperious.

Rebecca leaned in. "Some people try."

Waters started to say something but I waved, turned, and readied to leave. As I put on my overcoat in the hallway, I could hear Rebecca warning Waters about too much running around town, too many days spent up in Harlem. "After New Year's, it's back to school. You need to finish high school," she emphasized. "Next year college." I smiled. I heard Waters grumbling, a dutiful son talking to his concerned mother.

Ordinarily I thrilled to sit in the seats or pace the aisles or linger backstage at Broadway theaters. There was something about the rattling, hissing steam pipes, the odor of well-worn and stacked costumes, the hum and bustle of crews with their hammering and sawing and painting, the cursing and hilarity, the sudden shriek of humor, the garish lighting, the cacophony of instruments being tuned. Above all, the electricity of movement, the jagged flash of lightning in the dim-lit sky. But not that day. For some reason theaters have a kind of eerie quiet the day of the opening, a holding of a collective breath, some last minute surrender to Fate. The stark, flattened conversation and the heartbeat calm before a dreaded storm. A purple aura covered the stage, perhaps illusionary. Within hours, there would be deafening applause or, everyone's nightmare, deafening silence.

No one spoke to me. A crew member, adjusting an electrical cord beneath a rafter, stared down at me as if I were Marley's ghost, come to wave a bony, skeletal finger at him. Worse, at the Selwyn, Jed Harris bounded in just after two or so, unshaven, his fedora crumpled, glassy-eyed. When he spotted me standing there, looking lost as a Pilgrim on a wilderness shore, he turned on his heels and stormed backstage. Immediately, I could hear his raised, censorious voice, followed by a woman's apologetic and teary response.

No place to be today, so I left.

I sat with an untouched coffee at a counter in Clark's Deli, just off Eighth Avenue, and waited for something to happen.

Then, white with an anger I couldn't define, I hailed a cab that pulled in front of the deli to release a gaggle of midwestern sightseers. The cabbie sputtered at me in a coarse Neapolitan dialect and balked at an afternoon fare up to Harlem, though one glance at me through his rearview mirror told him Mount Edna was ready to erupt. He had no idea where the Spider Web was located and seemed intent on dropping me off anywhere up there. He cursed and belched. But a simple query to a young man waiting to cross the street directed us up Seventh Avenue. The cabbie squealed his tires pulling away, and I complained loudly. Finally he dropped me off in front of the nightclub and seemed displeased with the meager tip I deposited into his grubby hand. I was in no mood for anything less than pure and medieval chivalry.

Even before I opened the front door, I could hear the hum and tinkle of piano and saxophone. It jarred, as when you sense a bumblebee or nagging wasp flitting near your head. It made me wary, tentative and unsure, with a sense of foreboding.

Yet inside the cool, shadowy room there was a relaxed, peaceful feeling. I felt it at once, a wave of ease covering me. Ellie stood on a small stage back from the door, waiting, a piano player hitting a key, the sax player reading sheet music in a corner. Ellie muttered something about a chord, her tone pettish and whiny, and tapped her foot. The piano player hit a note, and waited. She was still complaining. Down front, sitting together at a table, were Waters and, to my surprise, Freddy.

Ellie spotted me. "Miss Ferber." Hardly a welcome, her voice tremulous.

Waters and Freddy jumped up and faced me.

"What happened?" Waters asked.

I approached them. "Nothing." A pause. "Well, maybe everything."

Confused, Waters took a step toward me, though I noticed Freddy sat back down, his body turned away.

I tucked myself into a seat, but my eyes were focused solely on Ellie, who'd stepped forward, away from the pianist, and was eyeing me cautiously. I stared back. The piano player, oblivious, hit some keys, as if he expected her to sing the line she'd complained about. He was a chubby man in a flashy blue tuxedo shirt worn out of his pants, and long hair so excessively conked it caught the overhead light and seemed, grotesquely, some polished plum. He hit the chord again, and Ellie, looking back, actually yelled at him. "I need ten minutes, all right?"

The man shrugged, stood up with difficulty because of his overflowing bulk, and lit a cigarette before lumbering off, followed by the saxophonist, who swung his instrument back and forth, a lance at a joust. Out of sight, they laughed raucously, and Ellie, glancing back toward the disappeared players, frowned. She walked toward the table where the three of us sat. "This rehearsal stinks," she announced. "I don't know what I'll do tonight."

She was paying me scant attention, which rankled. So I cleared my throat and blurted out, "How about you begin by telling me why you came to my apartment, a guest, and lied, straight faced, to me. You lied."

She actually trembled, dropped into a chair, and sobbed. Waters immediately reached out and touched her wrist, though I saw Freddy bristle, twist away, his mouth skewered into a tight, disapproving line.

"I didn't mean to lie to you."

"Well, that's the most disingenuous response I've ever heard in defense of a blatant fabrication."

She faltered. "I mean, well, yes, I lied." A deep gasp of breath. "But I *had* to. People would think I killed Roddy." Fresh tears, perhaps genuine.

"Tell me," I demanded.

"How did you find out I was there?"

"Ask Waters. Ask Freddy." I shot them both a dark look. "Waters was there when the upstairs tenant said he sensed a woman in the hallway headed to Roddy's apartment."

Waters defended her. "But it could have been someone else."

"Well, true," I agreed. "We know it wasn't Bella. That girl was still on her way, headed to the alley at the side of the building. Before she arrived…well, you were there."

Freddy looked squeamish. "I'm sorry, Ellie, but I told Miss Ferber I saw you at the subway stop that night. I'm sorry. I didn't mean…"

She shot him a harsh look, then turned away. She looked defeated. "All right, I was there. At the apartment."

"But why lie about it?"

She waited a moment, then shut her eyes. "After Roddy was found the next day, I got scared. I was in his building. I couldn't admit that. Yes, I'd told Lawson I was headed there. Roddy told me to stay away, but I needed to see him. He called me from his job, whispering because he didn't want his boss to hear him. We fought. He said some nasty things to me. I was going there to see if…if Bella was there. In my place. Maybe she was back…"

Freddy was fretting. "He was a sissy boy."

Ellie erupted in anger. "No, he wasn't. That was just some nonsense you came up with. Maybe…"

"No, I'm not a fool, Ellie."

She watched me carefully. "Roddy was, in his own way, a cad. I know he came off as caring and kind and gentle, but Roddy could be mean. Icy cold. He could go into a rage. He'd flirt, you know. Then he'd be like ice. We saw each other a few times, you know, romantically, but then he stopped. Just like that. But we still had our long talks, and he walked me home at night sometimes. I loved him, Miss Ferber. And I knew he loved me."

Freddy fidgeted. "Shut up, Ellie." But the words were said gently. Freddy, Ellie's dogged pursuer with his blind and juvenile infatuation, the man who hid behind cars and spied on her.

Ellie looked at him, pityingly. "Freddy, it's true. I know you don't want to hear it."

Freddy slumped back in his seat, arms folded, his lips drawn into a thin line. Bested.

"But you went anyway?"

"I *had* to. I knew Bella was jealous and when he begged off that night, I thought, well, *she's* back."

"Did Lawson know about Bella fooling with Roddy?" I asked.

Ellie laughed. "He encouraged it, I think. Not that he could have stopped her. Bella does what she wants."

"Have you two always disliked each other?" I asked.

She nodded. "I'm afraid so."

"So," I continued, "you went there anyway?"

"Stupidly I rushed in, came in by the front door and not the back, which I never did at that hour, and then I thought I heard Mr. Porter banging around his apartment. I thought he heard me. I didn't want to be caught. For a second I stood by Roddy's door, expecting music. He played music on the radio when he stayed up late. Or maybe Bella was with him, I thought. I put my ear against the door, just for a second. Then I could hear Roddy talking, I think, harsh, but like to a person he knew. Little periods of silence, so I figured he was on the phone. I couldn't tell what he was saying but he sounded angry. Then I heard banging from Mr. Porter's apartment. Lord, I didn't want Roddy to catch me there, standing in his hallway, outside his door, eavesdropping—or Mr. Porter. If he was drunk, there might be some tirade. I had trouble with him before."

"Like what? You seem frightened of Mr. Porter."

She sighed. "I came there one afternoon and he, you know, made moves, flirted, a little drunk, still with that fool Bible in his hands, but drunk. 'Come on in, sit, rest, baby, baby.' That sort of line. I had run away from him. So I was afraid he'd open the door, see me there so late, and, well, you know…"

Freddy spoke up. "Did you tell Harriet this?" A rasp in his voice.

Ellie nodded. "I shouldn't have. She hates her father, but after that she didn't want me around."

My mind was racing. "You say Roddy was on the phone?"

"Sounded like it. I thought it was strange, so late at night."

Waters spoke up. "Well, Ellie, it was only around midnight."

Ellie looked perplexed. "No, it wasn't."

"But the tenant heard you—or a woman, someone—around twelve," I insisted. "Just before Bella arrived outside."

Ellie spoke in a low gravelly voice. "Well, then, that wasn't me. There are other tenants on that floor, you know. I know that I arrived around two in the morning, real late. I'd planned on going earlier, but then felt silly." She looked at Freddy, frowned. "I guess you saw me at the subway stop around midnight." He nodded. "I was at Small's Paradise, hanging with Mary Turner, the singer that night, backstage, in her dressing room. We talked between her sets, had a few drinks. Then, leaving around two, I decided—why not? Go see Roddy." She smiled. "Make him angry at such a late visit. Disturb him and Bella, maybe. I'd had too much to drink. Phony courage." A pause. "No, it was two o'clock or so. I know that for a fact."

I looked at Waters, then back at her. "So Roddy was alive then. You didn't tell this to the police?"

"They never talked to me."

"But you could have volunteered the information."

She looked surprised. "For what reason? It had nothing to do with Roddy's murder. He certainly wasn't talking to some homeless person who just broke in. That must have happened right afterwards. Skidder Scott must have come into the hallway right after I got out of there. I wanted to stay far away from the police, you know. It wouldn't look good, me there so late...so close to the...you know...murder. The next day they nabbed the bum and that was that."

"But now perhaps it's not so easy as that." I tapped my finger on the table. "Perhaps there's more to the story."

"How?" Freddy asked. "Ellie said she didn't *see* Roddy."

"I don't like to get messed up with the police," Ellie reiterated. "I have a career. So I went home."

"And then Roddy was murdered," I said. "Probably within minutes."

Fear swept through her pretty features. "If he'd opened the door, I might have been a victim, too." A heartbeat, the face wide with alarm. "But no one could know I was there. Or people would think I killed him."

"Is that why you lied to me? Came to my apartment with the express purpose of lying to me?"

She bit her lip. "Foolish, that. I just thought, in case anyone asked, you would…you know…" She stopped, then blurted out, "I wanted it to be true. I wanted *not* to have gone there then." She shrugged her shoulders. "I'm sorry, Miss Ferber. It was stupid, but…I didn't want you to think I killed Roddy."

"It's a possibility."

Ellie said nothing for a moment, then stood up, turned swiftly and fled the room.

That evening, encouraged by Rebecca who fretted and *tsk*ed, I got ready for the *Show Boat* opening. Much too early. Hammerstein and Kern had sent a bushel of flowers, including the gaudy orchid I'd wear. I'd be sitting between the two men, third row center, as the curtain rose. But, though Rebecca kept nudging me, imploring, I couldn't budge: a *lumpen* in the wing chair, an exotic bird frozen in her elegant cage. The purple orchid pinned to my dress.

"Miss Edna. Joseph just called. The cab is here."

I didn't answer.

"Miss Edna…"

The cab in which Jerome Kern sat, waiting. Or was it Oscar Hammerstein? Or my editor at Doubleday? I couldn't remember who would be squiring me to the theater.

I waved Rebecca away. "Tell Joseph to make my apologies."

Baffled, Rebecca didn't question, but I could hear her on the phone, her voice puzzled and a little annoyed. This just wasn't right, she was thinking. And she was right, of course. I should be there, my mouth positioned into a happy grin, my eyes blinking from the flash of the photographers.

But almost immediately, as though I were a sleepwalker moving through murky waters, I draped the ermine over my shoulders, nodded at Rebecca, and headed for the elevator. Joseph, surprised at my showing up in the lobby, sputtered that Jerome Kern and the waiting cab had left. I shook my head. "A cab, Joseph." Nodding, he hurried to the curb.

Of course, I was headed to the opening, but somehow I knew I'd never get there—or *want* to be there. I didn't need to sit in a darkened theater, especially one that introduced my melodramatic characters to the world. No—I needed to be out on Manhattan streets, the spit and juice and pulse of the workaday city. People around me, getting me thinking, jazzing me, pushing. A flow of walkers would tell me something I needed to know.

I directed the dour cabbie down Fifth Avenue, now jampacked with cars, bumper to bumper, and we idled there. Wispy steam rose from manhole covers. Buses belched out blue-gray spumes of thick smoke. People laughing, talking, yelling to others, watched their breaths form little clouds. Sleet was falling, and the sidewalks glistened with reflected light: splashy shafts of translucent gemstone. The sleet beat against the cab's windows as the wipers slapped an irregular rhythm. Fifth Avenue, garish with red and green and silver Christmas garlands, store windows roped with twinkling lights, evergreen boughs laced with rainbow lights. A parade of eager tourists probably in the city for New Year's festivities in Times Square. A parade up and down Fifth Avenue. Here Manhattan sang out.

Suddenly the sleet stopped. A chain reaction as umbrellas closed and people stopped rushing for shelter. Folks huddling in store entrances moved now out onto the sidewalk. As the cab signaled to turn, headed toward Central Park and toward the

West Side theater district, I tapped the driver on the shoulder. "Let me off here."

"Ma'am?" He hesitated, his backward glare taking in the gaudy purple orchid on my breast.

Standing on the sidewalk, I was immediately disoriented. Uptown? Downtown? Where to head? My mind sailed to that old tune—*all around the town…East side, West side…boys and girls together…*

Boys and girls together…Bella and Roddy and Lawson and…

A young man in a hurry brushed against me, turned to face me, and apologized. I didn't answer. I stood there on Fifth Avenue and thought, crazily, of the celebrated Easter Parade. I'd never attended that wonderful spectacle of flowered hats and springtime bonhomie. Winter is over…April showers…

Walk, I told myself. Move. So I began walking downtown with purpose, my strides confident and sure. Not a strut, truly, but the swagger of a determined woman. A city of walkers, my beloved Manhattan, cement landscape navigated by the longitude and latitude of cross-town streets and long avenues that covered the length of the island. New Yorkers walked as though they knew where they were going, a performance not always believable, but necessary. I walked. As I expected, no one paid any mind to the fussy lady in the open coat, buffeted now by the breeze and a slight annoying mist. The purple orchid was squashed into unlovely torn petals. But I walked. The crisp winter air invigorated me as I strode through slicked-over puddles on cracked sidewalks. Everything glittered now under the thin layer of sleet: a fairyland of flickering light and mother-of-pearl reflection. Wispy haloes circled the streetlights. There were few shadows here, only the wash of yellow and white that reflected off the cars and buses, off the plate-glass windows with their luminous Christmas displays. Fifth Avenue: every day is a parade.

Fifth Avenue didn't end. No, not true. It was Broadway that never ended—the storied avenue went on and on, up through Morningside Heights, through the Bronx, through Harlem, then into the nether sylvan lands until it got lost in everybody's dream world. The boulevard of broken…schemes.

Jigsaw puzzle: Ellie's admission. Two in the morning at Roddy's apartment. That rattled me. Bella's admission. Lawson and Bella and Roddy—dead-end dreamers. The element of chance, removed. What is guaranteed every human being on this earth— chance. We all suffer chance, though we all don't have a *chance*. But taking away chance was itself chance—the chance we all take. My thoughts got muddled, foggy. Chance removed. Blotted out. Cancelled. Nullified. Something else: Roddy's notes, those scribbled observations. What? What?

It was starting to sleet again, ice crystals that tingled on the skin. I didn't care. I stopped to tighten the collar of my fur, buttoned it close to my neck, and glanced into the doorway of the Godiva shop. A stooped old Negro, dressed in faded denim trousers and a railroad cap, was hauling a bundle of bound card-board to the curb. He nodded at me. I watched as he lumbered with the trash: a pitch-black wrinkled face, sparse curly white hair, and a scar at the corner of his mouth. Wildly, I swung around. The parade of folks pushed past me: white folks all, dressed for dinner or theater. Across the street, at the Concord, a residential hotel with a Gothic façade, a middle-aged Negro doorman stood with his arms at his side, unmoving. Dressed in a brilliant red beefeater jacket with gold braid epaulettes, with an absurd ornate cap on his head, he stared idly into the busy street, at attention, a statue. A frolicking white couple sauntered past, laughing. Honeymooners perhaps—the way they clutched each other. The man's sleeve brushed the doorman, but nothing was said. For a second the doorman flinched, his head flicking toward the offender, but then he resumed his stoic stance.

Suddenly a blast of chilly wind swept across the avenue as a spray of rare hail covered the sidewalk. A boom of thunder in the sky. For a moment everyone stopped, a stage double take. Then someone near me laughed and rushed under an awning. The parade shifted as folks scurried and hid, everyone staring at the bouncing hailstones, though I remained planted there, my coat ruined, my shoes sodden, my eyes tearing from the cold.

What I saw were quick, static snapshots: that old man with the cardboard bundle looked up. The doorman looked up. Next door a young ashy man in a white apron sweeping an entrance paused. A bosomy woman in a maid's uniform stopped walking. All black folks, dotting the street, frozen there. Seismic, the shift of the earth's axle. They waited. Around them swirled the bustling, frantic white people. A curious portrait, that, and I realized who could not march in any Easter parade.

Wet now, bedraggled, I stumbled to the curb and hailed a taxi.

I gave him the address of the theater but then I snapped, "Cabbie, turn back." A policeman on a horse crossed in front of us. Staring up at him, I started to tremble. I knew I couldn't face the crowds, the well-wishers, the friends, even my family. It couldn't be done. "Cabbie," I sputtered, "turn back."

Turn back: home. Turn back: something in my apartment. Something. Turn backwards. That night.

Around midnight I slept, though off and on. Yet I must have fallen into a deep, rumbling sleep because at four o'clock—I glanced at the alarm clock on my nightstand—I struggled awake and stared into the shadowy darkness. I closed my eyes, rested my head down on the pillows. But at that moment, with the jackhammer force of an awesome epiphany, it was there: the answer.

So palpable, tangible...I could reach out and touch it in the dark.

In the morning I forced myself to take my walk before breakfast, though I avoided the kiosks where the *Times*, the *Herald Tribune*, and the other papers were temptingly suspended. But at the apartment, bathed and refreshed, I sat with breakfast as Rebecca laid the reviews before me: *Show Boat* was an unqualified success. An instant classic. A singular this and a spectacular that...Kern's score...Ol' Man River...cakewalk...Brooks Atkinson called it epochal...lines of people waiting for tickets. Bill...Can't Stop Lovin' Dat Man...Cap'n Andy and Parthy...Make Believe...

All morning, I fielded calls, telegrams, and bouquets of flowers. Jerome Kern: *You were missed last night, dear Edna, but you were obviously present throughout the glorious evening.* Oscar Hammerstein: *Your words touched every heart last night, and for generations to come.*

So I was happy, in my fashion.

But my mind was elsewhere: a kaleidoscope of fragments. Something there: my reporter's instinct, never diminished, the curious fact sheltered in the corner of my brain.

The evening of *The Royal Family* opening. Again, Rebecca, the mother robin, fluttered, hovered. A quick call from George Kaufman, who'd meet me in the lobby of the Selwyn with his wife Bea. The late-night supper afterwards at Enrico's downtown. Guests included the stalwarts—Dorothy Parker, Robert Sherwood, Robert Benchley—as we waited for the early editions, word of mouth, suggestions of failure or success. I refused a call from Jed, and Rebecca announced that he sounded furious, harried, a man not happy with the night to follow. Again, the dressing up: my stunning pearl-colored dress. The pungent gardenia that made me dizzy.

Bella…with the cloying gardenia perfume…the alley, dark and…

Somewhere in the vast, dreadful city was a murderer, and it wasn't that hapless hobo, Skidder Scott.

The long black Lincoln town car idled in front of my building, the dapper chauffeur standing at attention, his cap pulled rakishly low over his forehead. The doorman Joseph, perhaps anticipating a reprise of last night's equivocation, hesitated as he nodded toward the young man, who then rushed to open the back door. "Mr. Harris sends his regards," the driver said evenly. Of course, it was Jed's idea to send such a lavish car for me. Doubtless George and Bea Kaufman were being squired from their apartment in a similar monstrosity. "My name is Howie, ma'am." He bowed. "At your service. A pleasure, Miss Ferber." It was almost comical, his earnest delivery, though his voice cracked when he told me his name. A fair-haired farm boy, this Howie, thirtyish, red cheeks and a gigantic Adam's apple.

On the rain-slicked streets the car moved seamlessly into traffic, headed toward a cross street to the West Side.

"A change of plans," I said to his back, and I noticed his neck stiffen, the fair skin darkening.

"Ma'am?" The car slowed.

I waited a heartbeat. "I need to go elsewhere."

"But…"

I ignored that impudence. Instead, leaning forward, I told him, "At my service, didn't you say?" He winced. I gave him the address of Roddy's old apartment, up off Seventh Avenue, deep into Harlem.

He hesitated, uncomfortable, doubtless dreading Jed Harris' blown-fuse wrath, but he smoothly maneuvered the town car onto a cross street, then turned north on Lexington Avenue.

"Miss Ferber…Harlem?"

"I'll explain it to Mr. Harris. He won't understand, but he'll not crucify you. If he does berate you, they'll be witnesses. He likes to do all his torture in public."

He turned his head slightly, a sliver of a smile on his impassive face, and I realized, triumphantly, that I'd unwittingly found my Sancho Panza for the night's questionable adventure.

"Howie," I said to his back, "I'm not certain what I'm up to. I'm not going to a jazz club up there, certainly not, but I'm probably going to make you a little bit crazy."

The car stopped at a red light, and Howie's head swung around to face me. A wide boyish grin, feckless. A strand of blond hair escaped the chauffeur's cap, dangled over his forehead. Huckleberry Finn and me. Tom Sawyer. Maybe even runaway Jim on the inevitable raft down the Mississippi. He hesitated. "Mr. Harris *warned* me."

That tickled me. "Warned you? Tell me."

"He said you're…fierce." He leaned back toward me, warily. "I'm sorry. I don't mean to…"

But I laughed out loud. "I am that. Especially so when I'm on a mission."

The light changed and the car slinked forward, moving up Lexington, past busy storefronts—Clark's Luncheonette, Andy's Automat, Freddy's Steak and Chophouse, a pawnshop. Idlers hung in doorways, red dots from their cigarettes shining in the dark. I didn't know Lexington Avenue this far north, this ragtag neighborhood.

Howie was enjoying himself, I could tell. "We're on a *mission.*" He stressed the word, savoring it. His hand slipped off the wheel and fiddled with a pack of Lucky Strikes on his console.

"Yes, we are." I smiled. "I do like your use of the word 'we.'"

But my spirits flagged as we drove into Harlem, cruised up Seventh Avenue, and then turned onto 138th Street. Roddy's block was dark and shadowy at night, closed up, a horn blaring one street over, a woman screaming at a crying child. At the end of his block, we sat behind a cab dropping off a young couple, and, leaning to the side, I spotted Roddy's old building. No front stoop lights on, the first floor dark, an upper apartment with one light on. Silent. Dead.

A line from Shakespeare haunted me. *Night and silence. Who is here?*

"Pull over here," I directed. We were still several buildings away, but I wanted to watch the dead apartment building.

"Ma'am?"

"It's all right," I insisted, and he got quiet.

What did I expect? I had no idea, though I believed my being on the street, approaching that somber entrance, peering at that dark alley where Bella hid, would somehow let me understand something. Nighttime: I'd only been there during daylight. At night the street relaxed, sagged, seemed to fold into itself. A few cars sputtered by, but only now and then. A man in work dungarees clutching a lunch pail dragged himself by the car, stopping to stare into the fancy town car that should not be on his street, especially with a white woman's face pressed against the window. Yet there was no curiosity in his face—just a lazy boredom, something to do as he walked to work.

"Have a cigarette, Howie."

He quickly lit one. "You, ma'am?"

I shook my head. "No thanks."

As he smoked, his head went up and down, and I surmised he was playing a jukebox tune in his head. His fingertips tapped the steering wheel.

I started when a light popped on in Harriet's apartment— Mr. Porter's apartment—a rectangular block of murky yellow that looked menacing and even revelatory, though of course it wasn't. For a second I saw a shadow move past, pause, and then the light was switched off.

Perhaps this was how the street looked the night of the murder, I told myself: dark, shadowy, and still.

"Pull up across from that building," I told Howie.

He stopped the car directly across the street from Roddy's building, and I faced that dreaded dark alley. At night, I realized, it was pitch-black there—impenetrable, threatening. Or, rather, it seemed threatening to me, so forbidden, this black hole of Calcutta that loomed at the heart of the murder. I was convinced of that. Bella hid there, albeit for a short time. Ellie would sneak down the alley to the back. Bella, too. Others? The murderer must have gone that route—I refused to believe the murderer entered by the front door. No, the alley was the channel to that hideous stabbing. An unlocked back door, most likely. Roddy perhaps left it open—but not for Ellie. For whom? A tapping at the window. I'm here. Let me in. No, I told myself—no. Roddy lay in bed, sleeping. Someone stealthily moved down that alley. Someone who knew…

"Ma'am." Howie was pointing behind me at the sidewalk. "There."

I turned to see a figure bundled against the cold in a long black coat, someone who'd been huddled on the stoop of the boarded-up building directly across from Roddy's apartment. A homeless person, perhaps, but someone now rushing away from us, hunched over, stumbling.

"Howie, what?"

"Well, I glanced out the window and seen this movement in the dark there, someone hidden there. In the cold. Real strange. When I looked closer, whoever it is pushed back into the shadows. When I tossed out my cigarette, I heard a cough. He's running, see?"

The dark shadow was rushing away from us, weaving, dipping behind a parked car, bent over, shuffling.

"Don't want you see them," Howie said.

I glanced back at Roddy's building. All the lights were now on in Mr. Porter's apartment. That jarred, though I didn't know why.

"Did you see what he looked like? A face? A man? A woman?"

"I couldn't tell. Too bundled up, bent over. But a head wrapped in a bright red scarf or hat. Like a lady would wear. Maybe."

I rushed my words. "Can you follow?"

A slick grin covered his face. Coolly, his shoulders forward, he jerked the steering wheel, maneuvered an impossible U-turn on the tight street with rows of double-parked cars, and zoomed to the corner. But our elusive shadow was nowhere to be seen. At the corner of Eighth Avenue there was too much congested traffic, too many bustling people out in the cold. A cop's shrill whistle caused two drivers to blare horns. Jaywalkers shuffled and blocked cars. A man banged on a fender. Howie quickly moved through the intersection, running a red light—I gasped and he swore under his breath—and the car pulled to the opposite curb. I looked up and down Eighth Avenue, a vain pursuit, surely, but Howie was madly drumming his fingers on the steering wheel.

"You know, he figures we'd cruise the avenue." He bit his lip. "*This* avenue." He banged the steering wheel. "He's running the cross streets, avoiding the avenues." He placed the car in gear and moved through the cross street, narrowly missing the open door of a yellow cab. In the middle of a block of shabby brownstones he stopped so quickly I bounced forward, grabbed the seat in front of me. "There."

I saw nothing. "What?"

"You gotta watch the dark doorways, ma'am. Not the lit ones. Or the open sidewalk. There."

Night and silence…

A shock of red on a dark figure who was pressed against a doorframe.

I strained to see in the darkness—and then imagined there was no one there. Crazily, Howie flung open the door, though I yelled for him to stop, and he jumped out. "You!" he yelled into the darkness.

…Who is there?

But, through some nighttime sleight of hand, the red scarf disappeared, though in seconds I spotted the figure hurrying toward the corner. "There!" I screamed.

Howie slipped back into the driver's seat and the car sped on.

"Foolish, this chase," I sputtered, but Howie was having none of my reservations now. His hands fumbled on the steering wheel, his back stiff, his face beet red. Somehow, he managed to slip a cigarette between his lips and light it. I'd missed that trick, too. It bobbed up and down as he whistled softly. "Howie, enough." But he wasn't listening, and I realized I wanted this pursuit to go on, Howie and I gallivanting madly through the darkened streets. Wyatt Earp and Annie Oakley. He sped west, maneuvering around cars and walkers. At one point, dead-ended, he turned onto 141st Street and crossed Convent, then nearly collided with a taxi cruising up St. Nicholas Avenue.

"We may be ahead of him!" Howie yelled. "He's headed west."

"To where?"

He didn't answer. The elusive figure, I knew, could be anywhere now, sheltered in an apartment, hidden in a park. Anywhere. But Howie was resolute. "Howie…"

He broke in. "West," he blurted out. "I think I know…"

We stopped at a red light on Amsterdam Avenue, and Howie flicked his ashes into the ashtray. Finally, nodding, he pulled over to the curb, and we waited. "This avenue, maybe. He's running away from us. A busy street, a place to get lost." He smiled at me. "We wait."

The town car blocked part of an intersection. Behind us a horn honked, but Howie raised his arm cavalierly in the air, shrugged. The car squealed by us, the driver shaking his fist at us.

We waited. The light went red, then green, then red again.

A half-hour now, at least, this chase, and…nothing.

My mind reeled. "That could be…anyone…"

He cut me off. "Not a chance. Somebody was watching that building, ma'am. You know it. And when they seen *you*, they run off. No reason to *run*, you know."

"But…"

His voice erupted. "There!"

I saw nothing, though he pointed across Amsterdam, down a cross street. Shadows, headlights, the rumble of a car on the bumpy pavement, the distant whine of a bus stopping. The blaring horn section of a jazz record on someone's gramophone.

"That fool is hell-bent toward Broadway. I should have guessed it. The subway, maybe. Lots of people out tonight. Lots of…" His voice trailed off as a taxi behind us leaned on a horn.

Howie careened onto Broadway, tires squealing, heading north, weaving around cars and jaywalkers, his head twisting left and right, frantic. A chaotic street, this Broadway, uptown in Harlem, crowds on the sidewalks, venders still hawking wares this late at night, newsstands with lines of people, buses chugging by, a pack of jazzy young men in purple suits, their bodies bumping one another and blocking the intersection. Howie leaned on his horn. I didn't know where to look. We drove up three or four blocks, then down six or seven, up and down, crazily—all around the town, boys and girls together—crazy, crazy. Then, suddenly, we idled by the subway stop. Nothing. No red scarf.

Howie swore under his breath.

"What?"

"I used to track folks for Pinkerton's. In Chicago. Five years back."

"And?"

"And I like to believe I *think* like a runner from the law."

"We're not the law."

"Hey, you're acting like it, ma'am."

I grinned. "Well," I began, sitting back, "this is a big city… here…and…" I sighed. "Enough, Howie. This little adventure is over, foolish though it might have been. We'll never know."

Howie pointed to a black-clad figure rushing by, a floppy scarlet cap covering the face, the body stooped against the cold. But the figure paused and stepped off the curb, turning in front of us. A young woman clutched an infant protectively tucked into her chest. A gust of wind hit her face and the scarlet hat flew off. The hat slammed against a brick wall.

Howie laughed. "If she didn't have no baby…"

"No," I said emphatically. "No."

The town car merged into the flow of traffic on Broadway, headed now back downtown, moving slowly. We stopped at a red light. I glanced back. A city bus pulled up to a stop, and a rush of frozen folks bustled from behind a kiosk and hurried onto the bus. Within seconds the bus chugged away, backfiring once.

Darkness shrouded the kiosk. But, surprisingly, another bus unexpectedly appeared, pulling over and illuminating the dark space. Standing back against the kiosk, bent away from the wind, was the elusive dark figure with the brilliant red scarf, caught now unawares under the sudden stream of powerful light.

"Oh my God," I whispered. "Oh my God."

Chapter Nineteen

"Welcome. Happy New Year."

My voice was scratchy and hesitant.

At three o'clock on New Year's Day everyone gathered at my apartment for tea. I'd thought of an early brunch, but Rebecca reminded me that young folks usually went to New Year's Eve revels and doubtless would stagger bleary-eyed from bed late the next morning or early afternoon. Then a simple tea, I told her: with chicken salad sandwiches, fluffy blueberry muffins, and one of her trays of mouth-watering lemon chiffon cookies. Simple fare, nothing to upset the hangover or indigestion. Frankly, I'd provide the bile and the acid in the belly.

"What are you up to, Miss Edna?" Rebecca questioned, but I shrugged her off.

It had been a hectic few days since the successful opening of *The Royal Family*. The bouquets and accolades still poured in, floodtide, and everyone wanted at me. But I made myself available only to family visiting from Chicago. My mother had returned to the city from Connecticut for the openings—"Edna, what's the matter with you? You weren't *there*!"—but now was headed back to Chicago with relatives—my real Christmas present, indeed. And I saw George Kaufman and Noël Coward and Dick and Mary Rodgers, dinners or lunches with these friends. Other than that, I was busy. I had my homework to do, and I did it studiously, methodically, hidden in my workroom, out of sight of Rebecca. I had to be certain my late-night revelations were on target, and of course they were—for the most part—though I hated to qualify that statement. I had motive, guessed at but logical; I had evidence, grim and stunning. What I lacked was the *how*—because that seemed impossible, given the facts as amassed, digested, debated. But I trusted my instincts.

Chomping on a muffin, Waters innocently commented, "Here we are again. All of us, just like a couple weeks back. Sitting here in your living room." He waved his hand around the room.

"Except," Harriet smiled, "there were more of us. Someone named Roddy is missing."

Waters looked sheepish and stared into his lap.

He had spent the morning in the kitchen with his mother, the two laughing and leaning into each other, familial and warm. He was relieved when Ellie arrived, a half-hour early. Doffing her coat and gloves and rubbing her hands over her chilled face, she spoke to Waters, "So Langston Hughes is coming today?"

The question surprised him. "No, not that I know of."

Overhearing her, I came in from my workroom. "Not today, Ellie. I hope you weren't misled." I paused. "Langston Hughes did say he'd talk to the group but…not today."

She looked perplexed. "Then what?" She stepped back, as if planning to flee.

I didn't answer, and Ellie went to the sideboard, eyed some water chestnut and bacon canapés Rebecca had just placed there. Her lips were drawn into a severe line, and I noticed that she kept glancing at me, wary. Dressed in a spangly dress, cut above the knee, very flapper, with a bodice pulled tight across her chest, an attempt to flatten what nature had abundantly provided, she also wore sparkly drop earrings, ruby-colored ovals. The total effect of her look was New Year's Eve, dance hall, jazz cabaret, Clara Bow "It" girl—and not, obviously, a sobering and questionable afternoon tea at Edna Ferber's sensible abode.

When I employed Waters and Rebecca to engineer the invitations to this gathering, I'd been purposely mysterious, though

Rebecca, sly dog, had grimly nodded, suspecting something. For the past couple of days she'd spied me scurrying about, a dervish in the apartment, note taking, reviewing, staring out the window, becoming at times unnecessarily testy and abrupt with her. So she knew something was up. Waters, ready to return to classes in Maryland after the holiday, piddled about, an annoying lap dog at times, though he relished this gathering of his friends; yet, at times, prescient, he paused and quietly watched me, ready to ask me *why*. Why now? What was I up to? His mother's wariness clued him in a bit, but Waters knew better than to probe the feisty lady novelist who paid his boarding school fees.

Dressed in a pale blue shirt tucked into dark gray woolen slacks, with an oversized vaudeville red bowtie, with black tie shoes so shiny they seemed glass, Waters, as always, looked like a runaway from a British public school, a boy seemingly removed from the decade's oh-you-kid frivolity and *outré* costume, as evidenced by Ellie, the chanteuse with the sparkles in her hair. Joe College meets the cat's meow.

I knew it had taken some maneuvering to assemble the crowd, but, though no reasons were given other than a casual New Year's Day tea, they were all assembled in my living room. No one dared refuse the invitation. Bella had come alone, a few steps ahead of Lawson, and I suspected they probably rode up the elevator together but chose not to talk.

Bella, the temptress, looked ready for battle. She wore the opposite of what I'd expected, the negative to Ellie's glossy print: a burlap-textured smock belted around her hips with a thick round cord, an outfit that made her look like a chic Benedictine monk, her dress cut short above the knees, but high in the neck. A dramatic turquoise necklace draped down the front. She wore high heels with thick, shiny red ankle straps, patent leather, and on her head a black cloche of coarse material pulled so tight across her forehead her face seemed meshed into it: shadowing her light-skinned black face. Very dramatic. She looked, well, warrior princess. It both attracted yet jarred, the beautiful face stark now, bold, without lipstick or rouge. She snuggled into the end of the sofa, nodding at Waters who seemed mesmerized by her, yet I noted she did not acknowledge Ellie, who sat away from her. The coldness filled the room like a low-hanging cloud.

Lawson looked better than I expected. The last few times I saw him, days after the murder, he'd been shattered, pale. Now, dressed in a double-breasted charcoal gray suit with a snazzy blue tie, he looked debonair and alert, though his eyes betrayed melancholy and unease. How freakish that his persistent grief somehow enhanced his beauty, a kind of *Sorrows of Werther Weltschmerz* perhaps, the vagabond poet, lonely and aimless. He shook Waters' hand, graciously thanked me, and sat down next to Ellie, who was unhappy with his proximity. She turned her body away, but only slightly, as if to make a point but not too much of one.

Harriet and Freddy came together, standing so close in the entrance that their shoulders touched. They looked a couple, save for one thing: Freddy's possessive eye immediately focused on Ellie, glittering there on the sofa, though she purposely ignored him. Sad, that doomed romance, one-sided, blighted, though a little scary, too. Harriet acted oblivious, nudging Freddy to a wing chair. I recalled Harriet's comment about her discomfort in my apartment, it being so removed from the hardscrabble, workaday Harlem street life. And yet, Waters told me, of them all she was most eager to come to tea. She wore a simple dark brown smock, unadorned, but in her straightened hair she'd tucked a large silk magnolia blossom, so emphatically at war with her pouting face and drab attire. Yet when she shook my hand, I noticed her fingers were resplendent with rings: silver filigreed pieces imbedded with cheap stones. Only her thumbs were free of the ornaments.

Freddy wore a Sunday-go-to-meeting broadloom suit, a size too large and two decades out of fashion, though his necktie was a jazzy cobalt blue, wide and popular. I assumed he'd borrowed the suit, given how ill-fitting it looked on him, his reluctant concession to New Year's Day tea on the Upper East Side. Rebel though he might be, and rightly so, he nevertheless understood where he was headed that day.

Talking with Rebecca in the kitchen, I could hear the nervous buzz and hum of the voices—small talk, with long spaces in between. Where'd you go last night? Was Mabel singing there?… I hear that Valaida Snow was…Did you read that poem in the *Mercury*? Have you…well…should…I thought…maybe… well…well…

The only person missing was someone I had insisted be there: Jed Harris. The other night I'd phoned him, only to learn that he was packed and headed to Idlewild for a morning flight to Florida. I'd avoided talking to him after the opening, largely because he'd skirmished with George Kaufman about the play, which had been well received and gloriously reviewed. But only decently attended. Because ticket sales were sketchy, Jed insisted he'd close the play after New Year's. Horrified, George explained that openings right after Christmas had limited exposure, and that the audience would grow. If Jed insisted on closing the play, George had told him, he would take him for an unpleasant spin into the New Jersey hinterlands, probably with me riding shotgun. Jed had hung up.

"You're going where?" I'd demanded the other night.

"Florida. I've worked too hard."

"Jed." I was not certain how to approach the subject. I told him about the tea on New Year's Day. He *needed* to be there.

"Why, for God's sake? I have nothing to do with that maddening crew."

"You have everything to do with them. Bella, Lawson, Roddy."

I could hear him chuckle. "Miss Edna, the detective."

"I know what happened, Jed." A pause. "I *think* I do." I hated equivocation, not in my character, but there were loose ends…

"Tell me."

"No, not yet. And you are part of this, Jed."

"No, I'm not. I didn't murder that young Negro."

"True," I said. "You slaughter people in another, much more lethal fashion."

"What does that mean?" A snarled response, though whispered.

"I don't want to get into it now, but your treatment of Bella and Lawson and Roddy, for one." Again I could hear his nasty chuckle. "Jed, really! You tried to destroy Lawson's career, purposely so, dismissing his obvious talent. You mocked Roddy, scuffled with him. And Bella, well, you used her body with the promise..."

"She used me," he interrupted. "Me! They're all a bunch of ambitious Negroes. Bella is a cutthroat. Lawson is, well," a pause, "that was just pure fun for me. The boy takes himself too seriously. Messing with him was like a chess game that is too easy to win. People let themselves be manipulated, you know. When people want something from you, you can get them to jump hoops. And Roddy was a buffoon. I told Bella to drop Lawson, and she did. If I'd told her to kill that Roddy, well, she would have. Maybe she did, in fact. Maybe she misunderstood me... In any event, Edna, I'm not to blame."

I drew in my breath. "Jed, in some ways you are responsible for everything bad that has happened."

"I'm going to Florida, Edna," he seethed. "Goodbye." He hung up on me, something that I prefer to do to people.

So Jed would not be at my afternoon tea, but I figured his presence would be painfully and colossally felt. His malignant spirit, dark and bitter, hung in the room, splashed against the backdrop of a sleety, windy Manhattan afternoon. *People let themselves be manipulated.* Mantra for a devil's afternoon. Delightful, indeed.

"Why are we here?" Harriet finally asked when the last of the sandwiches disappeared and Rebecca returned to the kitchen to brew more tea. The presumptuous question hung in the air, stifled the small talk, and every head turned, as though mechanized, toward me, sitting there on the edge of my favorite rose-colored wing chair, a cup and saucer demurely poised in my lap.

I cleared my throat. "Obviously, as you guess, not just for a social tea."

Ellie started to say something, but it came out a thin whistle, for which she apologized.

"I have questions," I began. "And maybe a few answers."

Waters, standing in the kitchen door, said the words every-one was thinking, "Roddy's murder." Said by the young boy in a tremulous voice, the words seemed to punctuate the room, a stage announcement proclaiming the start of Act Five, the awful *denouement* to a Shakespearean tragedy.

"Well, yes," I answered him. "I wanted to share my thinking with you and…"

Bella interrupted. "You want to name one of us the mur-derer." She stopped, gasped. "Preposterous. Skidder Scott, the homeless man…"

"Didn't kill Roddy," I concluded for her.

"Proof?" yelled Freddy, who seemed surprised at his own raised voice.

I stood and walked to the edge of the group, watching their upturned, eager faces, and for a moment, light-headed, I wavered: a circle of young, bright men and women, creative, driven, yet removed from America. What price did these young people pay for wanting to succeed…to achieve…to get their rightful place? What? They struggled against their own blackness. Against the white world that looked right through them. Hated them. Worse, perhaps, was indifferent. Yet one of them was most likely a murderer of a young man who also wanted his chance.

I breathed in, held onto the back of my chair. Rebecca had come in from the kitchen and stood near me, concern in her eyes. I noticed she repeatedly glanced toward Waters, who had sat down on the sofa next to Lawson, her mother-eye cool yet covetous. "Some things bothered me," I began. "Just the other day, talking with Ellie during her rehearsal, she confessed that she'd visited Roddy that night—against his wishes. He'd told her to stay away. She came as far as his apartment door."

"So?" Ellie said.

"What I found interesting was that everyone assumed you'd been there, but given the upstairs tenant's remarks, everyone also assumed it was early, minutes before Bella hid in the alley." Bella grunted. "And Freddy had seen Ellie at midnight at the subway stop. What I learned is that Ellie admitted going there later, at two in the morning. She never told the police because she just assumed Skidder Scott arrived shortly afterwards, bungled the burglary, and stabbed Roddy. But you told me you heard Roddy on the phone, angry, talking to someone. He wasn't on the phone, Ellie. They'd had their phone cut off. Didn't pay the bill. Waters told me that." Waters nodded vigorously. "He was talking to someone in the apartment. True, you only heard—or thought you heard—his voice. You were nervous about being there and you left quickly, so you didn't hear the confrontation during which Roddy was stabbed."

Silence in the room. "You don't know that," Harriet said in a low voice.

"True, it's speculation. And something else is speculation: Bella and Lawson talking about how Jed Harris, a man without a conscience, had taken away the element of chance from some of your lives. That word—*chance*—held me. Failure or success, the toss of the dice, Dame Fortune's hit-or-miss game. Yes, Jed played God, destroying careers or threatening to destroy careers. And he has it in his power, unfortunately. But it got me to thinking about desperation, last-chance despair. The house of cards tumbling down. What happens when you believe everything is now gone—everything you've worked hard for, believed you deserved? What happens?"

Waters, spellbound by my words, mouthed the words: What happens?

"What happens are acts of desperation, irrational behavior, changes of character or acting out of character."

"I don't understand what you're talking about," Bella hissed. She wrapped her arms around her body. She was trembling.

"I think Jed Harris, who is not here, set in motion a path of destruction and murder. A game to him, but life-and-death to another."

"Miss Ferber…" Bella began, pleading in her voice. "You misunderstood what I told you. I mean, what I told *him*. Jed Harris. That thing about taking away chance, well, it…"

I held up my hand. "Stop, Bella. You're also a culprit here with your game-playing, manipulation, attraction."

She started to protest. "I never…"

"Oh, but you did." I took a breath. "The other day I took a walk on Fifth Avenue, not certain what I was doing. A busy avenue, that one, and I found myself thinking of…the Easter Parade each spring. It's always a parade there. But a street filled with white folks. The Negroes are in doorways, hauling trash, sweeping floors. Not *their* parade. They *watch*. I recalled that scene in Lawson's novel, *Hell Fighters*, the Negro doughboys back from France, marching up Fifth Avenue, filled with pride and joy, back into Harlem. Yet nothing changed—that burst of heroism in France, on the front lines, altered nothing. Negroes are excluded from the parade."

"We parade up in Harlem." Freddy's voice was a whisper.

A pause. "A curious tableau, that moment on Fifth Avenue. People talked to me without saying a word."

"Miss Edna?" Waters questioned.

"Let me go on." I walked to the dining room table and returned with a small sheaf of papers. "Roddy had started writing an essay called 'Letter to Mr. P,' an attack on old-style negritude, folks who mocked the young generations. He also jotted down a scattered bunch of ideas, including some remarks about Americans in exile in France, even a French quotation about keeping a horrible secret. He, too, remembered the doughboys on Fifth Avenue. A muddle of ideas, but probably reflecting Roddy's recent confusions. Roddy did, indeed, have a secret that was bothering him. He made some quick notations in a little spiral notebook, mostly concerning his fears about Harriet's father, Mr. Porter."

"What? Wait just a minute!" screamed Harriet.

"Wait, Harriet, wait. Give me time. Roddy was concerned that Mr. Porter was going into the apartment, rifling through his possessions. Three pages, two with just a line or two. One of the pages said simply, 'I don't trust him.' Another: 'It was not a good idea to talk about it,' followed by an attack on God. The third page was filled with anger at Mr. Porter. Now I assumed all these lines referred to Mr. Porter, but perhaps not so. Perhaps Roddy was sending a different message."

Harriet was fuming. "Railroading, that's what this is."

I ignored her. "A few years back, Roddy submitted a juvenile short story to *Opportunity*, and Langston Hughes just returned it to me. A sophomoric piece called 'Time to Die,' a stale Civil War costume drama, a young boy's playing with themes well beyond him." I held up the sheets. "Unwittingly, after his death, he has told us the name of the murderer."

Everyone in the room reacted, Ellie actually screaming, Freddy standing and bumping into a table.

"Let me read you a little of what Roddy said." I shuffled through the pages. "A couple revealing lines. 'At night, insects buzz above the tents, dizzy from the light of the lanterns.' Another line. 'The soldier lay on the ground alive, I thought, because I saw an eye flicker, yet when I reached out to him, white maggots slid off his face and I stared at the black stare of a dead man.' And one more…"

Bella grunted. "For God's sake, Miss Ferber…"

I went on. "'When I pulled my hand from the back of my head, I found myself bewildered. The wetness that I thought was sweat was crimson, sticky.' And: 'Now I hear the chorus echo: got no time to die, hear me, Jesus…Jesus…now I got no time.'" I paused, dramatically. "Oh, I'm sorry. I've made a mistake. I'm not reading from Roddy's short story now. These are some notes I scribbled on another sheet of paper. I get confused…"

"Never mind." A thin, metallic voice, almost inaudible rose from the sofa. "Never mind." Louder. I looked down at Lawson, who was sitting there with tears steaming down his cheeks, his hands pressed against the sides of his face. He blubbered, "Never mind."

"I don't understand," Harriet whispered, staring at Lawson.

"No, don't," Bella cried out. "Impossible."

Lawson was shaking his head. "I'm sorry. I truly am. It wasn't supposed to end like this."

"Lawson?" I asked.

He nodded. "I killed Roddy." A soft voice, wispy, shattered. "I'm so sorry."

A humming swept the room, a low rumbling of question and confusion. I held up my hand. I pointed to the dining room table and all the heads turned. "There," I said. "There. The last line I read to you was taken from Lawson's novel *Hell Fighters*, which Waters had rescued from the apartment. A beautiful novel of Negroes fighting in France in the Great War, its sentences stayed with me. The other night I read Roddy's failed short story, 'No Time to Die.' Later I realized I'd heard echoes of many of its lines. And then I remembered where I had read them."

"Lawson," Bella called out. "No."

"That got me to thinking. Why would Lawson steal Roddy's manuscript? How could he get away with it? And why? Why? Then I remembered Jed Harris and what he did to Lawson. Taking away chance. Taking away a future. Especially from such an ambitious, driven life."

Lawson whined. "He said I was finished. No acting, no writing, no plays. Nothing." He stopped short, looked around. "I was finished in this town. I had to have a future."

"But you can't blame Jed Harris, beast that he is," I said.

Lawson was sobbing now, rubbing his wrists into his eyes. "I just got...obsessed."

Bella sputtered. "But he couldn't, Miss Ferber. I drugged him. He was sleeping on the sofa..."

"Tell us, Lawson," I demanded.

Lawson breathed in, looked into my face. His lips trembled. "I didn't think you saw me, Miss Ferber, the other night. Across from our apartment."

"Why were you there?"

Helpless, sobbing now. "I couldn't stay away. I was like...like I could *undo* what I did. I was so depressed, hurt. Night after night I stood there in the cold. I wanted a different ending. But the ending was always the same. I couldn't *change* the story."

"Tell us," I repeated.

"It started as a joke in my head. Sort of a…mental game. Roddy hinted that he was working on a secret project, some novel. A great idea. He was going to surprise us all." Lawson looked at the others, but then faced me. "I'd told him about the Hell Fighters, showed him an article in the news. I was the one. I told him that I wanted to do a novel someday. He got excited, rushed to the library. He shared his poetry with everyone, but this was to be a surprise. He taunted me because I'd said I was going to use the Hell Fighters but he said maybe he was going to do it first. Someday. Maybe beat me to it. I didn't listen to him, he was always crowing about something; but he'd be in his room, typing madly. And I never got around to writing anything about them."

Ellie sputtered, "I don't…" She stopped, stifled a sob.

Waters looked confused. "He took the idea from you?"

Lawson nodded. "I started to wonder. Could he be stealing my idea? I sneaked into his room so many times, went through his stuff. One day he left the pile of manuscript on his desk. I'd not been around for a few days. Usually he locked his stuff in a drawer, made certain it was hidden. And I read it. My God, it was so good! I couldn't put it down." Lawson stopped, gulped, and wiped his eyes. When he started speaking again, his voice was stronger, with an edge. "I knew it would make his name. But so what? I wished it was mine, I felt it *should* be mine, and it got me to thinking. Not seriously, you know. It was supposed to be my idea."

I caught Rebecca's eye. Such sadness there.

Waters was watching her, too. "Ma."

But she held up her hand and shook her head.

Freddy glared at Lawson, and his fist smashed into his palm. We all watched him. "Christ, Lawson. Christ."

Lawson stared out the window. "Then my own life started to fall apart. Jed Harris rejected my play, and we got nasty with each other. He blackballed me—or threatened to. I felt my life spiraling out of control, and, well, I panicked. No more acting, in fact. My looks carried me, but no more. And my writing.

Nothing. *Nothing.* I got stupid. So jealous of Roddy. Then when he started sleeping with Bella, I got a little crazy. Ellie, then Bella. Then neither. He gloated about it. Everyone thought I was okay with it—after all, Bella and I kept starting and stopping—but it made me furious. *My* girl now. I wanted to *kill* him. I mean, it was the last straw. I knew he was planning to leave the apartment, he hinted at that, and I had nowhere to go. Belle was through with me. Nothing. Failure. So I thought—if *Hell Fighters* is *my* book, I'll be famous. I *want* to be famous."

"Lawson," Bella interrupted, but he held up his hand. I looked at her, expecting to see compassion in her face—what I saw was contempt, ice.

"You know, it was a game I played with myself. Getting rid of Roddy. I planned for him to, you know, kill himself with pills. I got some pills, saved them, and even typed a suicide note on his machine. *I don't like the way my life is going.* That kind of thing. I'd get drunk with him one night, feed him the pills in a drink, and leave the note on his dresser. I don't know if I would have gone through with it—it was a mental game, you know. But when he wasn't there, I'd go through his things—I didn't know he suspected and made that note in his notebook. Miss Ferber thought it was about Mr. Porter. But I know that he didn't trust me."

Lawson stopped for breath. "Well, I found the key to his desk. Secretly, over time, I typed my own copy of his novel. I knew where he kept his folder of notes, that kind of thing. He was real organized. It wasn't done, the book, and he'd put it aside, but… well, I loved the book. I thought I'd stage a break-in. We'd had the earlier break-in, and everyone suspected Skidder Scott, of course. We even laughed about it later, saying, 'You know it was Skidder. That drunk! It had to be him.' He'd dropped an empty pack of Camels on the bedroom floor, I'd noticed, and I hid it away. I'm not sure why, but I thought I'd use it somehow. And I did. I didn't know what to do about Roddy. I was gonna be left alone—with *nothing.* And he was getting colder and colder. I had nowhere to turn."

"But you were at Bella's that night," Waters said.

He shook his head. "Bella had this obsession with Roddy because he fooled around with her but then shooed her away"—Bella grunted—"and Ellie was mouthing the we're-just-friends crap that only Freddy wanted to believe, and I waited for a chance." He laughed sarcastically. "Chance, Miss Ferber. You hit the nail on the head. Jed Harris took away even a hope for a fair chance. But that night I didn't plan anything, not really, but I was mad at Bella who was mad at Roddy and Ellie. I knew she was up to something, right after I told her that Ellie was headed to Roddy's. I could see she was faking getting drunk and I did the same, but I was clear headed. Back at the apartment, she poured me a drink and I spotted her slipping something in. I wasn't stupid, so I acted drunk and drugged, and passed out. I *am* a good actor." A thin smile. "She beat it out of there, and I followed minutes later. Everyone was headed for Roddy's, even me, but I never saw Bella there—or Ellie. Of course, I avoided coming too close to the house. I walked the streets, looking for Bella, but nothing. I kept checking the back alley—I was getting nuts. Finally, late, I went in through the back door. I thought maybe Bella was inside, or maybe Ellie. Or both. No one. I was going nuts. But only Roddy was there, alone. In his bed. He heard me and I went into his room."

"And killed him," Harriet yelled, furious.

He ignored her. "He was awake, reading. He was angry, accusing me. 'Why are you back in the middle of the night?' he yelled. 'Now what are you up to?' The problem is that, suspicious, he'd gone through *my* stuff that day, and found my copy of *his* book. It baffled him. Then he actually pointed to my copy of his book. It was right there on a shelf. God, I jumped. I was so startled. He said it was over. I was done for. With my friends, everyone. He said he was moving out in a day or so, so what was I trying to pull? He made fun of me—so good looking and getting nowhere on the fastest bus in town. I was standing over him, shaking, and when he said get out, you thief, you're through going through my stuff and wait till I tell everyone, well, I lost it. You know, he kept that knife on the stand. I grabbed it, and I plunged it into his chest…" A gasp, a fresh wash of tears covered his face.

Ellie had started to cry.

Lawson watched her, bothered. "It was over like *that*." He stressed the word. "You know, at the moment I felt triumphant, but it didn't last. I felt this…this hollowness come over me. Frantic, I rushed around, faking a robbery. I put my gloves back on—they were in my coat pocket. I dropped the cigarette pack by the door, stole money from the dresser and some cuff links, and I messed up my room. I spread my copy of his book all over the floor in my room. I grabbed stuff from my bureau—that damn ring. I grabbed his copy of his book, even his folder of his notes. I knew where everything was, of course. I opened the front door, stepped out, closed it, and with my pocketknife I pried it opening, splintering the wood. The old lock just snapped. Easy. But it made a terrific noise. Within seconds, I heard someone coming in, the upstairs tenant, so I ducked in, switched off the lights but couldn't close the door. I ran out the back. I was carrying piles of stuff in a bag. Sweating, crazy, I rushed up the street. I knew where Skidder Scott slept nights—we all do—the abandoned building, out of the winter cold. He was near the corner, but drunk, begging, so I wrapped my ring and cuff links in some rags, and got out of there. I threw Roddy's papers in a trash bin. A mess, I headed to Bella's."

"But what if Bella had come back early?" I asked.

"I thought of that. She thought she'd drugged me—that was how I acted in the morning when I saw Roddy, of course—but I'd say I woke up and went looking for her at an after-hours club, staggering a little, slurring my words. But she wasn't there."

Bella grimaced. "Imprisoned by Jed Harris, thank you very much."

Waters spoke up. "But you and I, the next day, talked with Miss Edna. You agreed that it couldn't be Skidder. It had to be someone…"

Lawson held up his hand. "I *had* to agree with you, Waters. What choice did I have? You got so excited with the idea."

"Lawson, why didn't you tell someone?" I asked quietly.

"I thought I got away with it." A pause. "But it didn't matter. The next day it all hit me, leveled me. I lost all feeling inside me, I kept thinking—confess, confess." He gasped. "Every night I found myself back on that street."

"But the book…" Waters began.

Lawson looked at him. "The book didn't matter. Nothing did. I was hollowed out. When anyone talked of how great it is—how I am!—I got sick inside. I didn't care. I don't care. Not anymore. Something died in me. Something ripped out my insides, left me dead. That stupid act, so sudden. I realized I would never have followed through with it. But, strangely, I *did*. All my ambitions, dreams, hopes…dust. Dust."

Lawson started sobbing loudly now, a young man shattered. Freddy and Harriet stood up and were looking out the windows. I heard her say, "Now what?"

Lawson went on. "Doesn't anyone see what happened? I'd put my hopes on Jed Harris, and he squashed them. Worse, he stopped me from having a life in the city. Down here. Broadway. He…" He faltered.

"Lawson," I said, "stop this now."

He was looking into my face. "Dust, Miss Ferber. All I had left was dust."

Epilogue

A sad story for a glorious time. As the decade ended and the much-touted Harlem Renaissance blossomed and then started to fade, the lamentable tale of Roddy and Lawson and the other fledgling writers drifted into the spotlight and then quickly out, footnotes to the sweep and pull of American literature. American life. The Depression hit, and vast monies and innocent lives were lost or spent dancing to the pulse of uptown Harlem, but the clubs, the white-man excursions, and the jazz rhythms soon paled. Yes, the careers of Langston Hughes and Zora Neale Hurston blazed for years, but the decade that followed was a kind of Indian Summer of reflection, a bittersweet time of struggle and melancholy. The face of poverty was everywhere. It was easy to forget a world in which the lyric "I'm just wild about Harry" was replaced with "Brother, can you spare a dime?" The big bass drum beat of nightlife gave way to folks staring at the empty food slots at the Automat on Broadway. Flaming youth burned out. The cat's meow was suddenly the voice of the turtle crying in the night. Men in rumpled business suits sold apples on street corners. Gaunt faces waited in soup lines.

But not everyone forgot. At least I didn't. And I wasn't alone.

Some of you remember the sudden splash when *Hell Fighters* was published by Knopf in the first full year of the Depression: 1930, that fall. Some of you remember the name Roderick Parsons, though I still think of him as Roddy. It was published to wonderful reviews—Burton Rascoe in the *Herald Tribune* said "Negro narrative has found its Homer," hyperbolic but effective—though the economic woes and despair of the decade doomed sales and attention. It created a minor flurry among Negro intelligentsia, the avant-garde uptown, especially with Langston Hughes' brilliant preface and skillful editing. It won the Spingarn Award from the NAACP. I went to the ceremony at the Civic Club downtown on the arm of Langston Hughes and Carl Van Vechten, and felt out of place. And in the middle of the decade Knopf put out a small edition of Roddy's poems, *Twilight*, which was also nicely received, but quietly forgotten. I have both books in my library, and I often take them out, dip into them, remembering. I expect *Hell Fighters* will be rediscovered some day, in a more auspicious time, and then hailed as a minor classic. If there is any justice in the world…

Now and then some young writer or reader, energized, will make a sentimental pilgrimage to Roddy's apartment on 138th Street, but Mr. Porter, living alone now that Harriet has left, is none too kind—he has little patience with those who mourn the loss of the gifted young man. According to a piece in the *Times*, he actually slammed one pilgrim in the shoulder—with his Bible. The reporter also noted that the building was falling into disrepair and the city planned to condemn it.

Lawson was beaten to death in prison. Ironically, at last, he found the fame he'd so coveted when, in 1933, Harriet, working at the Lafayette Theater up in Harlem, discovered a copy of Lawson's play, the one so cruelly refused by Jed Harris. She mounted a production of *Harlem River* at the theater, where it flourished. Of course, the publicity surrounding the playwright, then serving time upstate, didn't hurt sales, though in the end it did have a darker side. Lawson had been maintaining a low profile behind bars, but reporters clamoring for interviews put him in the spotlight. No one knows the whole story, but his sudden celebrity—the pretty boy standing out in the cafeteria or showers, perhaps—led to a skirmish, and Lawson was found slumped over a lunch room table, his handsome face bashed in and a makeshift knife in his ribs. His notorious death simply meant even more tickets were sold for *Harlem River*. I hear it's being included in an anthology of *New Negro Plays*, edited by Wallace Thurman.

Ellie disappeared for a time, ignoring Waters' repeated phone calls, but then emerged a minor star in a revival of *Shuffle Along* on Broadway, reprising the Josephine Baker and Florence Mills parts. You'd see her photo in the tabloids, exquisitely dressed, but I always thought she had a scared-of-the-dark look on her face, as though she'd found herself in a wonderful place but feared someone would point and say, "You don't belong here." You also saw her in a revival of O'Neill's *All God's Chillun Got Wings* down in Greenwich Village. There was a photo of her riding in a Stutz Bearcat, her face veiled, at a reception for Duke Ellington at the Lincoln Theater. After that, I learned she migrated to Hollywood where she played fawning and comical maids in second-rate talkies, bit parts that had her in frilly French outfits. I saw one in which she played a scaredy-cat maid, mouth agape, hands fluttering, eye balls rolling. I left the theater.

Bella's destiny seemed written in the stars. For a while she plagued Jed Harris, who rebuffed her and finally threatened her. She even stopped in at his Ziegfeld office and created a scene, escorted out by the police. Her wildly exotic good looks no longer served as entry into cabaret society, and, according to Waters, she did a succession of minor roles in Harlem theaters, often playing the decadent *femme fatale* who comes to a bitter if obligatory end. One time she aped Josephine Baker's *la danse savage* in a silly review called *Black Manhattan*. But she had a reputation for being hard, unyielding, if not downright malicious, and the roles quickly evaporated. One of the last ones I saw was with Waters and Rebecca, a madcap comedy called *Flaming Youth*, staged in a backwater hall up on Convent Avenue, a theater group of youngsters. She played an older woman—she was barely thirty then—but the sloppy stage makeup exaggerated her brutally hard looks, and her voice was like hail on a tin roof. At one point she forgot her lines, and the audience hooted and howled.

Waters showed me a few of her short poems in *The Crisis*, but I never cared for them: terse, epigrammatic, and mostly enigmatic, meditations on the dark side of the moon, imitations of Stephen Crane's naturalistic snapshots of life. One was dedicated to Countee Cullen, though for the life of me I didn't know why. She'd always stated her dislike of his verse. When I last saw her, she was hostess at a Harlem nightclub. I'd gone with Noël Coward and Aleck Woollcott, against my will, to hear a favored drummer there, and Bella had seated us. Dressed in some oriental silk dress, with butterflies and sequins, chopsticks in her hair, she looked like a geisha girl without a compass. She nodded at me, but then turned her back, avoiding conversation. When we left the place hours later, she was not at the entrance. And I was happy that I didn't have to say goodbye.

Harriet and Freddy got married, which surprised no one. Once Freddy relinquished his obsession with the aloof Ellie—no one knows exactly how that happened, but Harriet obviously played a role in his reeducation—both settled into a good, productive life. Freddy, ever the social rebel, gained a reputation for his fiery, if beautifully written, essays for *The Crisis*, as well as his social-realism poetry of the long Depression, one of which was printed in *American Mercury*, and has been much anthologized. Harriet gained some fame as a columnist for the *Amsterdam News*, and wrote and performed some one-act plays for a small Negro ensemble in Greenwich Village. They bought an interest in a small Harlem movie house in the early days of talkies, struggled to make a go of it, but obviously did. A decade later, they moved into one of the grand Stanford White houses on 159th Street—Strivers Row. Very posh, indeed. They had one son named Macklin, a musical prodigy, and she sent me black-and-white snapshots, including a profile of the brilliant lad that appeared in the *Times*. Strangely, she is the one who keeps in touch with me over the years, with breezy, chatty notes arriving every so often. That surprised, but also thrilled me.

Always formal—*Dear Miss Ferber*, though I sign my notes back to her *Edna*—she talks of playwriting, of movies, of politics—she became a fierce FDR supporter, as was I, of course—even chats about her love of being a mother. Her devotion to Freddy—he published his book of essays under the name "Frederick Holder, Jr."—is unwavering and beautiful. They're a happy couple. A happy family. What she never mentions is Roddy, Lawson, Bella, or Ellie.

Show Boat and *The Royal Family* were huge successes. *Show Boat* ran for 572 standing-room-only performances, and was almost immediately revived. *The Royal Family*, though it struggled a bit at first, ran for 345 laudable performances and was soon made into an unwatchable movie. Both plays, I hope, are enduring pieces of American culture.

As for Jed Harris, I never stopped blaming him for his part in the tragedy, though, of course, he never agreed with me. But his overweening hubris, not only for his theatrical acumen but also for his attempt to use his suave good looks and charm to wheedle his way into the history books, ultimately faltered. His cold, hard worldview, his cutthroat dealings, his cruelty, led to a shipload of enemies, though I wasn't one. For years, he called me, talked like a magpie. His voice got more and more frantic, oily, demanding. Eventually I put a stop to it, which ruffled his feathers. But by this time his *wunderkind* star was fast dimming on Broadway, the hits suddenly faltered, and Jed Harris himself became a theatrical footnote to the helter-skelter decades before the Second World War. That vicious war changed everything, including me. That madman Hitler had a way of stunting my voice, though he broadened my heart for what was good and just and true.

Yet I end on a happy note. Rebecca's son Waters Turpin never lost sight of his own vision. Returned to school that January, finishing high school, he went onto college, though summers he was in the city and often helped me at parties and chores. For a while he worked in Harlem as a porter-clerk in a deli, then for the WPA, but by then Harlem, to him, was "a painted, glittering jade" that promised much and gave back so little. And in 1937, with no help from me though I sang his praises to everyone, he published *These Low Grounds*, a saga based on four generations of family memory and lore, life in old Maryland, though it looked back to the Old South, to slavery, lynchings, to…"these low grounds of sin and sorrow."

On the Sunday morning the *New York Times* bestowed tons of deserved praise on the novel, lauding its verisimilitude and its power and its evocation of real Negro lives, well, on that morning his mother Rebecca, humming to herself in my kitchen, routinely served me light and airy pancakes slathered in maple syrup and surrounded by plump strawberries, with piping hot coffee and fresh-squeezed orange juice. But she did such a culinary feast every Sunday morning. Yet that Sunday was special. You could tell it by her sprightly step, the tilt of her head, the dip of her smile. And by the song that came, involuntarily, from her throat. She was, after all, a proud woman.

O 5/19
H 10/19
W 4/20

To receive a free catalog of Poisoned Pen Press titles, please contact us in one of the following ways:

Phone: 1-800-421-3976
Facsimile: 1-480-949-1707
Email: info@poisonedpenpress.com
Website: www.poisonedpenpress.com

Poisoned Pen Press
6962 E. First Ave. Ste 103
Scottsdale, AZ 85251